DISTANT CHEERING

THE SOUND OF DISTANT CHEERING

K. M. Peyton

THE BODLEY HEAD

LONDON

Affectionately to my other three
legs, Micky, Tommy and Robin.
And to Peter who does
all the work.

British Library Cataloguing
in Publication Data
Peyton, K. M.
The Sound of Distant Cheering
I. Title
823'.914[F]   PR6066.E9
ISBN 0–370–30700–3

© K. M. Peyton 1986
Photoset and printed in Great Britain for
The Bodley Head Ltd
30 Bedford Square, London WC1B 3RP
by Redwood Burn Limited
Trowbridge, Wiltshire
First published 1986

1

The sun was low, bright in the sky. It was hard to see against it. The horses were bunched together on the far side, the sun behind them, shadows long across the cropped grass. A skein of geese was flying high above, and a soundless jet liner shone like a diamond.

'Midnight King, Greensward and Roly Fox,' intoned the commentator. 'Roly Fox moving up on the outside ... jumped the ditch well and gained two lengths on Greensward, who made a mistake....'

The girl, huddled in an ancient ski jacket, squinting into the sun, clutched leading-rein and horse-blanket with quivering fingers. Roly, my dear Roly, you are going to win this race. I can feel it in my bones.

She thought, I shall remember the geese and the silver aeroplane, the onset of cold with the sun sinking, the smell of trampled grass. Sometimes everything comes right. Once in a while Jeremy will smile; we can dance and shout in the stands, and Roly will stand there, steaming, in the winners' enclosure.

'You think you've got it, and they fall at the last,' the man next to her said.

Rosy smiled at him. 'He won't fall. Not Roly. He's the winner.'

Grace, watching television in the study to keep out of her mother's way (her mother never watched television in the afternoon, only for royal weddings), saw Jeremy's horse win and exclaimed out loud in surprise. Hugh said Jeremy was having a poor season. 'Proved you wrong,' Grace remarked to her absent brother, wondering if anyone in the village—Gin perhaps?—had put a fiver on. Roly Fox's price was fourteen to one. How easy to make money, if you chose the right horse!

Grace huddled into her cardigan, watching Jeremy, and that odd girl, Rosy, looking like a scarecrow, grinning as she led the horse in. If Jeremy looked like that when he won, whatever did he look like when he didn't? Something about Rosy's jacket struck a chord in Grace's mind, until she recognized it as once her own, bought for a skiing holiday in Val d'Isère one Christmas five years ago. There had been no snow and she had spent most of the week in bed with an Australian ski instructor, wearing the jacket hardly at all. Her mother must have put it in a jumble sale, and now here it was, appearing on television, fallen on hard days. Like me, thought Grace. Like the television, which distorted the picture strangely. Unbeautiful as Rosy was, her head was surely not that elongated shape? Rather, it was broad and short from hairline to chin, as Grace remembered it, the nose unimposing, the cheekbones flat and wide apart in the Mongolian fashion. Like Nureyev, if one wanted to be generous. She obviously did not realize that she was appearing on television as she flung her arms round the winner's neck and kissed him in a manner more fitting to a Pony Club event than the winners' enclosure at Wincanton. Such lack of sophistication was bad form, by Grace's reckoning. But what could one expect? She was only a village girl. Hugh had said Rosy was basic. She had defended herself with a pitchfork when he had made a pass at her. A pass at *Rosy*? Grace had been surprised. She had been away too long and forgotten how things were.

Not that anything had changed. The study she sat in was still the only warm room in the house. Filled entirely by a roll-top desk with a large sofa pushed hard against it, it served both as living-room and dining-room in the winter. The grate was small but the fire threw out enough heat to prevent chilblains, and dewdrops forming on the nose, as had been known in the sitting-room. The four of them tended to live in it in the winter, even eating their dinner watching the box, three on the sofa and one on the floor. It was very embarrassing if anyone called. They were considered quality by the village, Hugh having been to Harrow and herself finished in Switzerland, but they lived like pigs.

Mrs Cutbush, dozing on the sofa before her television set, awoke suddenly and cried out, 'The Tetrarch! The Tetrarch wins! Come on, Steve!' She sat bolt upright and stared, looking for the grey horse with white slashes over its flanks that was as clear in her brains's image as if it were present in the room. But nothing ... only a blurred picture on the screen before her—a horse, true, but not her father's darling. How vividly she remembered, in that second! Hugged it to her, because she knew her old brain would let it slip shortly in its present haphazard, unreliable way. She recalled the rare excitement in her father's face, his moustache twitching as he bent down beside the rails and said close in her ear, 'Watch that horse, child. You'll never see anything as fast as that again, ever.' And she lifted her eyes obediently—she did as she was told in those days— and regarded the wonder-horse, liking its ridiculous colour. It was a horse you could not fail to recognize, to remember, a circus horse, a giant, a clown, with a jockey to match its own charisma. The jockey smiled at her, nodded to her father, and rode on down the wide green river of the course, making for the horizon. The instant, some seventy years ago, passed in total recall through her waking brain and faded.

She looked at the television screen. Whatever had re-minded her of The Tetrarch, she wondered? The fire was nearly out, the racing dull, and she had fallen asleep again. It annoyed her if she fell asleep before evening. That's what they did in the old people's home, to be woken with cups of tea at four o'clock. Not her style, not yet. She had forgotten what she was about, but if she concentrated it would come back to her. Something about Rosy, as far as she could remember. Not that it mattered—Rosy would come again. In her confused mind, that certainty consoled. Not her grandson, Jeremy, nor Grace's mother, nor her umpteen long-forgotten god-children, but Rosy, and sometimes Gin, who neither of them had any claim on her at all, but came out of a casual kind of friendship. Not pity—she was sure of that—else she would have shut the door on them, as she had on the vicar and the WI women.

A girl like Rosy seemed to be dancing about on the television screen, holding a horse. But Mrs Cutbush had forgotten what she had put the television on for and thought her mind was playing her tricks. She got up painfully from the sofa and switched the picture off. Silence had become her friend. Not for her the eternal radio noise 'for company'; her own company was good enough. And Jasper's.

'Eh, Jasper?' she said out loud.

But the dog had died six months ago.

After the initial excitement, Rosy made a conscious effort to be cool about Roly's winning, slightly ashamed of her elation. She had been at it long enough, for heaven's sake ... but the thrill of it kept bursting through her bloodstream, making her shiver. She sat crouched up in the cab of the horsebox beside Gin going home, living it over, the vision of her horse coming up the straight with his ears pricked, his stride ever lengthening, going away in the fine, decisive style of a good horse. It had been so long, but she had never lost faith, unlike all the others. Roly had been given to her to 'do' when she was a new girl and the boys had made fun of them both: the dud horse and the art-student 'lass'. Jeremy had only given her the job because he was sorry for her father. He did not like girls in his yard.

'Time we had a winner,' Gin said. 'How long is it? Straw Top at Worcester? Nearly two months. It's the law of averages by now.'

Rosy would not rise to that. She stared out at the cold evening, disregarding the law of averages, watching the entirely appropriate magnificence of the evening sky, where heavy rain-clouds caught some strange, maverick stroke of sunset light on their ragged edges and for a few seconds rewarded her gaze. She was in the mood to take it in. She always liked going home, even without a winner, the cab growing fuggy and comfortable and the radio blaring. She loved motorways, their arrogant sweep across all the old, secret places, hurrying the hordes in their endless, mindless journeys from one end of the country to the other. Once it had taken a week to do what even the old horsebox could do in three hours. The ancient hoofbeats, heartbreaks, still lurked, to her mind—the flash of a crumbling inn behind a Little Chef forecourt, a medieval drain weeping into the new sewer, a stirring of ague and pain in bypassed lanes. She loved the new but was strangely aware of the old—got it from her father, no doubt, a biased pillar of the conservation bodies. The endless pattern of lights approaching on the opposite carriageway flashed and sparkled in her vision; she smiled into the evening, and Gin laughed.

'You are a nut, Rosy! Kissing old Roly, and on television and all.'

'Oh, God, was it?' She laughed too.

'Didn't notice the guv'nor throwing his hat in the air. I think winning hurts him more than losing.'

'Of course it hurts. Think, if it had happened to you—'

'I was never in that class. Can't guess—got no imagination.'

'You don't need much for that!' Rosy groped for the fruit gums under the dashboard. 'Mrs Palmer should've come. I could have told her he'd win today. It's not right, a horse winning and nobody to cheer.'

'The bookies cheered. Fourteen to one. I put two quid on.'

'Yeah, and me.'

In the second, third and fourth enclosures owners and friends had swarmed with congratulations, but Roly's owner had been in America. As far as Rosy was concerned, she was his owner. Nobody knew Roly like she did.

9

Glancing at her sideways, Gin said, 'It's dangerous, you know, how you love Roly.'

'Who's talking? You cried over Miracle Worker.'

'He was killed. That's different. I wasn't the only one.'

'But if you're not involved, you don't care, the job's nothing. Just hard labour for life.'

'For life? Haven't seen any old "lasses" of sixty.'

'That'll be me, one day. Can't see how I'm going to better myself. You need money to be a trainer.'

'You'll get married.'

'What for? That's just the same thing but for a man. I'd rather do it for a horse.'

'There's one you'd do it for.'

'Oh, shut up.'

'You scare 'em all off, Rosy, the way you are.'

'Good. That suits me.'

'Pity the one that gets you.'

'There won't be one.'

The banter was stock-in-trade. They both helped each other in the eternal quest for a mate, but neither took the other's advice. They had known each other since they were born, much too well for marriage themselves. Rosy knew Gin like she knew Roly, even better. Humans were more predictable. Gin had met a girl called Beryl in the betting queue at Newbury. He did his courting at occasional race-meetings, since he had no car and Beryl lived thirty miles away. It was slow going.

Gin flipped the indicator stalk for leaving the motorway and they heard Roly shift his weight behind them. The lorry rolled slightly and the anguished roar of its ancient engine eased to a kinder note as it re-entered the old order. The journey was easy tonight: no fog, no ice, not even rain. Spring was coming and there would be a couple of months of easier racing before the season ended, less to do in pitch darkness. Rosy had adjusted to the tough life, taking it in her stride. It was easier than London, where she had gone after she left school, where everything had been against the grain, the spirit out of its element. She had worked for

Jeremy now for three years; he had reckoned she would last no longer than three months. She was well up in the pecking order, giving way only to Hugh, the assistant trainer, and old Albert more through respect than anything else. The lads mostly came and went, the best of them aspiring to more successful stables. Rosy aspired too, but could not leave for many reasons, not least for her horse, Roly.

A car passed them, the driver giving a toot and raising an arm in greeting.

'What kept him?' Rosy asked.

'He was talking to a bloke—they went into the bar. Don't know who it was.'

'Talking? Jeremy?'

'The other bloke was talking.'

'A rich Arab?'

'A Yorkshireman.'

'More our style.' Rosy sighed.

The journey was nearly over. The grind up the last hill was a killer, why Jeremy said it wasn't worth getting a better horsebox, his perennial excuse. There was a hairpin bend half-way up like on some alpine pass and a drop into the rhododendron bushes that made the boys fasten the harness of their crash-helmets without being told. Hills made horses fit, not to mention men. The house was half-way up; there was no getting away from hills before or behind. Jeremy said the place discouraged unwanted visitors. He might have been thinking of owners, but it worked for useful characters like milkmen, newspapermen and charwomen as well. Brood House—it was well named—could no longer call the tune to the village below as it had in earlier times. More sensible people, Jeremy's parents, for example, had abandoned it for purpose-built yards in sunnier climes, but Jeremy, like the place, was washed-up and without a future, and Brood House suited. The trees scraped and soughed over the drive and in the headlights a barn owl flew away ahead of them, unhurried, lifting off from his perch on one of the stone globes that topped the gateway pillars. No acolyte nipped from the derelict lodge

11

to open the gates, for the gates had long gone. Gin had picked up a horse two days ago in a yard where the gates opened and shut electronically; he had been much impressed, and thought of them as he made the last awkward swing between the pillars. A driver from Brood House deserved danger money, he reckoned, but paradoxically they mostly got paid below par. Rosy was zipping up her jacket, shaking off the lethargy induced by the thick heat in the cab. A horse whinnied and Roly, recognizing home, whinnied back from the box.

'Silly old devil!' Rosy climbed into him, going to his head. 'You clever old stupid old horse, you. Come home a winner, have you, and about time too, you silly old beast, you gorgeous brute, you.' She gentled him with mindless words while Gin let down the ramp and opened the doors. Roly was always keen to get out when the engine died, anxious about where he was. 'I love you, Roly, you're wonderful. OK, I'm ready!' She raised her voice for Gin to hear.

The horse thumped down the ramp, whinnying some more. His row echoed round the walls, to send roosting pigeons crashing out of the nearest trees. He made for his box, ducking his head, and Gin dragged the door open while Rosy held him up. The straw was deep laid, haynet full.

Everyone had gone home. There was a light on in the house and Jeremy's car was parked outside the front door but he did not come out.

'Moody bastard,' Gin said to himself, crossing to the feedshed to fetch Roly's supper. Why did he stay to work for a moody bastard like that, he asked himself? He had the experience now to get a decent job, no ties at home, no wife and kids to move. What held him was the place, because he had never gone away; it was his anchor, his roots—his undoing. He had no stomach for pastures new, for people he had not known since he was born. He had no adventure in his soul. He was twenty-eight now. Life was passing him by.

'You needn't wait for me,' Rosy said when he went back with the feed.

'I don't mind.'

'No. I shan't hurry. I want to see him settle.'

'Okay, if you say so.'

He knew what was in her mind, why she wanted him to go, but he gave her no sign. She knew that he knew. They could hide very little from each other.

'It's not every day we get a winner.'

Stirred up by the excitements of the day, Rosy—unlike Roly Fox—had no inclination to settle down to supper and bed. The adrenalin lingered; a restlessness more common to adolescence than to the advanced adulthood she now considered herself in invaded her system. She leaned over Roly's half-door pretending that his win was a prelude to great improvements to the stable's fortunes—it happened that way, there was no denying it. Winning stables came and went for no obvious reason; their turn was surely due, overdue. Racing people lived on dreams, from the small breeder to the meanest punter. Every year the dreams came true for somebody, to encourage others to believe that next year it might be their turn. Winning was not the prerogative of the rich; the Queen had not yet bred a Derby winner, yet a Derby winner had been produced by a doctor who kept two mares for a hobby. Hope sprang eternal ... Rosy saw herself leading Roly in at Cheltenham, making him stand for the photographers. She would receive a couple of thousand from the grateful owners and buy herself a car...

Rosy, who never had enough for a new pair of jods, let alone a car, could weave dreams at the drop of a hat. Life was full of opportunities, she was convinced, if the cards were played right. The fact that in twenty-eight years not much had gone right for her was by the way. She was a born optimist.

Optimism kept her longer than was necessary. Did Jeremy have such trust in her that he did not come, or was he waiting till she went, to avoid her? She could see the light in his kitchen from where she stood. She leant on the door, smelling the cold air that came over the top of the downs with its scent of trodden grass and earth and winter dew. Brood House was cold as a tomb. The stables were warmer, with the hot blood of the racehorses in their tattered rugs leavening the draughts, the thick straw snug and the ancient stove in the tack-room ticking over through the night. Rosy did not answer her own question; she did not want to know that Jeremy avoided her when there was no one else around, although the answer was perfectly obvious. Jeremy avoided women full stop. While it was so, Rosy had no incentive to regret, for she knew she was closer to him than any other female, seeing him every day, even on Sundays. One could scarcely ask for more by Rosy's reckoning. She knew, quite frankly, that she was not in Jeremy's class, but while he insisted on leading his lonely, cheerless life she could dream of becoming his comforter, one day. Another dream. Rosy, as well as being an optimist and a romantic, was a realist, and could scorn her own dreams even while she was dreaming. Basically, if one thought nothing would ever change, that their horses would never come good, that one was going to go through life without ever meeting a congenial partner, that—at age sixty—she would still be earning her pittance for the same hard and unrelenting labour, life would hold very little appeal. Just as well I have a few incentives, she thought, translating dreams into something altogether more prosaic.

'I can't wait for ever, Roly, can I? He'll come and see you when I've gone and tell you what a grand fellow you are. Quite right too. You are a grand fellow.'

She gave him a kiss, a last feel under his rug to make sure he was dry, and went out into the yard. Her bike was in the hayshed, the old stone barn that had once been a threshing barn. Jeremy's yard, lacking all the latest gimmicks, glamour and paraphernalia of the up-to-date crack yard, looked austerely beautiful in spite of its dilapidation. In the dark the patches of corrugated iron over the roofs were hidden; only the elegant proportions were revealed against a star-spattered sky: the two rows of stables facing each other in an elongated yard inside the main gate, overhung by the vast, ancient evergreen oaks that grew in the garden beyond. The garden and the house, reached through an archway with a cracked bell-tower threatening life and limb to those who passed below, was generally out of bounds to the stable staff. Jeremy did not encourage communication. Once under the archway, his life was his own. The all-pervasive vegetation secured his privacy. A gravel frontage to the house and a modest acreage of mown lawn beyond was all that was kept clear of the rampant woods and shrubberies that had been planted in earlier times with a precision now unappreciated. 'You should have seen it in his grand-dad's day,' the old boys in the village said knowingly, and Mrs Cutbush sometimes said things unexpectedly to Rosy which gave hint of past grandeurs. Rosy looked in over the door of her other horse, a chestnut gelding called Villanelle bought with the Triumph hurdle in mind but so far having been a great disappointment; he was snatching happily at his hay and turned his head briefly. Rosy only had two to do; the boys had three each and any newcomer would come into Rosy's care. But it was over a year now since they had had a new horse.

Rosy fetched her bike, pulled on a battered balaclava and thick gloves, and wheeled it out towards the gates. Downhill all the way ... she knew each pot-hole intimately and could weave a fast and erratic course without danger. Walking up in the morning gave her time to think. Uphill and downhill—it was racing in a nutshell. Snakes and ladders. She reckoned Brood House was due for a ladder or two.

Grace said, 'That father of Rosy's—is he all there? Or a touch insane?'

'Good question,' said her father.

'Nonsense. Of course he's all there,' Mrs Maddox said sharply. 'Considering he's been a widower for the last ten years, I think he's coped very well. He's as sane as any of us round here could be said to be sane.'

15

'Nut list,' Hugh considered, 'Rosy's dad, Jeremy Cutbush. Borderline case, Colonel Maddox. Hugh Maddox going same way fast.'

'His back garden is full of weeds, all planted out in beds with labels. And his front garden is solid nettles, surrounded by a lavender hedge.'

'Wild flowers, not weeds. The nettles are for the butterflies.'

'We see him on the downs, often, on his hands and knees, gazing at the turf. Once he put a hurdle across one of the gallops, told Jeremy not to use it because an orchid was growing there.'

'What did Jeremy say?'

'We went round it.'

'Mrs Cutbush is senile.'

'Only when she wants to be.'

'She is so independent she's offensive. But one has to admire her for it.'

'Why did you include Dad on your loopy list?' Grace asked her brother.

'Look at him.'

Colonel Maddox was sitting on the back of the sofa, eating his dinner out of the roll-top desk. He wore brown dungarees and a polo-necked jersey and looked like a park attendant.

'Careful what you say, my boy.'

'You'd never think—believe—to look at you—that you liberated Caen single-handed in 1944.'

'Me and a few others.'

'When people get old, it's terribly hard to imagine how they were when they were young.'

'He was quite as nice as Hugh,' said Mrs Maddox. 'Much nicer, in fact.'

'Hugh's all right,' said his sister.

Only just, thought his mother, although she did not say it. Her two children were, so far, a disappointment: perfectly adequate, but not startling in a way, not clever or beautiful or witty or even successful. Some of her old

16

friends had amazing children—flawless young gods making fortunes in the City or girls of such appeal that eyes turned wherever they went. Or so it seemed to the jaded mother of Hugh and Grace. On the other hand they hadn't made off with the family silver or stuck themselves with heroin; one had to be grateful for the minor mercies. They came home a lot. Hugh, damn it, would not leave. Working at Brood House across the valley, a job he had fallen into by chance after being sent down from his minor university, seemed to content him. At thirty he was already thickening round the waist and thinning on top. At thirty her Hugh— old Hugh, as they called him—had been slender and slippy and constantly on the go, always game for the next lark, or war, or 'bloody excitement' as he termed it. Of course he had mellowed, but not to the extent the children implied. Children . . . he said she should not call them children any more, but there was no word for one's grown-up children. How dreary, that one's children should be nearly thirty. The cold springs got her down these days; she would feel better when the sun started to shine and they could eat properly in the dining-room. The little room was all right when there had just been the two of them, but now Hugh and Grace were both home it was grossly overcrowded.

'Do you remember Mrs Cutbush young?' Grace asked her.

'She was about forty when the war ended. I saw her a few times up at Brood House. She was very beautiful and very fierce. I was invited there once, so they could have a good look at me. There's a painting of her by Munnings in the hall, done when she was about twenty, on a horse— fabulous! I wonder if it's still there?'

'Jeremy would have sold it by now, if he's so hard up. It would be worth a bit by now.'

'Oh, no! Surely not! Sell his grandmother—'

'He would, you know.'

'No,' said Hugh. 'He's a mean bastard but he wouldn't do that. He's got a thing about his roots, the house and that. He'd have gone long ago, if not.'

'D'you think? He hasn't got much of a thing about his grandmother. He hardly ever sees her. It's very naughty of him.'

'Do you wonder? She's such an old harpy.'

'Well, you'd think it would be policy. She must have quite a pile to leave.'

'Oh, Grace, how cold-blooded you are!'

'Moth*er*, don't be so old-fashioned! That's probably why Rosy butters her up, and Gin. So she leaves them something.'

'That's very unkind.'

'Why else then?'

'I think, with Rosy, it's Mrs Cutbush's old mare, out in the field,' Hugh said. 'She's frightened the old girl forgets to feed her. What with Jeremy's roots and old Weeks's weeds, Rosy's thing is clapped-out racehorses.'

'Whatever do you mean?'

'She gets very neurotic about dud horses being sent to the sales—you know, when their legs have gone or they're just too damned slow. When they've tried their best, she says, and nobody wants them.'

'People like me buy them, to hunt,' pointed out the Colonel. 'What's wrong with that?'

'That's what I tell her. And she says darkly, "If they're lucky."'

'She's right, of course. But people get thrown on the scrap-heap too. That's life, as they say. Look at me, thrown out of the army in my prime. How about that?'

'Come off it, Dad. You weren't exactly left to starve.'

'That's true. There's a lot on the scrap-heap before they've left school these days. National Service would be no bad—'

'Land of hope and glory—' Grace started to sing loudly.

Maddox turned back to his dinner. His wife shivered at her daughter's crudeness. Not only were her children boring and without ambition, but quite often she did not even like them. Presumably the fault must lie with herself

18

somewhere, for she—and those expensive schools—had brought them up. She too, she accepted, could well be boring and without ambition, but she thought she was nicer with it.

'Have you finished?' She started to gather up the plates.

'Is there pudding?'

'Apple crumble.'

One would have thought, somehow, that they would have grown out of being excited about pudding by their late twenties. They had dreadfully infantile ways about them. For all they deplored Jeremy's unsocial habits, one could not imagine Jeremy being crass and insensitive in the way that they were. Did one have to suffer as badly as Jeremy to grow up with understanding and grace? No, Margaret decided, one didn't. Even village Rosy had more consideration than Grace. Margaret, going out to the freezing kitchen, decided her dark thoughts were part of her menopause. One blamed all depression on the female phenomenon; it became a habit and when one was out of it would the habit—of using the menopause as an excuse—stick? Would one really grow happy and optimistic after the hot flushes had died down? Perhaps one would merely drift out of it and never notice the difference. As one had drifted in, not realizing until a few years of it that one's nature had somehow changed.

The phone rang in the hall. She answered it.

'Is Hugh there?'

'It's Jeremy, isn't it? Wait a moment, I'll call him.'

She did so. Hugh came, startled. Communication from Jeremy was rare. Margaret dished up the apple crumble, listening to the one-sided conversation.

'Yes, all right. Who is he? A sheikh?... a Yorkshire-man? Oh, bad luck. You think she'll sell him?... if the money's right—some of these blokes certainly throw it around. Time some came our way ... OK, best bib and tucker. I'll be up early.'

'What's all that about?'

'Some tycoon chappie saw Roly Fox win today, wants a

19

racehorse or two. He's calling tomorrow. We've all got to pull our fingers out.'

'Good heavens!'

'Is there cream or custard?'

'Custard.'

'Good oh.'

Margaret thought, for an example of pure, honest lack of interest in one's career, Hugh's attitude was outstanding.

'Not tinned. I made it,' she said.

'Oh. Well, never mind. Good oh just the same.'

When Rosy got home she realized she had been so wrapped up with Roly's winning that she had forgotten to look in on Mrs Cutbush's mare.

'Oh, damn!' She hesitated in the kitchen door, in the middle of pulling off her jacket and scarf. The kitchen was warm and her dinner was waiting in the oven, and she was tired, cold and hungry. She groaned. Her father was in the front room watching television. She looked in the oven. A dish of some thick brown rice and wind-inducing white beans steamed gently, not a sight to arouse great enthusiasm. Her father was into vegetable living and was not an inspired cook, although well-meaning. Rosy always had a good appetite, but was used to a sad sinking of the spirits when sitting down to his cooking. Sometimes she went home with Gin and sat down to his mother's fantastic steak and kidney pudding or roast pork for a treat; they laughed at her predicament, but not unkindly. Her father was well liked, although considered potty. The slightly repellent dish in the oven prompted her to button up her jacket and wind her scarf back on. She put her head round the living-room door.

'Hi, I'm back. Just going to feed the old mare—I forgot. Roly won today. Did you see it?'

'Won, did he? Good for you. I've left your dinner.'

'I'll be back in five minutes.'

She fetched her bike out of the shed and cycled back down the road the hundred yards or so to Mrs Cutbush's

20

cottage. The cottage had a large garden round it and stood well back from the road. There was no need to disturb the old woman, just go in at the field gate beyond and walk up to the barn. Rosy climbed the gate, trying to skirt the mud, but the mare liked to stand by the road and the ground was churned up. Why on earth did she bother about the old nag? She wondered at times like this—interfering, Gin said, thinking no one could look after a horse like she could, thinking every horse that wasn't in her care was deprived. To prove him right she found the old mare happily munching at a large bundle of hay thrown down for her already by her owner. She hadn't forgotten. The horse had her ragged tail to the night. A thin moon shone in and cast cruel shadows along her rib cage and down her shoulders, delineating the fine bone-structure that had contributed to her past glory. Not for her a tin-pot novice chase at Wincanton; she had stood in winning enclosures at Royal Ascot and Epsom, at York and Goodwood and Newmarket, and had her photo taken against the potted hydrangeas to appear in the *Tatler*. Pure white in her old age, she had once been the unusual splashed grey of her great-great-great grandfather The Tetrarch, which is why Mrs Cutbush had kept her, past associations—her father's admiration of the unique flying colt of 1913—meaning more to her as she lost her standing in the racing world after her husband's death. The mare was called Silverfish; her grand-dam was Herringbone, a great winner in 1940, and Herringbone's sire had been King Salmon, second in Hyperion's Derby. For all her failing memory, Mrs Cutbush could remember the names and dates and relationships of all the great horses of the past and Rosy's fascination for horse history had forged the initial link between the two of them. Silverfish had bred six winning foals, but now Mrs Cutbush could no longer be bothered to send her away to a stallion. 'Bring one here, to the door, and we'll breed another,' she said to Rosy.

'They don't do that any more,' Rosy told her. 'It's the mares that have to travel now.'

21

'Stupid. I can't be bothered.'

The last twice she had been sent to a stallion Silverfish had not conceived. She was twenty, after all. But the potential in that gaunt frame never failed to stir Rosy, especially since Mrs Cutbush had said, once, 'You can get her served, if you're so keen. I've done with all that. But if you want to, you do it.' But the stud fees were beyond Rosy's pocket. She had discussed it with Gin, but he had no spare cash either. They had tried a few bets—certain winners—to go towards a stallion fund, but the certain winners had failed to win.

'What would you do with it, anyway? It'd cost you,' Gin said.

'We could train it here, give Jeremy a half-share.'

'You must be joking!'

'Well—' The practicalities were dismissed. Rosy thought that side of it would solve itself. She would be able to find enough money to feed the beast, certainly not to train it. She did not look that far ahead.

'When you think,' she had said to Gin, 'of all the useless mares that go to the good stallions, just because their owners have the money, it makes you weep to see her wasted.'

It had often occurred to her that, for all its outward show of big business and expertise, there was a terribly haphazard side to the production and racing of horses. Perhaps that was part of its fascination: for all the big names that did it scientifically, there were still people like herself, given the chance and the luck that everyone in racing needed, big or small, who had it in their power to produce a winner. Looking at Silverfish in the cold moonlight, she saw the opportunity within her grasp, yet she could not take advantage of it. She had the will, the knowledge, the devotion . . . but not the money. In a week or two, with the coming of the spring sunshine, the mare would come in season: the moment would be ripe. The opportunity would then pass, and she would be no further forward, only frustrated afresh. She loved the mare for all she represented, and laid her arms over the knobby spinal ridge, stroking her muddy coat, and could easily have wept with self-pity.

Gin said she was daft. He laughed at her. But kindly. He understood.

Silverfish turned her head and butted her affectionately, still eating. 'Wasting my time, you idiot mare!'

Rosy squelched back down the field, sniffing the cold air, damping her wild aspirations with the thought of the supper that waited in the oven. It was time she grew up and recognized her dreams for the rubbish they were. She had had these feelings as a child: a vision of some magic, paradisical world spread out in some heaven on earth for all to enjoy if they could find the key to enter it. 'Wanting' her mother had called it, simply, understanding her. In a girl it was acceptable, but in a grown woman it was in danger of becoming ridiculous. During the long journeys in the horse-box with Gin she sometimes talked about—or round— her muddled aspirations, knowing that Gin too, for all his phlegmatic exterior, was aware of missing out somewhere. In their not very articulate speculations on the nature of their daily round, they both appreciated more than was said. Rosy was afraid that Gin was beginning to think that his frustrations could be cured by marriage to Beryl, but she knew he was kidding himself. She could say nothing. Whoever he married, she was and always would be the closest friend he would ever have. There was too much history to change that. She just wished Beryl was more worthy.

She got on her bike and free-wheeled back to her house, one of the six council houses that stood in an ugly row beside the road. They were the only modern houses in the village: the rest were old and picturesque and lived in mostly by well-heeled 'incomers', only a few by the native elderly, like Mrs Cutbush. Mrs Cutbush was something of a legend, sitting uneasily on the village conscience, for she was downright rude, and ungrateful for any offers of help, yet was over eighty and had, like her horse, a glamorous past much bound up with the village history. Her strong personality made itself felt even now, for all she was little seen away from her house. Her garden flaunted her spirit, sloping conspicuously up from the lane to the cottage, an eye-catching tangle of bright flowers and strong, regimented vegetables amongst which her frail figure could sometimes be seen stooping, grunting and muttering, acknowledging no one. Rosy, interfering when the mare had got too thin for her to bear, had been accepted, bringing down ten bales of Jeremy's good hay in the lorry which had been received with a grace not accorded to the lady from meals on wheels. Rosy reckoned that Mrs Cutbush had once lived in the paradise she herself aspired to, but her old age was far from gracious.

Rosy, after the excitements of the day, was reluctant to finish it, to go in to the claustrophobic presence of her father and sit down to her brown rice. She put her bike away and stood in the garden, looking up at the dark ridge of the down that encircled the village and the luminous sky above it, too misty for stars and yet seeming to quiver with light. There was a moon somewhere, and the damp in the air was not harsh, but smelled of spring. Instinctively her eyes went to Brood House, swamped by the inky dark of the Victorian plantings, but—in winter—showing an end gable between bare branches, and the line of the wall. Occasionally a light gleamed from a window, and late in the evening a faint glow from the yard light showed when Jeremy was doing his last stable round, but tonight there was no indication of life. Once, old people in the village said, the sound of Brood House parties kept them awake at nights; there had been a dance band on the lawn and smart open cars tearing through the lanes full of the Cutbush set. Now there was always silence, except for the screech of the owls that nested in the rotting barns.

'Why?' Rosy wondered. Her father said, 'People make the wrong decisions.' She could see that. She had made the wrong decision, coming back; Jeremy had, for not going away. If he went, she too would be released.

There was no wind. She felt she was surrounded by the

bright stillness of death. Far away, on the main road, a motor-bike engine roared away into the night, receding—someone going somewhere. Fortunate man. She waited until the sound had gone, and waited some more, hoping to be visited by a revelation that would prove a key to paradise.

No such luck. She put the bike back in the shed and went in for her supper.

2

The following morning a Rolls came up the drive to Brood House and parked outside the front door. So it was true. They smirked at each other, unable to face the prospect with the cool nonchalance they would have preferred. The rawness of dawn had given way to a mild, sunshot morning. The thrushes sang over the wall and Rosy felt optimism lurking. She put Villanelle away and got to work on grooming Roly, to show him at his best. He was not, after all, a fantastic-looking beast, but workaday, powerful more than beautiful, and slightly old-fashioned looking: head large and eyes honest, nose a touch Roman. He did not know how to do less than his best, and worried if he thought he had failed. The race seemed to have taken nothing out of him. He looked as well as Rosy had ever seen him. Whether being sold to the newcomer or not would be to his advantage or not they none of them could know.

'He might buy you a smart rug, at least,' Rosy said to him encouragingly. A new bridle would not come amiss.

She was good at grooming, throwing all her beef into each brush-stroke to see the gloss on the light bay coat improve. The hard muscle flexed to her vigour, the horse standing quietly. Roly's nature was pathetically ingratiating. He had no will of his own, only wanting everyone to be pleased. He hadn't the flame of the great racehorse, but equally he had no guile, no nasty tricks.

'You're a great fellow, Roly,' Rosy assured him.

'Action stations,' Gin said, looking over the half-door. 'Our rich friend in view now, coming your way.'

Hugh, self-important, with a better shave than usual, hurried across the yard to take orders. Rosy looked out, pretending she wanted to see the new owner, knowing she wanted to see Jeremy. They were a contrasting pair: Jeremy's slight figure in the battered waxed jacket and well-worn cap dwarfed by the newcomer, a massive, ponderous man dressed in fine tweeds, with a naturally suspicious and scowling expression on his fleshy face, eyes very sharp and small and overwhelmed by their surroundings. Sparse hair was arranged tactfully and gripped down over the scalp. He did not smile when he was introduced, nor hold out a hand. A curt nod.

'Rosy, this is John Hawkins. He has come to see Roly Fox. Lead him out, will you?'

Jeremy, Rosy would have said, was on the verge of feeling happy, a rare condition. His pale and interesting—to Rosy, fascinating—face was a shade less drawn than usual, the eyes a hint livelier, more green than grey, with a touch of the old spirit that had once proclaimed him invincible. ('Cocksure bastard,' Gin had called him in those days, when Rosy had cut out his photo and pasted it on her bedroom mirror ... 'The cocksure bastard'll come a cropper, you wait.' So long ago, it seemed, that Rosy could scarcely remember; she had been a child in love. Now, the state apparently a permanency, she was as washed-up as he was but without his excuse. If she had taken herself seriously she could not have carried on.)

She went in to Roly Fox and untied him and led him out. She chucked him under the chin and got his legs square, and he got the message and held up his head and gazed nobly all round him, selling himself, the silly beast ... Rosy had a dreadful feeling that he would be much safer with Mrs Palmer than with Mr Hawkins who wanted to get his name in the papers.

'He likes the ground soft. We can't run him on hard going,' Jeremy was saying. 'He's had a spot of leg trouble in the past, but he's fine now, as long as he's treated right.'

'It's more often soft than hard in the winter, surely?'

27

'There are no rules. It's soft now but at this time of year it can dry out very fast. Then we'd run the ones that like it that way, give this one a rest.'

'But he's entered for some more races soon?'

'Yes, he is.'

A faint sun shone on Roly's bright frame, bringing up the shining muscle that Rosy had nurtured to the detriment of her own femininity: her muscles were as large and impressive as his. The dust she had brushed from his coat furred her own fine skin and eternally gritty hair. How could Jeremy be expected to notice her desirability, destroyed as it was by the work she did for him? She joined the men in regarding her horse as he stood out obediently, a touch anxious. His big rabbity ears flexed hopefully to catch the admiration in the voices of the spectators.

'He's very much the type I like. Stands over a lot of ground.'

Rosy suspected Mr Hawkins had picked up the phrases without knowing what they meant. Roly made an affectionate lunge towards his outstretched hand and landed some specks of slobber on the fine surface of the Yorkshire tweed. Hawkins withdrew a fraction.

'Walk him out,' Jeremy said. 'He's a nice mover.'

'I'm a nice mover too, Roly,' Rosy whispered as they went away down the yard. Had Jeremy noticed? Her quarters were as shapely, her fetlocks as springy.

'Thank you,' Jeremy said.

Big deal. At least, unlike some trainers, he was civil to his lads.

She put Roly away and saddled him ready to exercise, put his rug on and tied him up. Mr Hawkins looked at all the other horses and Rosy joined Gin in the tack-room. Hugh put his head round the door.

'The guv'nor's taking that guy up in the Landrover. Wants the second string got ready, and Roly Fox is to go too, Rosy, to do a canter. Looks like we've got an interested customer.'

There was no time for speculation; they got the horses

out and rode straight up on to the downs by the track that led out of the back of the stable-yard. Roly was as fresh as if he hadn't raced for weeks, and in the sharp canter over the crest of the hill before the watchers in the Landrover Rosy felt his eager spirit imbuing her with an optimism which, this time, she felt had its roots in something more substantial than her own natural whim. Roly pulled harder than usual and Rosy, perched above that smooth machinery with the wind of their passage making her eyes smart, looked to the gauzy sky ahead where some rooks were tumbling like wind-blown rags over the horizon and felt her spirits soaring in unison.

'Steady on, old Roly. We're not on a racecourse!'

The long ears switched back to her voice, and she laughed out loud. Roly, the way he felt, was laughing too. She took longer to pull up than usual: the feelings were too good to curtail.

When Jeremy was saying goodbye to Hawkins, standing by the open car window as Hawkins fastened his seat-belt, he felt not unhappy.

Then Hawkins said, 'You know, of course, that my own jockey rides all my horses? Young Mowbray. I don't want to change this arrangement.'

'Not if you prefer it that way. I have great faith in Dave, though. To my mind, there's none better.'

'He's too old.'

'Experienced.' Jeremy made himself smile, not to offend.

'Well, Mowbray rides all mine.'

'Will he ride work for us?'

'Yes, if I tell him.'

'Fine.'

'Cheers then.'

But it wasn't fine. Jeremy went back under the archway, silent and scowling, like the moody bastard they all said he was. He pushed open the front door and stood in the square, mosaic-tiled hall beneath the life-size picture of a young woman on a horse. Confidence and spirit radiated

29

from the portrait. The girl was slight, her bearing arrogant, her hands delicate. She had a bundle of untidy golden-red hair pinned up in ancient fashion beneath a shapeless twenties sun-hat that shaded half her face, darkened the brown, direct eyes. The face was beautiful, in sun and shadow, thin, the chin pointed and lips sensuous and curling, mocking. Her bearing was one of supreme self-confidence and pride, no sign of feminine docility, not a suggestion that she would wish to warm a husband's slippers by the fire and get his supper. The horse was as arrogant as its rider. Between them they made a dramatic impact upon the unsuspecting visitor coming in through the front door, as if the live pair were riding down the stairs en route for the downs.

'Oh, Gran,' Jeremy said out loud.

She laughed at him.

She was three minutes away by car, working in her garden. On an impulse he drove there, parked outside, and limped up the garden path. She was trying to nail a wind-blown climbing rose back on to the porch, wielding a huge hammer and a plastic bag of staples. Failing.

'Here, give it me.'

Surprised, she yielded up the hammer.

'What's brought you to see me then?'

'Sentiment.'

She didn't understand. 'Leave that. Come inside.'

'Go and make a cup of coffee. I'll do it first.'

He did not pretend that he was a devoted grandson. He was a swine to the old girl. She had all the courage that he lacked, facing crippling by age with a resolution he could not find in his own situation. She had ten times his guts. That was why he kept away, he supposed, not even having the guts to ponder on the comparison. He should have found her an inspiration, but in practical terms recognition of her qualities tended to depress him still further. But his mood today was uncertain, excited by the prospects Hawkins had expounded over the smoked salmon sandwiches, sickened by the thought of having to employ Mowbray to

30

ride. Mowbray the Boy Wonder, who had won the Gold Cup at the age of nineteen and had had much publicity proclaiming his genius.

The rose, an old-fashioned Caroline Testout which Mrs Cutbush had brought with her from Brood House, was throttled into subjection against the wooden posts of the porch and Jeremy stepped inside. It was so long since he had called that the dark, low-ceilinged room with its walls solidly packed with racing pictures and mementoes came as a shock. There had been no wall big enough for the portrait back at Brood House, but anything she had been able to fit in was there, from the little Stubbs, 'Horse and Groom in a Landscape,' to all the lesser portraits of horses her husband had trained. There was a whole wall devoted to himself, in photography (for he never sat still long enough in those days to be painted), riding winners at Cheltenham, at Newbury and Ascot and, as a boy, at point-to-points from Tweseldown to Cottenham. A morbid compulsion forced him to study them for a few moments. In all of them he looked fearless and arrogant like the rider in the portrait at home. At eighteen he had grinned at the camera, mud-splashed, victorious, obnoxiously cocky—not unlike Tony Mowbray. When his gran doddered in with the coffee cups on a tray, he tried hard to see in the stooped figure the girl in his hall, but it was as hard to reconcile the two as it was, in his mind, to recognize the young jockey in the photos as himself. The old claw-like hands, knotted with gardening, rheumatism and general wear, were the same that held those shimmering reins in his picture with such silken authority. That dirty bundle of white frizz was the same gleaming gold hair that escaped in artistic tendrils from the sun-hat. Oh, Gran! he wanted to cry out—lovely Letitia McAlister on Golden Harvest—where have you gone? And where the cocky rider of Gunshot, winner at Kempton on Boxing Day, triumphant behind a mask of mud?

Letitia McAlister had the excuse of sixty years passing; the rider of Gunshot a shattered pelvis, and disintegration thereafter. Nobody could escape the battering of age, but

31

better people than he had surmounted worse injuries than he had received and lived to be gracious, loved and successful.

'You look peaky, dear,' said his grandmother. 'Aren't you well?'

'Yes, I'm fine. How are you?'

She grunted.

But she could live on her memories, coast on past triumphs that no hardship now was going to eradicate. He was not sorry for her.

'I've got a new owner, a Yorkshireman. He's bringing me two youngsters off the flat, and he's bought Roly Fox.'

'A foreigner?' She pursed her lips. 'I don't like Jews.'

He groaned in spirit, having forgotten her eccentricities. 'A Yorkshireman is not a foreigner. Hawkins is not a Jew. Besides, Gran, Jews might not like us. What's the difference? A good guy is a good guy, whatever his breeding.'

Over her mantelpiece was a portrait of her husband, Peter Cutbush, an upstanding, clean-cut Britisher of impeccable antecedents, Winchester, Trinity and, later, the Gloucester Hussars. He had volunteered in 1940 and got killed for his impetuosity, leaving a stable-yard at Brood House with a reputation second to none. He had been a golden boy of pre-war racing. Whether his success was due purely to talent Jeremy had never been able to work out, or whether luck had been heavily on his side. Both, most likely. Jeremy thought his own talent reasonable, but luck had never smiled on him, and his temperament was hopeless. All round the cottage walls the evidence of Peter Cutbush's success was recorded, not only in pictures of his winners, but in charming snaps of him with his owners and friends. It seemed that the sun was always shining—of course, he had trained for the flat, not for jumping—and that his owners were all lovely people like himself. He and his wife had attracted owners because they themselves were lovely people to know; racing with the Cutbushes was fun and glamorous and Peter Cutbush's dedication did not affect his charm and likeability.

32

Genes being notoriously unpredictable, the Cutbush glamour had faded in the next generation. Jeremy thought his own father had perhaps been overshadowed by his parents' powerful personalities. A more stolid and altogether less showy character, he had taken on Brood House after the war at the age of twenty, taking out the licence in the name of a very efficient head lad who had nursed him through his first years. The stable had been moderately successful, but turned more and more to the jumping game, because young Cutbush liked to hunt and ride as an amateur himself. He had married an Australian girl, the daughter of an owner, and Jeremy had been their only child. Letitia Cutbush had been a terrible mother-in-law. Still living on the premises, she had tried to run the place as she was used to running it. Jeremy could remember the impressive rows during his boyhood, Letitia's powerful will smashing head-on against the growing doggedness of his father and his wife's loyalty. Between them they all taught him to ride, and fast riding had been his release, his passion. His triumph and his downfall. The photographs round the walls chronicled the life of his grandfather Peter Cutbush, and his own, and completely missed out the intervening generation. Five years ago his parents had emigrated to Australia, but he had refused to go.

'What you need,' said his grandmother, between noisy sips of her coffee, 'is a wife, to look after you.'

'Please, Gran, don't start on that.' He remembered now why he never came to see her.

'That gel—Judith Partridge ... was that her name? What became of her?'

'She went.' Hospital visiting had bored Judith. She liked her men in bed all right, but not hospital beds.

'That was a long time ago,' he said.

'Was it?' She looked surprised. She got her sequences of events much muddled these days.

'Seven—eight years ago.'

'When was your accident?'

'The same time—eight years ago.'

33

He had been twenty-two, the same age as Tony Mowbray. The thought of employing Tony Mowbray hurt dreadfully. That was the reason he had come. A back-to-the-womb instinct. Seeing Tony Mowray ride his horses was going to pull the scabs off the deepest of his wounds because—of them all—young Mowbray was everything he had once been. The Cutbush glamour had flowered again, briefly, when he had been riding and winning and everyone had wanted to know him. He had been brave and powered by an arrogant self-confidence—he could still remember the dizzy glow which illumined those days: life had been a party and he had been guest of honour. Until the day he got buried at the last of the railway fences at Sandown Park.

True courage would have seen him through all that, but true courage was not what he possessed. He had not coped. Self-knowledge was not a good thing. Seeing the photographs recalled those days with startling clarity. He assiduously avoided remembering those days normally, and had done so with considerable success, hence the shock. He got up and studied the walls again, taking the coffee cup with him. He found Judith Partridge, gazing up at him as he was led in at Newton Abbot, frankly adoring (or so it seemed), lustrous film-star eyes wide beneath a wild fur hat. She had promised to marry him. So much for promises. Painfully stirred, he moved on, and came to the Stubbs.

'This is worth a fortune, Gran. I hope you lock up well.'

'I never go out.'

'At night, I mean.'

'I've got Jasper.'

He didn't argue. 'Horse and Groom in a Landscape' was full of serenity, very beautiful. A stallion with eyes as lustrous as Judith Partridge's stood haltered by a boy in livery in a park filled with a golden autumn glow. The horse was perfectly proportioned, muscled and shining and pictured for posterity in a moment of poise, one foreleg uplifted, mane and tail stirred by an invisible breeze.

'That came from your great-grandfather's place,' Mrs

Cutbush said. 'That was his grandfather's horse. It was called Lionheart.'

Casually she quoted connection, kinship, with the great Stubbs. Did she know how valuable it was?

'I'm going to leave it to Rosy, she loves it so.'

Jeremy was deeply shocked.

'To *Rosy*?'

'Yes.'

'Have you told her?'

'I can't remember. I might have.'

Jeremy did not know what to say. He knew Rosy and Gin helped the old girl but had never suspected they were in it for money. Did not suspect it now, in fact. But the Stubbs...! It was probably worth half a million. Far more than a gift of friendship.

'It's worth an awful lot of money, Gran.'

'I'm not short, dear.'

'That's not what I meant.' But he hadn't the nerve to say what he meant. He prevaricated. 'Is it insured?'

'The contents of the house are insured.'

'Did you tell them you had a Stubbs?'

'I don't remember.'

He had a right to it. But what had he ever done to deserve it? Far less than Rosy. Or would all her estate pass to his father, her only child?

'Did you put it in your will, Gran? To leave the picture to Rosy?'

'I think I wrote a note in my desk. I know that you will see to it for me, the few little bequests. It's all quite plain.'

He did not know what to say. He did not even know if she had made a will, did not know how much she was worth anyway. He had never thought of her leaving him money, never even thought of the Stubbs until now. Money was a subject that did not interest him much—or so he had always thought, until now. But the thought of the Stubbs going to Rosy was very disturbing. It might be worth mentioning to Rogers, the family solicitor ... although what sort of a light did that put him in? Damn it, Jeremy thought, what an embarrassing situation! Just the sort he would go a long way to avoid. He knew at once that he was going to put the subject at the back of his mind, forget it; the old girl was obviously far from dropping dead, and he had Mr Hawkins to keep him occupied just now.

'Does Rosy come often?'

'Two or three times a week. She does my errands. She stays and talks.'

The visit gave him little comfort—he might have known! The thought of Rosy doing chores for the old girl, when he scarcely ever looked in, gave him a bad feeling, but he knew he wasn't going to change anything. If she got the Stubbs ... god dammit, half a million for running a few errands! Don't think about it, Jeremy said to himself, grinding up the drive to Brood House. It was as bad as having to employ Tony Mowbray.

He looked in the tack-room to give a few orders.

'We'll need two boxes got ready for the new horses. The two end ones, I suppose. They'd better be thoroughly scrubbed out and disinfected. Will you see to it, Gin?'

Gin was a good lad, entirely reliable, which was more than one could say about dreary Hugh, whom Jeremy felt himself lumbered with. Well-meaning and honest—but lazy—Hugh was thick, whereas Gin was sharp as a needle. Gin was short for Ginger. Whether because of the name or not, Jeremy always thought of him as the personification of Ginger Hebblethwaite, henchman of Captain Bigglesworth in the Biggles books which were all upstairs in his bedroom in Brood House. His father had loved Biggles, and Jeremy had read all the books during his long convalescence. Gin was Ginger Hebblethwaite matured, loyal and enthusiastic.

'When are they coming, sir?'

'Wednesday, he said.'

Without meaning to, Jeremy caught Rosy's eye, as she looked up from her tack-cleaning. She had a way of looking at him which he found slightly disturbing. Now, with the Stubbs in mind, it occurred to him that he ought to rethink Rosy; she was infringing on family, moving into another league. Up to now she had been a hard-working lass, entirely capable, not one to worry, even think, about. He had known her, as he had Gin, ever since he could remember. He could recall her following him about at the local point-to-points, as a girl of fourteen, fifteen; remembered the letter she had sent him when he was in hospital, the regret more fiercely phrased than in most, as if she had some knowledge of how it felt. Her dad, Weeks, a recently retired postman, couldn't be much of a rave to live with, his conversation rarely rising above the creeping habit of the procumbent cinquefoil. He was to be seen on the downs in his long ex-army shorts, 1940 vintage, muttering to invisible wonders in the earth or, sometimes, meeting other small, brown-skinned naturalists in unlikely places to look for gromwort and twayblade. In man's natural habitat, the pub, he was never found, although he was said to make a heady brew of parsnip wine to offer visitors. His wife, Doreen, a primary school teacher, had died of cancer. She had been taken ill when Rosy was in London at art college and Rosy had come home and helped nurse her. People had assumed that Rosy stayed after her mother's death to look after her father, but Jeremy always thought she had stayed because she had decided that country life suited her better than town life, and she had made the situation to suit her own inclinations.

Rosy was stocky and brown like her mother, with matching curly hair, cropped rather fiercely, and a strong face that could have been a boy's. The eyes that regarded Jeremy so steadily were calm and wide, not as striking as Judith Partridge's or Lionheart's, but more reassuring. They were blue-grey in colour and hard to read, Rosy being older than she looked and not given to much display of emotion, except where Roly Fox was concerned.

Feeling generous at the thought, he said to her, 'Roly ran a blinder yesterday—he seems to have got his confidence at last. All credit to you.'

She coloured slightly but said nothing. Last night, when it had mattered, he had gone indoors without a word and waited, until she had gone, to look at the horse. It was not

37

surprising he thought, that he had a reputation for being lousy to work for. It was hard to be gracious when the jealousies burned as deeply as they had yesterday, seeing Dave Perkins bring Roly flying over the last with a jump that could have cleared the Aintree Chair with still a foot to spare. Dave Perkins being as ungracious as himself, Jeremy employed him regularly for the main reason that, although extremely competent, he seemed to get very little pleasure out of his profession. Jeremy did not want euphoric jockeys. He feared that Tony Mowbray might prove a talkative brat; he was certainly young enough never to have heard of Jeremy Cutbush and his brilliance over fences before being cut off in his prime.

'You'll have to do one of them, Rosy. You can have first choice.'

She smiled, looking pleased at the prospect of more work, which none of the men would have done.

He shut the door on them and made towards the archway to the house, but Hugh was coming out of the feedshed and waylaid him.

'With the new horses coming—if you're short of anyone to ride, Grace said she'd come up. She's a pretty good rider.'

'Grace?'

'My sister. She's at home—at a loose end just now.'

'Oh—Grace—yes, sorry. Of course.'

That Grace . . . an ill-named female, by Jeremy's reckoning. 'Fine, thanks.'

He darted for home under the clock-tower, suffering suddenly from a surfeit of human intercourse. Letitia McAlister, back in her prime, watched him cross her track towards the large bleak kitchen and the remains of the smoked salmon sandwiches.

'Did you ask him?'

'Yes,' said Hugh.

'What did he say?'

'Oh, nothing much. You know him.'

'Not as much as I'd like to,' Grace said.

3

The horsebox from Newmarket made three attempts at clearing the stone pillars into the yard and decided to unload outside.

'Don't know how you do it, mate,' the driver said, noticing the resident horsebox safely parked within.

'It's knack,' Gin said carelessly, but was pleased all the same. The Newmarket box was worth about ten times as much as Jeremy's heap, which must make the driver some ten times more inhibited about grazing its sides.

Rosy, warm with Jeremy's promise that she had first choice of the newcomers, went out to help unload.

'Which is the best?' she asked the lad who was travelling with them.

'The best is Peppermill, the chestnut. The nicest is the Sagaro.'

They were a very classy pair, wrapped in dazzling rugs and thick felt bandages that seemed to be part of the deal. Installed in the newly prepared looseboxes, their handsome heads reviewed the new surroundings with the complacency of old hands, much-travelled. They were both superbly bred, out of winning mares who were by Busted and Habitat respectively. Peppermill was by Mill Reef, out of a mare called Peppercorn. They had been stayers on the flat and were now to be schooled over hurdles to see if they could make a new career for themselves.

'They're to learn how to jump hurdles, then they're to be cut and turned out for the summer,' Hugh said pompously.

It wasn't until Rosy was riding out for the first time on

Peppermill the next morning that the revelation came to her. Hugh had said take them through the village on the lanes first and do the long hack home over the downs, and Rosy was just beginning to get the feel of the skittery Peppermill—like a pony after Roly—when they came to the gate of Mrs Cutbush's field. Silverfish was at the top of the field and heard them coming. Rosy saw her lift her head and stare and, for a moment, look like her photograph in the *Tatler*: the shapely ears pricked up tight, nostrils dilated. Then she gave a plunge and a buck and came down the hill, with the beautiful flowing stride that had once seen her triumphantly round Tattenham Corner, pulling up at the gate at the moment Peppermill was passing.

Peppermill let out a deep-throated whinny and swung round, almost catching Rosy unawares. Silverfish answered him and presented her elegant posterior, winking furiously.

Rosy snatched up Peppermill and drove him on desperately with her heels and Gin, laughing, circled his horse and came up on her inside, driving the colt away from the mare. Silverfish let out a piercing whinny behind them.

'Get on, you brute!'

They trotted to get out of the danger area, and the boys behind laughed and jeered.

'Who said the old girl was past it!' Gin said. 'Love at first sight—at her age!'

'God, Gin—if only they could! Think of it!'

'No, I won't. And don't you either.'

'Hark at her!'

Rosy had never seen old Silverfish so steamed up, crying after them as they trotted down the village street. She felt a surge of frustration as strong as the mare's, that there was no way of getting her in foal. And yet she was astride a stallion as well-bred as any in the book . . .

'Christ, Gin, this boy—'

'You're mad!'

He was grinning as he rode beside her. They turned off on to the track up to the downs, and Peppermill started to pull, feeling the grass beneath his feet. Rosy tried to relax him, not wanting to get carted on her first ride. He felt like a time-bomb after Roly, bottled up and bursting. The lane curved uphill, steeply enough to make the colt settle, surprised at the hard work. Newmarket had nothing so steep. On the left they passed the lovely Georgian house belonging to Hugh's family, set in an old-fashioned, beautifully kept garden that his parents spent all their time in during the summer. Grace was going out for the newspapers and watched them closely as they passed.

'She's asked if she can ride out,' Gin said to Rosy.

'Whatever for? She's got her dad's hunter if she wants to ride.'

'She's after the guv'nor. Like you, Rosy.'

'You're joking!'

'Bet I'm not. Why else?'

The news disturbed Rosy, for Grace had a formidable will. She seemed to get what she wanted, and had never been short of men-friends in spite of her aggressive manner. Rosy had never thought her attractive, but perhaps her view was not shared. She had sharp features of classic proportion and her colouring was true blonde and rose, with sky-blue eyes. Hugh was a faded, fattened version of the same. Rosy liked neither of them particularly, but liked both their parents, sensible kind Margaret and her cheerful sporty old colonel husband.

'She's not what he needs, I'm sure.'

Sour grapes perhaps. Her aggressive drive might be the very thing Jeremy needed.

Rosy put the idea away, unable to contemplate the idea of Jeremy falling for Grace. He'd have more sense ... but the chemistry of love was a funny business. Silverfish now ... that was something to think about. If the old mare was in season so strongly, surely she would 'take' if she were given a chance? Astride the colt, the crazy idea took hold. Once on the downs and smelling the softness of spring in the breeze, feeling the power of the little colt as he strode out beneath her, nothing seemed impossible. These were

41

the moments that held her to this daft job: that one could do this and get paid for it! There were days when nothing went right—but enough like this, when the blood cart-wheeled in the veins, to put the drudgery into perspective. And the ambition flared: by God, but the little fellow had a stride and a spirit. He was passing Gin on old Drogo as if Drogo were pulling a cart, and Hugh was shouting at her from the Landrover where they met the track, but she knew he hadn't got away from her, and she was laughing as she pulled up. Hugh was swearing at her. But Peppermill dropped his nose and came back to her like a lamb and she had a feeling that she understood his ways already. She knew she had good hands; she knew that Jeremy knew too. But Hugh didn't know good from bad and only held the job because Jeremy hadn't the guts to sack him. Jeremy no longer wanted to collide with people. Once he had ridden them into the ground and not even noticed.

The idea, once seeded, would not leave Rosy.

Peppermill was a good sort, fitting mate for Silverfish. He was not big and rangy like Roly, but built very correctly, neat and powerful in a different sort of way, full of class. He was a very dark chestnut with no white on him save for a small star, a bit fierce in the stable, especially at feeding time, but nothing that Rosy couldn't handle.

'He's to be let down,' Hugh said, measuring his oat ration. 'Get the condition off him, then he can be gelded.'

'How long will that take?'

'About a month, probably.'

A month—no time at all!

'Just what are you proposing, for goodness' sake?' Gin asked, exasperated. 'Who is going to agree to it? The colt belongs to Hawkins, for God's sake. He's not standing him at stud.'

'All that lovely sperm going to waste! Another month—he gets the chop—it's enough to make anyone weep.'

'I can't see Jeremy asking old Hawkins on your behalf.'

'I wasn't thinking of asking anybody.'

'No?'

They were in Gin's kitchen, sitting at the kitchen table over cups of coffee. His parents were watching television in the front room and the kitchen was still full of the lovely lingering aromas of supper, fried bacon and onions and chops and apple pie. Rosy had just come from her father's speciality: curried eggs with bolognese sauce, and was grateful for the coffee to soothe her offended palate.

'There's still such a thing as nature. Silverfish thinks he's wonderful—you've only got to give them a chance! She'll come in season again in two weeks—take him down then and let them get on with it!'

'During morning exercise?' Gin's voice was sarcastic.

'There's afternoons when Jeremy and Hugh are away racing—there's no one about at all. No one need ever know. She's not a maiden, for heaven's sake—she knows how to behave. She never kicks. There's no risk at all.'

'Not much!'

Gin stared into his coffee. During the ensuing silence Rosy knew that he was impressed with her thinking.

'Mrs Cutbush told me—I could have the foal—own it—don't you remember? If I got the mare served. Any foal of Silverfish's is worth a lot of money.'

'But you couldn't register it—who would give you a covering certificate? You couldn't send it up to Weatherby's, as by Peppermill. What good is it without papers? Who would you say the sire was? Unless you can work that one out, the foal couldn't ever see a racecourse. It'd be worthless.'

'Oh, there must be a way round that. I'm sure we can think of one.'

Her airy dismissal of what Gin saw as an insoluble difficulty annoyed him.

'It's time you grew up! I'm not having a hand in such a crazy idea, and you wouldn't be able to do it by yourself.'

'It would be half yours, if you helped.'

Rosy was grinning. She did not really believe in the idea herself. 'We'd be pretty lucky,' she conceded, 'to get everything right—Silverfish in season and the chance to get Peppermill to her without anyone seeing. She might not come in season again before Peppermill gets cut.'

Gin looked relieved. 'You are a nut. Only you would get a notion like that into your head.'

'It's not so stupid—not if you could work out how to get it registered.'

'You'd have to find the right stallion owner and a crook vet—who'd sign the papers for you.'

'You know plenty of crooks,' Rosy said. 'I'd leave that bit to you.'

Gin, so derisive at first, saw possibilities in the idea, in spite of what he said. Rosy, carried away with it when it had first struck her, saw all the drawbacks on further reflection.

Rosy got up and made herself another coffee at the stove. She was always tired in the evenings, and it took more than two cups of coffee to keep her awake.

'It might be a daft idea, but no dafter than all that factory production in the States, and the prices they fetch at Keeneland. Bring 'em over here and three-quarters of the million-dollar touches never win a race. Ninety per cent of anything bred is duff. We stand as much chance as any of 'em.'

'There's supposed to be a science to it.'

'You could fool me.'

Rosy switched the kettle off and reached for the instant. 'Thing is, if the chance presents itself . . . you know, it's like an offer, from God. It's meant.'

'You're such a romantic!'

Rosy laughed.

She was in no hurry to go, at home in Gin's house more than in her own. It was a haphazard family—'feckless' her father said. Gin's father was some sort of a dealer in scrap and cars, but not the sort Rosy would wish to buy a car from. Sometimes he had a large roll of notes in his pocket; other times they had to buy on credit. Gin was considered the steady one of the family. There were several brothers

44

and sisters, all married but Gin. They came and went with many children that all looked the same to Rosy—and to Gin, she suspected, for he avoided calling them by name. They were all on at him to get married, and often told him to marry Rosy, in her presence. Laughs all round. 'She's been one of the family for years,' they said cheerfully. It was true that, right from being small, she had spent as much time in Gin's house as her own. The confusion, the crowd and the cooking had always attracted her, an only child from a quiet, tidy home.

'How's Beryl?' she asked.

Gin followed her train of thought. If romance came easily to Rosy, with her patient, useless infatuation for Jeremy Cutbush, it was an altogether different matter for him, more used to persuading horses than girls. He dreaded both the intimacy and the responsibility of marriage; he liked living at home, and having occasional sex when he required it with one of the local girls who supplied it for mutual pleasure, no strings. He did not know how to court and woo and did not particularly want to learn, but his family were increasingly nagging him to leave the nest. Beryl was the only girl who seemed likely to have him, the way he saw it. Whether he wanted her or not he never could decide. At least she knew racing, so she'd know what to expect, but going home to her every night ... the thought did not uplift him. But his mum and dad kept on at him. Nobody in their family had been unmarried at twenty-three, let alone twenty-eight. He'd have to get to know Beryl better.

He shrugged to Rosy's inquiry, and she laughed.

'You're terribly *slow*. Your ma told me she's going to kick you out if you've not got round to it by next Christmas.'

'I'm taking Hallmark to Newbury tomorrow. Beryl will probably be there. I'll try and make a date—borrow Dad's car.'

'That's a boy!'

'It's a pity...' He hesitated, considered, 'that you and

me, we know each other too well. But if we'd got married when we were kids—twentyish or so, it might have worked.'

'I doubt it.' Rosy did not encourage the thought. There would be time for regrets when she was fifty, not yet.

When she went home, two houses away, she looked up the hill and saw the light shining through the trees. She glanced at her watch. It was ten, the time Jeremy did his round. The old lad, Albert, who lived in what had once been the gamekeeper's cottage just outside the yard, told her the guv'nor never missed and was punctual to the minute. He went in each box and stayed a while, looking and talking. Rosy wished she were Roly Fox with that to look forward to every night. She reckoned Jeremy was a good trainer, but he did not attract new owners with his introverted disposition; he did not go looking for them, and they were a rare breed in any case, requiring to be sought out and tempted and offered delectable horses. Jeremy never bought horses as other trainers did; he just trained the ones he had, which were nearly all owned by elderly people who had had horses with his father or even his grandfather. He did not deserve any better, the way he was. Hawkins was the first new owner she could remember. It was something of a wonder that Jeremy had taken him on, not sent him away with a flea in his ear. It was as if he desired obscurity, to do no more than tick over, the years spinning by. What a waste it all was! His old gran at eighty had more resolution than Jeremy. Rosy would have despised him if she did not remember his glorious youth, the fire and the courage he had shown before his accident. Sometimes Rosy feared that her love for him was maternal. Certainly it was ridiculous.

The next day Grace came to ride out. Hugh gave her the Sagaro colt, who was quiet and kind and called, perversely, Needles. Grace was made-up as if she were going hunting and wore white breeches and boots and a black velvet riding hat. Gin insisted that she wore a crash-helmet, which annoyed her. Hugh should have insisted, but took no notice, and Gin was angry at having to ask her, and have her reply to him in a curt, patronizing way. Rosy watched, interested. There could only be one reason for her wanting to ride work; she was not known to have a passion for horses, only men. When Jeremy came out to see them mounted he merely nodded to her, not even a smile; he was his usual dour self.

Grace rode well, better than Hugh, who always rode the hack, Brown Ale. Brown Ale had been Jeremy's own brilliant point-to-pointer, had never fallen in his life. The two lads, Simon and Trev, were embarrassed by Grace and steered well clear, not knowing whether she was in the same pecking order as themselves or, being Hugh's sister, some one to be kow-towed to. Rosy found Grace settling in beside her mount, Villanelle, as they climbed the wide track through the Brood House forest up towards the bare crest of the downs above.

'What does he do?' Grace asked her, nodding at Villanelle, 'Not much by the look of him.'

A true estimation, it offended Rosy deeply.

'He's a novice hurdler. He's done nothing wrong so far.'

Not much right either, but criticism of her charge made Rosy defend his unprepossessing looks. He tried; he was well-disposed—just not fast enough, like all horses that failed to make the frame. Jeremy came up behind them in the Landrover and they made room for him to pass.

'Does he never ride now?' Grace asked.

'No. He can't.'

'I don't see why not, if there was some one to encourage him—to motivate him—'

'He couldn't race, so there's no point, is there? He never rode for the sake of it, even before.'

Rosy saw at once how easily she could be trapped into revealing her feelings. If she rose to defending Villanelle, how difficult not to rise to the bait concerning Jeremy. Was Grace doing it on purpose, suggesting he only needed motivating? By the love of a good woman, presumably. Thinking she could see the suggestion of a smile on Grace's face, she fumed.

'Do you do much for Mrs Cutbush?'

The new tack was confusing.

'Just a bit of shopping. I look in, see to the mare. She's only across the road.'

'Did Jeremy ask you to?'

'No! Why should he?'

'He hardly ever goes himself. It seems strange—that he doesn't trouble. She could go back there, to Brood House, now the rest of the family has gone, you'd think. She's really too old to live on her own now, by the look of her.'

'She's very independent. She'd drive him mad.'

'You'd think Jeremy would go out to Australia to join his parents. Hugh says they're doing very well out there and love it. They want him to go out. Perhaps as soon as she dies, he will.'

Rosy felt she could well do without Grace's conjectures, and her probing. Everything she said Rosy found disturbing, slanted in some way.

'Unless he marries, of course.'

Rosy stuck her heels into Villanelle and trotted on, passing the boys. If Jeremy married Grace, it would be she—Rosy—who would be doing the emigrating.

When they got to the top of the steep slope they trotted on the level to where the Landrover was waiting. Gin had made Grace shorten her stirrups and Rosy was pleased to see that she looked none too comfortable, not used to rising from the unfamiliar position. Jeremy beckoned Rosy over. Grace came with her, but when Jeremy got out he said sharply to Grace, 'Ride on,' and turned to Rosy.

'Villanelle is not going level.'

In her distraction, Rosy had failed to notice. She hated to be found wanting. She stroked the gelding's neck while Jeremy picked up his feet. A stone was wedged against one of his frogs, and Jeremy worked it free with a hoofpick. Rosy looked down on the back of his head and had a great urge to caress the curling dark hair that lay close against his neck, to take her hand from the horse's neck and lay it against his. The instinct was so strong it gave her a qualm. Damn Grace! She spent her whole working life damping the ridiculous sparks Jeremy's presence ignited in her system; she had thought the precautions of a lifetime had made her proof. When he straightened up and declared the horse fit, she nodded coldly and looked into his eyes for signs of irresolution, cowardice, meanness and bad temper, but saw only the grey-green independence of his old gran, wanting his own cussed way, not wanting pity, sympathy or even, it seemed, the human face of friendship. 'Oh, damn!' thought Rosy again—damn Grace, for setting off the old weary cycle of frustration. She thought she had got sentimentality beat, thought she was a hard old racing hand, a bit soppy over horses, true, but proof against the human male. A sign of competition, and she was all on edge, as bad as Silverfish.

Surprisingly, he smiled, patted Villanelle's neck, and said 'OK.' Rosy interpreted it—to suit herself—as a conspiracy against Grace, to whom he had not yet extended either smile or word. She did her working canter in high spirits, and went home. In the tack-room on the calendar the week's likely events were pencilled in. She was surprised to see that Roly Fox was to run again in five days' time, and three days earlier Hugh was taking Drogo and Straw Top to Worcester—the day after tomorrow. Jeremy would go, and she and Gin would have the place to themselves, if they so desired. Silverfish was due to come in season again any minute now. While these conjectures were going through her head, Hugh said, 'The vet's coming to cut the two colts on the fourteenth.'

Ten days' time. The chance was coming up, the only one there would be. Rosy stood dumbly before the calendar, in a world of her own. If Silverfish showed tonight, or tomorrow . . . God meant it to happen.

'Are you deaf?'

She blinked.

'I said Mowbray is coming to ride work on Tuesday. Tomorrow.'

49

'Who's Mowbray?'

The boys were laughing. She came to, pulled herself together. 'Oh, *him*. The Boy Wonder. When did you say?'

'Jesus!'

Wednesday was the day that mattered. She wasn't interested in Tuesday.

'To ride your blooming horse. He's its jockey from now on, or is it news to you?'

'He's not like Perkins. He's whip happy,' Trev said. 'I'm glad he's not riding mine.'

'Even he wouldn't make yours move.'

The banter continued but Rosy wasn't listening.

Grace, having delivered Needles back to Simon to put away, tossed her crash-helmet in at the tack-room door and walked firmly under the clock-tower and across the gravel drive to the door of Brood House. Jeremy's Landrover was parked outside. She paused for a moment with her hand on the door-knob, then gave it an experimental twist. It opened the door, and she took a step into the hall.

'Coo-ee! Jeremy!'

The portrait that dominated the hall took her by surprise. It was almost as if one were being ridden down, the action of the horse so strong, the figure so vibrant. Grace, having heard of the portrait but never seen it, stopped in her tracks to consider. This painting, unlike many of Munnings's large portraits, had all the liveliness of his sketches from life; she had never seen a Munnings so impressive. Whatever was it worth, she wondered? Nobody knew whether Jeremy had money or not. By appearances, he had none, save that he owned the decrepit Brood estate and its buildings. Yet Grace knew that his grandparents had made a lot of money and, as far as anyone knew, it was still around. Old Mrs Cutbush, if appearances were anything to go by, hadn't spent a penny of it. Grace liked money. Grace, looking at the portrait, was not at all averse to the idea of taking on Brood House and modernizing it, letting in the light and air both inside and out. She thought Jeremy would benefit from the same treatment. She had no desire to start yet another job, depending on a little typing, some stylish cooking and the right connections, which led nowhere. She had been educated for marriage, in the pre-war deb style, but life wasn't like that any more.

The house was colder inside than it was out. It had a musty damp smell and was as cheerless as an unused church. Yet it retained, somehow, an innate style; it was not at all hard to see it in its pre-war splendour. Grace, not inhibited by a decent reluctance to make herself at home, crossed the hall and opened the door into the drawing-room. She found herself looking right through the width of the house and out through vast french windows on to neglected lawns. The room was an inspired blend of chic twenties colouring and design imposed upon the natural Georgian order, a mix of fine, pale *Vogue*-ish draperies and sophisticated jazz-inspired patterns upon the classical shapes of nineteenth-century furniture. It should have looked brutal, but was strikingly successful; even brash Grace—who knew a thing or two—was impressed. It was the sort of room one paid to see, and admired from a barrier of red silk rope in a hushed whisper. There were paintings on the walls of racehorses and sporting subjects, but none as striking as the Munnings in the hall. All the same, Grace thought, I would gut it and modernize it; one could not possibly live with so strong a flavour of somebody else. That the somebody else was Letitia Cutbush Grace had no doubt. The recalcitrant old granny had had rare taste in her youth—or the money to buy it. She had impressed her style on everything she had had to do with: this house, her cottage garden, even Jeremy himself.

She withdrew and shut the door, and set off in the opposite direction, trying another 'Yoo-hoo!'

Jeremy, phoning a Clerk of the Course to check on the state of the going, tethered by the telephone cord to the kitchen wall, was outraged by Grace's audacity. She appeared at the kitchen door and stood taking in his sanctuary, apparently unaware that it was out of bounds. Even Hugh had never come further than the hall. He turned his back on her and spun out his conversation, shrinking from having to cope with her. But soon there was no more to be said; the Clerk of the Course was busy and rang off. Jeremy was forced to replace the receiver and, eventually, turn round.

'I'm dying for a cup of coffee,' Grace said.

The look on Jeremy's face she chose to ignore. Or perhaps—and it crossed Jeremy's mind—she was too thick to notice. But she was supposed to be the bright one of the family; her brother the slow-witted one.

'Shall I make you one?' Her nerve unnerved him.

'Do what you please.'

He meant to be deeply sarcastic but she took the invitation at face value and crossed over to the stove where the percolator was standing. Jeremy pretended to study the racing calendar, intent on his entries, but his mind seethed with indignation. He had built and nurtured his sanctuary with care over several years and entertained nobody at home, except the most persistent of his owners. Most visiting owners he took to the local pub for a drink and a meal if he could; only the very old ones came in for a drink in the drawing-room, because they liked to reminisce. No doubt they shook their heads over the pass Brood House had come to on the way home in their carefully driven cars, but Jeremy was not afraid of spent forces. He was at home where spent forces were concerned. It was the young and active he preferred to avoid, especially the aggressors like Grace. And Tony Mowbray, due to introduce himself tomorrow.

'I like riding out, if I'm of use to you,' Grace said, spooning out the coffee as if she had lived at Brood for years. 'Hugh said you were short-handed.'

Too mean to employ another lad, Jeremy knew Hugh meant.

He grunted, pretending to read attentively.

'It's very cold in here, colder than outside. Haven't you ever thought of putting in central heating?'

She busied herself looking for china in the glass

52

cupboard that he hadn't opened for years. She was setting a tray, putting milk in a jug as if she was still passing exams in her expensive finishing school.

'No,' he said.

'You're just the same as Dad. He says it's healthy to be cold. It's a very old-fashioned attitude.'

If nothing else, Grace was certainly healthy. She had strong bones and fine, taut flesh and if she had been a horse she would have been a certain winner. But her assurance crucified Jeremy.

'Do you take sugar?'

'No.'

'No, *thank you*.'

'It's my sugar. Why should I thank you?'

'You need sweetening, Jeremy. Why are you so bitter?'

Her retort, her cheek, was astounding. Her eyes glittered with bravado. She wanted him to respond, ready to pounce again.

Like a fool, he responded.

'Why did you come in? I didn't ask you. Nobody comes in the house, not even your brother.'

'I'm not surprised. It's such a morgue.'

'They're not invited.'

'No, I can see ... but why? You may not like me, but you used to have plenty of friends. Why the hermit act? You never used to be so fond of your own company. You have chosen to make your life very dreary, you must admit.'

She carried the tray to the table, pushing his racing calendar to one side.

'I know it's very out of place for me to talk like this, but what a waste, Jeremy!'

'I think you'd better go. I've a lot to do.'

'It's a platitude that you only live once. But it's true. You're living just like your old gran. But she's eighty.'

She poured milk into her coffee to cool it, drank it off quickly, and turned to go.

'I want to help you, Jeremy. Please don't be cross. I'll

53

come again tomorrow and do as I'm told. I won't come in again. Goodbye.'

And she turned and pranced out, full of self-assurance, leaving Jeremy livid and ashamed, and deeply disturbed.

4

On her way to work the next day Rosy called in on Silverfish and confirmed that she was in season. Her mind was
completely occupied with the God-given opportunity
which was presenting itself and she went in to do her horses
in a daze. She knew that if she did not manage to engineer a
meeting between the mare and Peppermill the lost opportunity would haunt her to the grave. The melodrama in the
situation was not lost on her. She was intoxicated with the
idea, to such an extent that Hugh thought she was ill and
Simon asked her what sort of a party she had been to the
night before. Gin, recognizing what it was all about, told
her not to be crazy, but then became somewhat abstracted
himself.

'Christ, you're not serious?' he hissed at her when they
were fetching their tack.

'Oh, I am! Gin, you must—*must ...*'

It was not a job one could do single-handed. Gin looked
at Rosy and felt himself growing pale.

'For heaven's sake!'

'It's the chance of a lifetime. You must see that!'

'Chance of getting the sack, yeah.'

There was no chance to discuss it then, with the others
listening, and the first lot to be tacked up. The others were
all agog for the arrival of the Boy Wonder who was to ride
Roly Fox on the gallops. At any other time Rosy would
have been anticipating this even more than most, but as it
was she scarcely noticed when the dark blue MG pulled
into the yard and its driver inquired for Mr Cutbush.

Grace, arriving right behind him in her battered Mini, got out and, before the approaching Hugh could say anything, said, 'Come with me. I'll tell him you're here,' and escorted the newcomer away under the archway. Hugh shrugged, grinned, and turned away.

Gin said tartly, 'I would have said that was your job.' He was not in the habit of treating Hugh with much respect and Hugh was too weak to demand it. 'Your sister won't be very popular here if she carries on like that.'

But Grace returned almost immediately, leaving Mowbray to enter the hallowed portals alone. Hugh tacked up Needles for her, and Rosy, on Roly Fox, avoided her company as they rode up on to the gallops, not much wanting to talk to anyone. She was so preoccupied with planning how she could get Silverfish in foal that she was not even aware of Roly Fox's new jockey until she was on the gallops and Jeremy was beckoning her over. The lad was sitting beside him in the Landrover.

'Get down,' Jeremy said briefly. 'Mowbray is having your horse.'

Mowbray was a vision in silver-grey, his anorak fur-lined, blond hair artfully highlighted, a gold chain necklace showing at his throat. Rosy gawped. Ice-blue eyes took in her shabby figure, thawed faintly in acknowledgement.

'Give him a leg-up.'

Mowbray settled his helmet and raised an elegantly-booted ankle into her hand. He went into the saddle like thistledown, gathered up the reins. Rosy noticed his whip, a cutting, well-worn affair, and remembered the talk in the tack-room.

'He won't need that. He gives everything. He's absolutely genuine.'

'Fine then.'

She had seen him before at races, but in the jockey uniform his personality had been shrouded. Jockeys came to ride work often, but none of them looked a fraction as beautiful as Tony Mowbray.

She looked at Jeremy. 'Cor,' she said, and grinned.

56

He actually smiled.

'Hop in.'

She hopped. They drove up over the crest of the down and sat in silence to watch their new jockey. Rosy, now faced with it, felt a deep unease at the thought of her darling now owned by an uncaring businessman and ridden by a whizz-kid who had a name to make. Jeremy felt every bit as bad as he had foreseen he would, taking in Mowbray's youth and confidence and natural flair. It occurred to them both that under the new arrangement they were likely to win more races, but this fact made neither of them happier. Mowbray did his gallop and took Roly twice over the three schooling fences and came back to the Landrover looking happy and cocky, and very young.

'He's fine.'

He got down and Rosy got out to take the horse again. The boy held Roly for her and gave her a leg-up back into the saddle, slapped Roly's neck and said, 'Cheers. No problems.'

If only, Rosy thought.

By teatime Gin had accepted the inevitable. The following afternoon the stables would be empty. Even old Albert was going racing: Hugh was taking him because it was his seventieth birthday. Simon and Trev would go home after lunchtime feeding and not be back until four-thirty. Silverfish was magnificently in season and Peppermill had nothing else to do.

'It'll only take half an hour—ten minutes' walk down, ten minutes back—we can use the big barn, Silverfish's barn—no one will see. No one will ever know.'

'What about Mrs Cutbush?'

'I'll go and talk to her—now. She'll like the idea, I swear she will.'

'Gawd! What if—'

'Oh, Gin, shut up! It's such a little risk, compared with what might come out of it. I'm going down to talk to the old girl.'

One mating—if she conceived it would be a miracle ...
Rosy walked fast, half ran, down the dusking lane to Mrs
Cutbush's cottage. When she got to the gate she paused,
catching Gin's panic. Over the fence at the top of the
garden, Silverfish stood waiting to be fed, a white ghost
against the rain-dark sky and the bare, purple-twigged
hedgerow. The smell of rebirth came with the rain; the old
girl's bulbs were thrusting out of her overfilled flowerbeds
and her broad beans, pale and innocent, patterned the
black beds dug for the vegetables. Spring ... it's what it's
all about, Rosy thought, calmed. Mrs Cutbush would like
the idea.

She banged on the door. The old girl came. 'It's open. I
left it. You can walk in.'

Rosy kicked off her boots and went in, shutting the door
behind her. The poky little room, crammed with its pictures, fire smoking, always enchanted her with its stamp of
past glory. She had minutely studied all the photographs,
mostly when Mrs Cutbush was pottering in the kitchen,
and knew where to look for Jeremy on his horses. If—
when—their study was too painful she turned always to
the eternal golden afternoon of the 'Horse and Groom in a
Landscape' where everything was as it should be: in a
word, perfect. Contemplation of the Stubbs never failed to
soothe. Even now, one glance gave courage. Riches, of
achievement as much as money, did not come to faint
spirits.

Letitia Cutbush was delighted with the idea.

'A Mill Reef colt? Splendid, splendid! Lots and lots of
Nasrullah blood—he'll be grandsire on one side and great-
grandsire on the other.'

'Is that a good thing?' Rosy had heard dubious stories of
Nasrullah blood, the great sire transmitting his tempera-
mental defects as well as his speed.

'Who knows? Nasrullah was third in the Derby the same
year my husband was killed. I remember him well. I took
two horses to that meeting, and won with both of them. I
thought Peter would have been pleased, but I don't think he

ever knew. He was killed four days after the Derby. Can you see my glasses anywhere?'

She could remember every date of fifty years back, but lost her glasses all the time, and never knew whether it was Sunday or Thursday. Rosy retrieved the glasses from the top of the china cabinet and passed them over.

'If I don't like him, mind you, I won't have it. He's not a weed, I hope?'

'No, he's got lots of substance. He's beautifully made, not big, but compact.'

'That's what we want. Will you bring him up in the morning? I'll have her ready for you.'

'No. The afternoon.' Rosy hesitated.

She did not know what exactly to tell Mrs Cutbush, and what not. The old girl got things so muddled, and might easily mention the mating to Jeremy—save that she saw little of him.

'You said—you said—' Rosy was embarrassed, but knew she had to get it right. 'If I arranged it, the mating— you said the foal—' She could not say it.

'Would be yours,' Mrs Cutbush said.

'Yes.' Did she only remember what mattered, and forget what didn't? It didn't matter to her at all whether it was Sunday or Thursday, as she never went out.

'Yes, that's right. I want you to have it. Like the picture.'

Rosy had no idea what she meant by the last sentence but was too relieved to inquire. It was of no importance to the old girl's acquiescence in what mattered. She was touched by the spark that she had fanned in Mrs Cutbush, with mention of breeding again, as if she had opened a door and let a crack of light into what must be—when one was so old and declining—a sort of tunnel's end. Rosy found it very hard to envisage what it must feel like to be eighty.

She was half convinced that something would happen to upset the plans the following day, but Jeremy and Hugh departed for Worcester at the appointed hour, taking Albert with them, and at one o'clock Simon and Trev went home on their motor-bikes. Rosy sat shaking in the tack-room.

The quiet of the stable-yard, disturbed only by the steady munching of the horses over their midday feeds, meant that all was in order. Rosy had planned to bridle Peppermill and lead him down but had an attack of the panics, and could not start.

Gin came in. 'I'm on my way. By the time you get down there, I'll have her ready and waiting. What's the matter, gel?'

He, the unwilling partner, was now calm and objective, Rosy nervous as a hare.

'Come on, idiot—' but kindly—'You can't back out now. I'm off.'

'OK.'

He departed, and Rosy unhooked Peppermill's snaffle. He had finished feeding, and had his head over the door, ears pricked. He was a handsome devil and deserved his propagation. Rosy's courage came back, and she slipped the bridle over his ears, talking to him kindly. If she'd had a choice of them all, she would have been happy with this colt to do the job. Many of them were not as likeable in fact as they were on paper. But Peppermill was worthy of the favour he was getting.

They walked down the long drive together, the colt curious, Rosy happy now. A warm breeze ruffled the tree-tops but it was still below, the vegetation undisturbed, thick and burgeoning on either hand. The tunnel under the trees gave several of the horses the spooks, but Peppermill was not rattled, kind to Rosy's restraint. They came out on to the road, but met no one. The village was asleep, the only sign of life Mrs Cutbush waiting by the gate into Silverfish's field. She wore her ancient gardening jodhpurs, with the old-fashioned winged upper parts, and an even more ancient suede jacket and felt hat so that she looked like one of the Bloomsbury set who created gardens, trug in hand.

'If I don't like him—' she said, jutting out the famous chin.

'Look—how can you not?'

Rosy unbuckled his surcingle and pulled back his rug, to show the splendid slope of the shoulder and brave heart-room. Mrs Cutbush groped for her spectacles. Silverfish whinnied from the barn, and Peppermill threw up his head, startled and excited. He flung himself round in a circle and the rug fell in a heap under the open gate.

'Oh, very nice!' Mrs Cutbush leapt into action like a girl. 'Yes, he'll do splendidly. Come along.'

She slammed the gate shut, gathered up the rug and they hurried up the hill towards the barn. Rosy had her hands full with the horse and had no time to bother about the old girl. Gin came to meet her, grinning.

'Here, wait.' He clipped a long rein on to the snaffle rings. 'Give us more room. You go and handle the mare—I'll take this end.'

Rosy ran. Silverfish was tied up and churning the deep straw, nostrils wide. Rosy undid her.

'You sexy old beast! Old enough to know better! Hold up, old girl—there's no hurry.'

Silverfish thought otherwise, and plunged round to face the entrance to the barn. Peppermill came in, amazed, the sweat rising, making deep whickering noises in his throat.

'Get her behind the bales,' Gin called out. 'Keep her back!'

He ran Peppermill round in a circle and the colt threw himself up on his hindlegs, striking out with his forelegs. There was a fence of straw bales piled across the centre of the barn, and Rosy knew that the idea was to introduce the mare to the stallion with the barrier between them, to save any possible injury, but in this case the two animals had no intention of delaying their act. As Peppermill advanced, mainly on his hindlegs, and roaring, she dragged the mare's head round to present her backside, and heard Gin cry out, 'Watch yourself!'

Peppermill's front feet missed her by inches. He mounted the mare at a bad angle and fell off sideways, roaring with excitement. Rosy kept the mare in place, rear on, and at the second attempt Peppermill mounted her properly, forelegs

61

on either side, and started to bite her neck quite savagely. The mare backed up under him and they danced about unsteadily. Rosy jerked on her headcollar to keep her still, and saw Mrs Cutbush dash in at the far end like a little dervish, reaching down to direct Peppermill's masculinity in the right direction.

'Let me! Let me!' Gin pushed her out of the way. 'Hold her tail!'

Mrs Cutbush caught it up smartly, agile as a monkey. Peppermill thrust at the mare, shoving wildly, pedalling with his front legs and grunting with excitement. The mare stood like a rock, ears flat back, stoic in obedience to nature's pattern. Rosy had seen it before but this time the creation was as much hers as the two animals'; she was playing God, and felt it.

'That's it,' said Gin. 'You won't get another chance, old girl.'

Peppermill slithered down, sweating and blowing as if he was standing in the winner's enclosure. Mrs Cutbush was smiling, having shed about thirty years.

'When will you bring him up again? I'll have her ready.'

'We can't. There's no chance of doing it again. We borrowed him—nobody knows about it, only the three of us.'

'Jeremy doesn't know?'

'No.'

'Oh, that's good! I like that!' Mrs Cutbush grinned again, her old gums bared in alarming fashion. 'Our secret, eh? Well, I like secrets. That's good.'

Gin threw Peppermill's rugs on and buckled them up. The two of them felt a great anxiety to have him back home now the deed was done. Silverfish must take her chance. They turned her loose and watched her walk away towards the best of the spring grass that was coming through down by the stream, taking on the way a satisfying bite of the rare *torilis arvensis* that Rosy's father had marked with a bamboo stick. The field, in spite of Silverfish, was one of his dearest, but Mrs Cutbush was to be avoided at all costs, as she screamed from the gate as if she owned all nature when trespassers came her way.

'I got Rosy to bring me down a haybale from the racing-stables, and when I opened it out I counted thirty-three species of grasses and broad-leaved plants in that one bale. I asked her to find out where the hay came from but Mr Cutbush said that Potters supplied it, and they collect it from all over. I'll go down and discuss it with old Potter himself one day. Are you going to try this elderflower? It's too sweet, but otherwise quite good.' Mr Weeks, entertaining the chairman of the local naturalist society, became talkative on his brew.

'You'll miss your Rosy when she gets married. Has she got a boy-friend these days? I always thought myself she'd set up with that neighbour of yours—Gin or whatever he calls himself.' The chairman of the local naturalists liked a bit of gossip over the elderflower.

'He was Ginger at school. They were at school together, more like brother and sister, I suppose. No, I wonder at Rosy sometimes. Seems to me horses is the only love in her life, like children. I can't see her giving all that up to stay at home cooking and cleaning. She goes around, she meets people. She went to Ireland a year or so back and she travelled all round, met lots of people you hear about, and when I asked her about it, "What did you see, Who did you meet," she said, "I saw Meld in a field, and stroked her." Apparently Meld was a great racehorse in her day and won all the big races going, the Oaks and the St Leger and what have you and since then she's foaled a Derby winner. But after all, it's only a horse. But Rosy said, "She took an apple from my hand, and I talked to her." She didn't say anything about the places or the people, only Meld. She's odd like that. I mean, that horse she does, Roly Fox or whatever he's called, she's potty on that horse. I say to her what happens if he gets sold or goes away, or killed even. I've asked her what she'd do if he gets killed and she says it would be terrible but he loves racing and he'd go happy, he wouldn't know. But if he broke down and was sold away and got into bad hands, she says it would kill her if that happened.'

They gazed deep into the elderflower wine.

'Funny girl.'

The chairman of the naturalists said, 'It's a good thing she's got you to look after her.'

'Aye. I've thought that.'

5

Three days later Rosy went to Newton Abbot with Roly
Fox who was running in a handicap chase in his new
owner's colours. Tony Mowbray was to ride him and Rosy
was worried. Driving down with Gin she was remembering
Simon—or was it Trev?—saying Mowbray was whip-happy.

'Is it true?'

'Probably. All the young ones are. Anyway, Hawkins—
he's in it to win, not like Mrs Palmer. Things are changing
round the old placc, or haven't you noticed?'

'I didn't really think about it.'

'Had too much on your mind, didn't you?'

Gin had Beryl on his mind and wasn't bothered about
Rosy's new problem. Beryl had told him the last time he
met her that she was fed up and wanted a new job. What if
he proposed marriage, just like that? She was a betting
lady, and might take a chance. His mother was going to
turn him out and he didn't fancy doing his own cooking.
He liked his food. There was a cottage on the Brood
estate—it had once been the lodge at the bottom of the
drive, when the drive had boasted gates at both top and
bottom—and Gin reckoned Mr Cutbush would let him
rent it for the time being, until a council house came up. It
was a bit ramshackle but nothing he couldn't tart up with a
few evenings' work. Summer was on hand, and it would be
handy to live on the estate itself. He had thought about it
and liked the idea more and more. He had visions of calling
out to Beryl as he rode past in the morning, nipping down
for lunch and coming in at the door to find her waiting in a

pretty apron, table laid in the window, covered with the sort of dishes the women's magazines taught them to make. She would kiss him gratefully, glad to be delivered from riding out fractious chasers on frosty mornings and bumming round the race-tracks, doing her runner. She would love him for looking after her, not like Rosy with her wild ambitions, now brooding over Roly Fox and the possibility that he might have to wake up his ideas.

'I'm going to see Beryl today. She's got a runner in the three o'clock.'

'Huh.'

Perhaps she was jealous, Gin thought. The idea pleased him. She'd had her chance, after all. He couldn't wait to find Beryl. The sun was shining, the air clear and bright, perfect racing weather. The flat boys were taking over and the old chasers were due for their annual holiday, nosing into lush pasture and putting fat over their lean hides. As soon as the weather firmed the ground, Cutbush would shut up shop. May ... June ... that was the ideal time to get married, get some fun in before the season started again. They roared down the Exeter bypass and smoother, smarter horseboxes from Lambourn skimmed past outside them.

'I'll kill that Mowbray if he punishes Roly.'

'I've told you, Rosy, it doesn't get you anywhere, caring too much.'

'The guv'nor wouldn't let him though.'

'Old Hawkins calls the tune now.'

Steeped in dark thoughts, Rosy unloaded Roly and saw him into his stable. He looked as good as she had ever seen him, his spring coat gleaming over hard muscle. He was fit to run for his life, and would not need a whip's encouragement—but when she looked at the card she saw that he was up against some good horses. The firming ground was against him too. He walked round his strange box in his usual nosy, poky way, and put his head out to take everything in. He looked happy and keen, and Rosy would have put a tenner on if she had had one to spare.

'Tell Beryl—when you're proposing—he's worth her while, whatever the price is. Her trainer must pay better wages than ours.'

'She says she *makes* money betting.'

'I don't believe it.'

'Well—' Gin wanted to learn her secret.

He found her amongst the bookies, screwing her eyes up to study their chalked figures. She was a small, skinny figure, too thin, Gin thought, with smudged shadows under over-large eyes and a rather repulsive ex-punk hair-style, the spikes growing out and the blonde dye starting two inches from the roots. He thought he would have to change the hairstyle. That apart, he saw her as attractive, like a little bird, cute and perky.

'Hi, Beryl. Will you marry me?'

She stared at him. 'Have you been drinking?'

He was deeply hurt. Having had the idea, he had been thinking about it with such concentration that he had forgotten how very limited their contact had been up to now. The vision of the little lodge-house and Beryl in her apron had carried him away.

'Thought you said you wanted to change your job?'

'Why, you going to pay me?'

'Oh, come off it. It's a good offer.'

'Bit sudden. Sorry. You gave me a fright. I was just putting a fiver on Gunfleet.'

'Our horse'll come good today. Roly Fox. Put it on him.'

She studied her card. 'He won't beat Gunfleet.'

'Why not? He's never been better.'

'He likes it softer, I thought.'

'Please yourself.'

The betting was a mug's game, Gin thought; that was something else he would have to change. 'If you've got a spare moment—before they run—we could go down to our horsebox—you know. If your horse isn't in until the last.'

'Yes, OK. Just let me put my bets on.'

She was easy to manipulate, not like Rosy. How old was

she? She looked barely out of school, all thin bones and wrists, hard-edged. She was a lightweight compared with Rosy. He could train her in proper ways, deliver her from the rough world she found herself in. She was always complaining of the cold, and the hours and the hard work. Gin was soft-hearted like his mother, not shrewd, far-seeing and dishonest like his father.

'Come on. You spend too much time in this department.'

'The only bit of excitement I get.' Beryl giggled.

'I'll give you a bit of excitement.'

'All right. I'm coming.'

Rosy saw them, knew what they were up to. Sighed angrily. She knew she was not jealous of Beryl, but felt it, in that moment. She went and got a cup of coffee by herself, watched the first race, and went back to Roly Fox. He was restless, but in a let's-get-on-with-it mood, not nervous, and there was no sweat on him. He liked her to be around, she knew, and stood quietly while she talked to him. She was more nervous than he was, afraid of Tony Mowbray and his winning ways.

'You're potty,' Gin said to her when he came back. He was very jaunty.

'No. That Mowbray—he'll put himself before the horse.'

'We're all in it to win, twit. Are you bringing him out?'

The second race was starting and the first runners were back and being washed down. The weather was fine, a warm breeze blowing, and the ground hardening by the minute. The favourite for Roly's race, a grey called Gunfleet, walked by in a navy-blue rug trimmed with yellow; Rosy stripped off Roly's mothy day-wear and flung on the Hawkins's finery with its woven initials and sharp, bright trim, and was glad her horse looked as smart as he deserved. She led him out and followed Gunfleet down.

Hawkins was in the paddock with a glamorous henna-headed lady by the name of Artemis. Roly Fox, it appeared, was a birthday present for Artemis. Artemis thought he was cute. Tony Mowbray came out and Hawkins said,

'You must win for Artemis,' and Mowbray said, 'Sure, we'll do our best.'

Rosy looked to Jeremy to give his instructions, but Jeremy said nothing, legging the jockey into the saddle in tight-lipped silence. Rosy led him away, appalled. Once out of earshot she turned and said to Mowbray, 'This horse doesn't run any faster if you hit him. He gives everything without that. He's really honest.'

'Fine. No problem then.'

He gave her a cool smile which told her to mind her own business. Rosy, disregarding, said, 'The ground's too hard for him—remember his legs aren't too marvellous.'

'Too bad.' Cooler still. With his fashion-touched hair and gold jewellery concealed by the jockey's apparel, Rosy noticed that his face was harder than most and knew that his ambition was dangerous. This was a boy on the make, not an old-fashioned horseman in the trade for love of it. There were still plenty of those around, but Roly Fox had struck unlucky. His former owner, Mrs Palmer, had been one of the old girls thick on the ground at winter meetings, the woolly-stockings brigade who had hunted as gels and knew horses like young men knew motor-bikes, with love and admiration. Artemis was a far cry from Mrs Palmer.

Rosy unclipped her horse and he bounded out eagerly on to the wide green course, ignorant of the change in his fortune. Rosy shook off her pessimism and made for the stands to find Gin and Beryl. She had never formally met Beryl before, but now Gin introduced her and said, 'If Roly wins, she's going to marry me.'

Rosy thought he was joking.

'The way I see it, getting married carries the same risk as money on a horse. So I've decided your horse shall decide.' Beryl giggled happily.

Rosy was appalled at such irresponsibility. When she thought of her undying rock-fast love for Jeremy Cutbush, like something out of a Victorian novel, Beryl's joke decision was by comparison so carefree that she felt done down, mocked, shelved, ridiculous. She knew immediately that she should have married Gin herself. Loving Jeremy was far more ridiculous than Beryl's bet. She tried to be equally flippant.

'He's in with a chance. Good luck.'

It was Gin who was going to suffer, she could see, flushed and excited as a schoolboy. He, who scorned her infatuation, was crazily in love with the idea of getting married; Beryl happened to be available. Oh, Roly, Rosy thought darkly, what a lot of weight you are carrying today!

There were ten in the field and five were good horses. Roly had jumping and courage on his side, but not the turn of foot that Gunfleet could produce after the last. They went away fast on the firm ground and Mowbray kept Roly well up. Rosy could not dispute that he rode well and with brains, losing no ground and placing Roly to perfection, but on the second circuit, where Rosy judged he should give Roly a bit of a breather before asking for his effort, he gave him a reminder instead and took him to the front. Gunfleet at that point was some five lengths behind, a group of three on his heels, the others tailing, but Rosy saw Roly switch his tail, a sign that he was tiring. As they approached the home bend Gunfleet began to make his move, and two of the other horses went after him, all three of them catching up on Roly. The gap between them began to close. Mowbray glanced behind, pulled out his whip and gave Roly a real stinger behind the saddle. Roly lengthened but Gunfleet was travelling very smoothly and catching him fast. As the last jump came up Mowbray gave Roly another belt and booted him into it; he crashed through the top and Gunfleet jumped into contention beside him, so that they picked up together. Both jockeys started to ride for home, whips flailing, and the two tired horses galloped desperately neck and neck up towards the finish, neither being able to pull out any more. Gunfleet's rider dropped his whip, knowing the horse was doing his best, and rode out with heels and hands, but Tony Mowbray beat Roly all the way to the post, getting there a head in front of his rival.

The crowd roared, Gin picked up Beryl and hugged her and said to Rosy, grinning, 'Congratulate us, Rosy—we're going to get married!'

Rosy was sick with rage against Mowbray. Winning was one thing—but winning like that... She pushed past Gin and Beryl and ran down the steps to meet the returning horses. With the pace so fast, all the horse had had a hard race; Gunfleet passed her, head down, heaving. Roly was behind him, so tired that he stumbled, and his jockey pulled him up sharply. Rosy took the rein. She had never seen Roly in such a state, his eyes showing acute distress, nostrils distended into red caverns, flanks working like bellows.

'You didn't have to use the whip like that! You've half-killed him!' She could not stop herself flinging the words at Mowbray.

He did not answer, in much the same state as Roly, with no breath for a retort. The crowd liked tight finishes, but Rosy hated them when they came at the end of a long hard race and were ridden without any regard for the horse's future. Many horses never came back after such an experience.

'He didn't need it—you could have won without!'

'Oh, shut up,' said Mowbray.

Back into the crowd Rosy did so, and made for the winners' enclosure, normally a happy place. Hawkins and Artemis were waiting, all smiles, and Jeremy came forward to greet Mowbray as he slid off. He did not smile or congratulate him but put a hand on the trembling Roly's neck and let the effusive owner shower her jockey with compliments. Rosy had to position Roly to have his photo taken with Artemis at his head, great lipstick smile to appear—no doubt—in gruesome contrast to the horse's exhaustion, which she hadn't the wit to notice. Gin appeared with the rugs and his late exuberance at his sudden engagement changed to genuine concern as he buckled up the surcingle.

'Poor old bugger!'

Hawkins pressed a note into Rosy's hand, which she

stuffed without a word into her pocket, resisting an instinct to shove it back at him.

'Horses away!'

She turned Roly for the exit and as she left Jeremy came up to her and said, 'Sorry about that.' He put his hand for an instant on her shoulder before turning back to the owners' party, who were inviting him to go and share in a bottle or two of champagne to celebrate. Rosy did not know whether to laugh or cry.

'Bloody Mowbray! Dave would never have done that to him.'

They took the horse back to the stable and washed him down tenderly, working together with the ease of long custom. It wasn't until he was dried off and rugged up again that Rosy came to and remembered what the win was responsible for.

'Were you joking—about marrying Beryl if he won?'

'No. She agreed! She's a real betting girl. I said afterwards would she go back on it and she said no. She said she'd marry me whenever I liked.'

'You won't have second thoughts?'

'No. I really like her. She doesn't care—worry ... she likes a bit of fun. Suits me fine.'

'I hope so. Congratulations then. I hope it works out.'

'Well, why not? It's all a toss-up, however you go about it.'

More a toss-up this way than most, Rosy thought, but didn't say. Gin was obviously very pleased with life, and went to kiss Beryl goodbye before they loaded Roly for home. While she was waiting for him, Rosy put her hand in her pocket and discovered the note Hawkins had given her. It was for fifty pounds. She turned it over bitterly, wishing it had been the usual fiver, and Roly the jaunty winner as in past, happier days.

Jeremy, aware that he had had too much champagne, drove with the extra confidence the condition gave him, too fast and yet with what felt like extraordinary skill and care. He knew that the feeling was an illusion, that he was stupidly close to the legal limit, that he despised people in his condition ... yet, what the hell? Everything was panning out as badly as he had feared. He was unhappy, yet assured of a more optimistic future than he had had for years. Hawkins was thrilled with the afternoon's miserable win and had told him over the champagne that he had made an offer for a chaser called Spinning Wheel which was unlikely to be refused, and that Spinning Wheel was destined for Brood House, a classier horse than the old place had boasted since his grandfather's day. This was the sort of break he had once dreamed of. To have Spinning Wheel in his string ... the reporters would come down and interview him, the Racegoers Association would ask if they could make a stable-visit, he would go to Cheltenham with confidence, the rich races at his mercy, and aspiring stable-lads would write and ask for jobs.

Jeremy, flying down the fast lane, thought of all the conditions he should have made over the champagne, and had failed to do. If he had Spinning Wheel and Hawkins dictated when and how he was to run, he had nothing to look forward to at all. Hawkins knew nothing, yet expected to give the orders. Jeremy was used to owners who sent their horses Christmas cards and said kindly to their jockeys as they left the paddock, 'Make sure you both come back in one piece. Enjoy yourselves now.' Hawkins's parting words to Mowbray had been, 'Remember, there's a lot in it, if you win.' Artemis had made a packet, and not in the prize money. Mrs Palmer had always had a pound on to win with the Tote—'The money goes back into racing, dear, not like the bookies.' Her thrice-yearly pound had not noticeably enriched racing, but her character had. It was just his luck to have landed himself an ignorant rich bastard out of the blue, whose wealth was exactly what the stable wanted, but whose attitude was completely unacceptable. Yet, so far, he had accepted.

Hawkins had said, 'That was a great win! How soon can the horse run again? A week? Ten days?'

'We'll have to see how he comes out of it.' But Jeremy already knew, as Rosy had done. Hawkins had put a fifty-pound note into Rosy's hand. How much did money sweeten the unlovely afternoon? Fifty pounds was a real windfall for Rosy, but Jeremy knew she would have preferred her darling horse home spry and cheerful to having such a tip. Rosy was sentimental over her horse, which did not do in racing, for racing was a hard game and the knocks could break faint hearts. Jeremy did not agree with the afternoon's work, not for love of Roly Fox but for the common-sense knowledge that such a race would knock all the confidence out of the horse, for he was a horse who did best when humoured and encouraged. A nice second, instead of a punishing win, would have been of far more value, more likely to line Hawkins's coffers in the future than what had happened today. Some horses would make light of such a race, but Roly was not one of them. His owner never inquired as to his horse's mentality, constitution or preference, thinking that if he paid out good money for known winners he would reap more in return, merely by running them, knowing nothing of the skill, guile, luck, intuition and sheer hard graft that went into making runs winning runs, even with the best of horses. Jeremy did not like heavy-betting owners, as it made the game so tense, the horse so vulnerable, yet it was a commonplace in racing. Mowbray had beaten Roly home in front because, financially, it mattered a great deal. Jeremy, having expected to greet Mowbray back after the race with the old, consuming jealousy, had felt not jealousy but contempt. The boy rode beautifully, but was greedy for both recognition and money. Jeremy had not ridden for money. To be fair, he had had no need to. He had been brought up in the old school, his family grounded far back in the way to treat horses. Mowbray's father was a garage mechanic, and Mowbray rode like a motor-cyclist.

At this gloomy point in his meditations Jeremy looked at his dashboard and saw that he was doing close on a hundred miles an hour, and swerved out of the fast lane, slowing to a mere eighty, to prove that he was thoroughly sober. The motorway exit loomed. He slowed down and proceeded home at a pace reckoned not to disturb the local constabulary. Having been kept some time talking to his new owners, he was home no sooner than the horsebox. Gin and Rosy were unloading. Old Albert, out from his cottage at the sound of the engine, was saying, 'What's up with him then?'

It showed, even in the dusk. Roly's uncharacteristic exit down the ramp, shivering and nervous, his cockiness knocked out of him. He had sweated up, and there was lather on his neck.

'That bloody jockey—' Rosy launched into a diatribe against the new constitution that Jeremy felt bound to check, although he agreed with every word.

'Get him comfortable, and I'll come out and have a look at him.'

Gin, about to park the horsebox, said, 'Sir, can I have a word?'

'Yes?'

'I want to get married, sir. I wondered if there was any chance of renting the lodge-house? Until I can get a council house.'

'The lodge-house? I thought it was derelict.'

'I could do it up, sir.'

'What girl would want to live in that, for heaven's sake?'

'I could make it OK, sir. She wouldn't mind. She'd ride out, if you'd like. She works for Mr Ackroyd now.'

'I didn't know you were courting, Gin?'

'Yes—no, it's a bit quick, like.'

Jeremy grinned. 'I hope—' But it was no business of his. Gin, young, strong, good-hearted, was the marrying sort. His family all bred like rabbits. Gin had no inhibitions.

'Yes, I see no reason not. Not if you think you could make it habitable. I wouldn't fancy it myself.'

'That's great. Thank you, sir!'

If only life were so simple, Jeremy thought. Why on earth wasn't it like that for him?

On the way home, in the almost dark, Gin stopped his motor-bike at the bottom of the drive outside the gate of the lodge-house. In the sudden silence he sat for a moment, his whole being suddenly shaken with a happiness he had never experienced in his life before. It was as if everything came together, this very place that he had known all his life, this house where he had played as a lad, surrounded by the woods whose every track and glade he had explored minutely during his life: playing, rabbiting, petting girls, and now to be his home, with Beryl. A couple of hundred yards away was the yard where he had his job, the job he had enjoyed since he had left school and which was all a part of his small, enclosed, precious existence. Life was exactly how he wanted it to be: secure, full of promise, utterly familiar. He saw himself as blessed: Beryl promising, on the result of the race, old Roly winning ... it was all meant; God was on his side.

He sat there, and the owl came down the drive under the trees, unafraid, the owl that was always there, year in, year out. And in the headlight of his motor-bike he could see the patch of wood anemone, beloved of Rosy's dad, unfolding its tender leaf to the spring on the edge of the drive, just where it always did, always had, the habit of a lifetime.

A car sped past on the road just ahead of him. It was too dark to go over the cottage now, but tomorrow he would come up early and see what had to be done, before work. The sooner he got it shipshape the sooner they could be married. Beryl would be waiting for him when he got home each evening ... life was just starting.

He opened up his throttle with a triumphant roar and surged out of the drive.

6

'Do you think she's in foal?'

'Yes, oh yes,' said Mrs Cutbush. 'Look at her.'

Rosy looked, but could not see what Mrs Cutbush could see. The mare grazed in the soft evening, switching her tail at the midges.

'How do you know?'

'She tells me.'

The old girl was batty but—Rosy hoped—sound in her intuition.

'A filly. She will have a filly.'

'How do you know that?'

'She's due for a filly.'

If only, Rosy thought, you could tell what was true and what was not out of Mrs Cutbush's ramblings. Having delivered what sounded like a judgement based on all the experience of a lifetime, she then turned and called her old dead dog.

'Jasper! Come along! I'll get your supper.'

She bought dogfood and put it down on the kitchen floor in the evening, scooped it up the next day and scraped it into the rubbish bin. She kept talking about Rosy's picture. Every time Rosy looked at 'Horse and Groom in a Landscape' Mrs Cutbush said, 'That's right. That's your picture. You like it, don't you?'

'Yes, I love it. It's not mine though. It's yours.'

'No. It's yours. I told Jeremy. You're more interested in old times than he is. I told you, that horse was in our family. He belonged to Peregrine Cutbush who asked

Stubbs to paint him. Stubbs was his neighbour. My grandmother told me. That horse, Lionheart—he was by
Highflyer. You know who Highflyer was, don't you?'

'He belonged to Mr Tattersall who founded the Tattersall fortune. He sired three Derby winners.'

'There!' said Mrs Cutbush in admiration, 'Jeremy
wouldn't have known that. Of course you should have the
picture.'

Rosy did not see what her general knowledge had to do
with it. The subject disturbed her, because she had an idea
that the picture was worth a lot of money. It belonged by
right to Jeremy. The fact that Mrs Cutbush might be willing it to her disturbed her: the whim of a near-senile old
lady willing family treasures to passing strangers was a
classic bone of contention, and she had no ambition to get
tangled up in such an embarrassing situation with Jeremy.
It would be embarrassing enough if he found out about the
foal.

'Well, he will, if it's born,' Gin said, when the subject
was broached.

'Mrs Cutbush seems to think the mare is in foal.'

'Fine.'

'If she is, I was leaving it to you, remember—to make it
legal. To earn your half-share. We want a covering certificate from somewhere to register it with, otherwise it might
as well not exist.'

'I did think about it—there's a friend of a friend—you
know—of my father's whose got a couple of quite decent
stallions over Marlborough way somewhere. We might
come to a deal with him, agree that his stallion covered her.
He's pretty deep in debt, I understand.'

'We can't pay him.'

'No one'll do it for nothing! Talk sense. He'll have to
have a share somewhere, for taking the risk. It's fraud, after
all.'

'No one'll ever follow it up.'

'I suppose we can worry about that when it wins the
Derby.'

'The Oaks. Mrs Cutbush says it's a filly.'

'Funny old bird!'

'You won't tell anyone about it, will you? Not even Beryl. Don't tell Beryl.'

'No.'

Gin had spent a weekend with Beryl at Bournemouth, and brought her home to meet the family. The wedding date was fixed for May, and Gin was spending all his spare time trying to put the lodge-house in order, browbeating his dad and his brothers into helping out. The roof leaked, the floors had fallen through, the windows were broken.

'What do you think of it?' Gin asked Rosy anxiously.

Beryl had found it wanting, apparently, on her visit.

'We've done a lot to it since then. I think she'll like it a lot better next time she sees it.'

Rosy was not so sure. The cottage was quaint, sweet almost, but not—Rosy felt convinced—of the type to appeal to Beryl, who liked things fashionable. It was very small, a sort of clover-leaf of three rooms with a bedroom above, nestling under some rat-ridden thatch. Doing up the thatch was something Gin could not afford. He filled it with rat-poison until the scuffling stopped and fixed some heavy-duty plastic sheeting over the apex so that it no longer leaked. One of his brothers was re-wiring the place and another had installed some slightly battered kitchen units and a sink in one of the downstairs rooms. Gin was reboarding the floor.

'It's better than what she lives in now. She lives with her mother in a flat in Newbury and they quarrel all the time. Her mother has boy-friends in and Beryl has to keep out of the way. I met her mother. She's a right slag.'

Like mother, like daughter ... Rosy hoped not, but hadn't Gin's faith. Beryl was a lightweight, too flimsy for foursquare Gin. Rosy, visiting the cottage on her way home, standing in the living-room with the smell of fresh wood-shavings and paint, recognized its utter tranquillity. The trees that surrounded it, planted in the valley, reached high in competition with the others ranked above, and made a green veil of light through every room. On a spring evening it was magical, the outside world blurred, only the thrushes fluting to the sky, the smell of growth out of the dank earth filtering in through the open windows to mingle with the carpentry. It was a poet's cottage, a philosopher's haunt, where one communed with nature—for there was nothing else. Whatever would Beryl make of it, when the November rain came, and the branches above scraped in the wind? Rosy was filled with foreboding for Gin.

'How old is Beryl?'

'Eighteen.'

'Baby-snatching—'

'Ah, you're jealous!'

Rosy grinned, thought of living in the green paradise with Jeremy, scoffed at her fancy. It was a perfect love-nest, but Beryl would never see it as that. Beryl wasn't in love. Beryl was marrying on a whim. I'm in love, Rosy admitted, I want it; I would die of bliss to live here with my beloved. She rode her bicycle out on to the road in a dream, spinning down the lonely valley where nothing stirred save the sky-larks in the water-meadows, no action threatened, no clouds loomed ... *nothing ever happens* ... Rosy groaned out loud. She would soon be thirty and nothing came her way but peace and security, and nourishing food.

Grace, in whom spring was rousing much the same gamut of emotion that was seizing Rosy on her bicycle, suggested to her mother that she might ask Jeremy to dinner.

'Summer is coming. Declare the dining-room open.'

'Good heavens!'

Margaret, clipping the grass round the dead daffodils because it was too soon to mow over them, looked up at her daughter in surprise.

'Jeremy never comes here.'

'You never ask him, so no wonder. I want to marry him.'

'Oh, really, Grace. Does he know?'

'Of course not. Have you seen inside Brood House? It's palatial, it could be quite stunning. I could do it up, and

80

become an interior decorator. People would admire it, and ask me to do theirs. It's terribly wasted at the moment.'

'I understand it's never been touched since Letitia did it. What do you know about interior decorating?'

'It's only colour sense. I've got a good colour sense.'

'How do you know?'

Grace looked irritated. 'People say so. Ask him to dinner, Mother.'

'I don't mind having him, but the invitation will have to come from you. Poor Jeremy,' she could not help adding.

Grace had great determination; she had always been single-minded in getting what she wanted.

'If you cut all the trees down below the house, you could paint the front a pale colour and it would look out right across the valley. It would be terribly impressive. You would see it from here, with all the dark trees behind it and the line of the downs above. I'm sure that's how it was intended to be. Not smothered, as it is now.'

'Mm, perhaps. But Jeremy has rather a private nature.'

'He needs bringing out.'

'Perhaps.'

Grace needed doing down, but it did not follow that this would happen.

'He must be worth an awful lot of money. That place, and all the land, the gallops and everything, not to mention the paintings, and Mrs Cutbush's stuff. She is supposed to have a Stubbs, you know.'

'You have a very avaricious nature, Grace. I'm sure you didn't get it from either your father or me. We married for love, you know. There's a lot to be said for it.'

'Things are different now,' Grace said kindly, as if to a child. 'I've loved lots of men without wanting to marry them. But I want to marry Jeremy, whether I love him or not. I would be very good for him.'

'Perhaps he would rather be the judge of that.'

'Well ...' Grace shrugged. 'At least we can ask him to dinner?'

'Yes, if you arrange it, of course I don't mind.'

She liked Jeremy—too much, really, to wish him married to Grace, pleasant as it would be to have him for a son-in-law.

Grace asked Jeremy to come up. She told him her father might be persuaded into having a chaser for a bit of fun. Old Hugh had no idea that he wanted a chaser; Jeremy was told not to mention it outright, just spend the evening in idle racing chat. As it was put to him in the nature of a job, the evening out was accepted, young Hugh also applying some pressure. The dining-room was aired; its long, stately windows looked directly across the valley towards Brood and in the spring evening, as Jeremy stood looking out, a very good sherry in his hand, he saw his own home in new perspective, hunched in shadow under the highest brow of the down, while the last golden light from the west flooded across the smooth lawns of his host so that one half-expected to see the Horse and Groom appear, lustre-eyed, in the Stubbsian evening. The silent valley lay between the two stately homes as Jeremy never saw it from his own windows; it appeared fresh and new and strange and it was hard to realize that he knew every inch of it, the valley he had been born in and never left. He liked the new perspective. That, and the shock of realizing that he had accepted an invitation out to dinner, kept him musing while Grace made her entrance in a dress she had bought in Covent Garden, marked down from a hundred and eighty pounds to thirty-two. It was a difficult shape, given to revealing the bra straps—and even the whole bra—if she wasn't careful, and she had to make a conscious effort to stop herself plucking anxiously at the neckline. It was a stunning fuchsia pink. She could tell her father didn't like it, as soon as he saw her, by the glazed expression that came over his face. He had an old cardigan on that could well have been from Letitia's wardrobe; it disgusted Grace. Her mother had fished out her Jaeger (also bought in a sale) and looked much less attractive than she usually looked in her old cords and pullovers. Hugh, her brother, was too lazy to change out of his under-trainer's wear, but Jeremy wore a dark grey suit and a lemon yellow shirt with a white collar and a dark yellow tie, which was very taking indeed. Grace was impressed. Jeremy had instinctive style, which she supposed was inherited from his autocratic Cutbush forebears. If she married him, they would make a smart pair between them. She was now committed to the idea, and intent on carrying through the conquest.

Jeremy—rather to Grace's relief—was nicer in the social context than he was at work. Of course, he could not appear as a moody bastard to his owners, as he did to the staff at Brood, so one assumed that he could switch on affability to order, as a requirement of the job.

In fact, having made the initial effort to switch on affability—just as Grace surmised—Jeremy found as the evening progressed that he had no difficulty in maintaining it as old Hugh and Margaret were just so damned nice. A pity about their children. Grace had an amazing capacity for picking as subjects for conversation exactly those he least wanted to talk about.

'Have you never ridden at all since your accident?' she inquired, as Margaret stacked up plates after the soup. She did not appear to help her mother at all.

'No.' He had tried it, but wasn't going to tell her anything of his pains, humiliations and lonely tribulation.

'Is there actually any reason why you can't ride now?'

'Probably not.' Lack of the necessary grit to accustom his complaining, cock-eyed pelvis and rebuilt thighbone to the harsh facts of life aboard a thoroughbred was not an answer he cared to spell out.

'I understand that, actually, if you get over the first agonies it's generally OK. If you persevere.'

'No doubt.'

'Honestly, Grace, what do you know about it?' asked her brother.

'I know people. Mary Anstey broke her back in two places and was riding within six months. Hunting in eight.'

'I bet you wouldn't.'

Hugh and Grace conversed between themselves like eight-year-olds.

'I bet I'd try.'

Old Hugh, looking glazed again, said to Jeremy, 'Can I top up your glass? Have you had a good season? I suppose it's nearly over now.'

'Not very marvellous, no.'

'But it'll be better next year,' said Grace knowledgeably. 'With Mr Hawkins's horses.'

'Perhaps.' Jeremy felt deep foreboding regarding Mr Hawkins. Not to mention Artemis—unless she was a passing fancy.

'Who is Mr Hawkins? A new owner?'

'He's a tycoon,' said Grace.

'He bought Roly Fox and two more horses, and is trying to buy Spinning Wheel. If he's successful, we shall have Spinning Wheel at Brood.'

Even Colonel Maddox had heard of Spinning Wheel.

'That must be good, surely?'

'Yes—fine. As long as I can see eye to eye with Mr Hawkins about a training programme.'

'And his jockey,' put in Grace. 'Mr Hawkins insists on having Tony Mowbray. You don't like him, do you?'

'What gave you that idea? He's a very good jockey.'

Grace shrugged. 'Oh, they said—' Her voice tailed off. 'How has Mr Hawkins made his money?'

'In fertilizer, I understand.'

'Oh, *that* Hawkins? Better not tell Rosy's dad,' said old Hugh, amused. 'Arch poisoner of the British weed—as well as making fertilizer, he makes Killit Plus—it clears whole forests, I understand, let alone a weed. Friends of the Earth call him Public Enemy Number One.'

'Oh dear.' Mrs Maddox had returned with the casserole. 'I'm on Mr Weeks's side in that. All the life you find in a dead log—just think what he must kill—'

'Mummy kneels in the hearth for hours rescuing the woodlice when the logs go on the fire,' Grace said. 'And spiders in the bath—she—'

'We only live once. So do they,' said her mother mildly.

'This pork in here,' said Grace, lifting the casserole lid, 'was a live pig last week. You love pigs.'

'Yes, but it had a lovely life before it was killed. I'm not a vegetarian. If we were all vegetarian, there would be no animals in the fields, which would be very sad. Mostly, they enjoy themselves before they die. You've only got to look here, in the valley. Sometimes I sit here in the window and watch the lambs through the binoculars. They always make me laugh.'

'Funny you should say that—I was watching a hunting owl through the binoculars a month or so back and I saw something very strange,' Grace said.

'What was that?'

'I saw Rosy leading Peppermill down the road from Brood. Gin met her at the gate of Mrs Cutbush's field and let her in, and they took him up to the barn. About ten minutes later she led him away again and back home.'

There was a long, thoughtful silence. Mrs Maddox started to dish up. Jeremy, hating Grace, was fascinated by her information. He had to know more.

'When was this?'

'One afternoon, when you were at the races.'

'My grandmother—was she there?'

'Yes.'

'This was before—I take it—Peppermill was cut?'

'Mmm, I think so.'

'And Silverfish—where was she?'

'I didn't see her.'

'In the barn, obviously,' said young Hugh. He looked stunned. 'What a colossal liberty!'

Jeremy didn't pass comment. He was full of admiration for the ingenuity, the utter simplicity, of the operation—a stroke of genius, to use what was at hand.

'I wonder if it's been successful,' Colonel Maddox said. 'Odds against, I'd say, the mare that age.'

'But how on earth is Mrs Cutbush going to register it at Weatherby's?' said Hugh.

Margaret laughed. 'I can't see a detail like that daunting her. Was it her idea? Or Gin and Rosy's?'

Jeremy considered. He thought Rosy's, but did not say so.

Grace had rather thought he would be angry but if he was, it did not show. She would quite like to get Rosy into trouble, disliking Rosy's tie with old Mrs Cutbush and the strange possessive attitude she betrayed towards Jeremy. She watched Jeremy closely, trying to judge his reaction, but he had a way of closing up, a touch of the moody bastard expression that defied the observer. Having decided that she would like to marry him for the lifestyle, the house and the money, not to mention the good she would do him, Grace studied him to decide if she were likely to fall in love. She fell in love quite easily as a rule, or thought she did; she fell out as quickly. Jeremy had plenty going for him, being slender and fit and hard, a touch elfin with his sharp features, rather pointed nose and hard-edged cheekbones—not unlike the Munnings's vision of the young Letitia McAlister. His dark brown hair showed no sign of thinning, but had a touch of grey in the forelock which was distinctly becoming. His eyes were greenish, and cool; he did not smile easily, nor talk overmuch. Grace remembered how cutting he had been when she had gone into the house—lucky she did not take offence easily. He was far from being a fun person—'sense of humour' being the most required characteristic in the lonely hearts columns, Grace had noted—count Jeremy out there. But eligible, yes; and yes, she thought she could well fall in love.

To her disappointment, Jeremy made no comment at all on the exciting news she had passed on, although she suspected that he had been very surprised—even shocked— by the revelation.

But the evening had been a success in that it hardened her ambition to marry Jeremy: he had fitted very easily into the social background of her own home. Her parents liked him, and Grace had no desire to go away and earn her own living again.

7

Roly Fox ran twice in April and won each time. Rosy assumed the third race he ran in Mr Hawkins's colours would be the last for the season but ten days after the third race he was declared for Worcester.

'There's still heat in his off-fore,' she said anxiously to Jeremy. 'You've never run him so soon before.'

It was the nearest she dared come to telling Jeremy his job.

'He'll be out of novice chases next year. Mr Hawkins wants to make the most of it.'

'He'll break him down.'

'I'll be the best judge of that.' Jeremy was sharp. Rosy knew he was being overruled by Hawkins.

'Yeah, well, the guv'nor's had it easy up to now, training for all these old ladies. Hawkins is a different kettle of fish,' Gin commented. 'He wants his pound of flesh.'

Roly, hard-raced, had become anxious, and now left a good deal of the feed he had so eagerly scoffed in the past. The silly old devil ran his heart out under Mowbray's urging; large sums of money passed hands and Rosy got a fifty-pound note each time. She accepted it, with murder in her eyes. The 'lad' was not in a position to pass comment, or to speak at all unless spoken to. The 'lad' was of no account. Mr Hawkins did not even know her name. The ground was getting hard and Roly liked it soft, but Rosy was not supposed to care.

Tony Mowbray turned up to ride work the day before the race, and Rosy saddled Roly and led him out.

'Aren't you going up in the Landrover?'

'No, I'll ride up with you. It's a nice morning.'

Catch him hacking the days the rain came in horizontal lines over the top of the hill, Rosy thought ... all right on a spring morning of soft sunshine, the skylarks whirring, the ramblers with their rucksacks bulging strung like targets on the skyline.

'Cheer up, darling. You'll soon be dead.'

Mowbray grinned, chewing gum, his pale blue eyes like the sky showing through his skull ... could have been, for all the brain there was to get in the way. Tony rode by instinct, natural balance and brute strength, but knew little of science and how horses ticked. Horses did what he asked them to because of the strength of his command over them, but they did not relax with him, or trust him, or seem happy in his hands. Rosy, riding alongside on Villanelle, noticed Roly's anxiety. She knew if Dave Perkins had come to ride work, Roly would have gone blithely out over the hill, even though Dave looked like a pensioner monkey in the saddle. Dave had a natural rapport with his horses, and rode sympathetic races, but did not win as many as Mowbray.

'Second's no good,' said Tony. 'Winning is what counts. These fellows have to earn their keep, you know.'

'You can keep a good horse winning for years if he enjoys it. Your way—beat the hide off 'em to get a nose in front—they pack it in after a season.'

'There's always youngsters coming on. Trouble with you girls, you get sentimental. Owners want a return—can't pay out these training fees and get no return. It's a business.'

'It's a sport. If everyone thought your way—you might as well play a fruit machine, or put it in stocks and shares. The whole attraction of racing is in the nature of the beast. It comes first. It ought to come first. If you get that right, the money comes.'

'Haven't noticed it in the dump you work for. Not till us businessmen arrived on the scene.'

Rosy, having got heated with righteous indignation, now had difficulty in keeping her temper. Mowbray was grinning and chewing, Roly's long stride beneath him breasting the chalky path that cut in sweeps up the shoulder of the down. With the spring in his coat, the warm breeze lifting his mane, Roly looked, if not beautiful, workmanlike and strong, radiating health and well-being. To his owner, surely, he was more than a mere business proposition? Mr Hawkins never came to the stable to visit, and the last time Roly had raced, Hawkins had had to have his own horse pointed out to him in the paddock. Gin had told her. Imagine Mrs Palmer, short-sighted as she was, not recognizing her own horse!

'If you're a businessman, don't break this horse down tomorrow. He's not a hundred per cent in his off-fore. It would pay to pull him up if there's any doubt.'

'Christ, since when do I take orders from a lad?' The grin vanished. 'I take orders from Mr Hawkins—he pays me, doesn't he? Very well, I might add—I'd be a fool not to, wouldn't I?'

Being a heavy better, Hawkins paid his jockey a good per cent of his winnings as well as the normal ten per cent prize money—so Gin had informed Rosy. Mowbray was shrewd and getting rich fast.

He grinned again, scornfully. 'You ought to run the Pony Club, not mess around in racing. Racing's for men.'

'Excuse me while I'm sick.'

'You got a boy-friend?'

'What's that got to do with it?'

'It's what you need—you're too uptight. I'll take you out, if you like. I like mature women. A good screw'll do you the world of good.'

If he hadn't smiled again, the sky shining brightly through his head, Rosy thought she would have taken her whip to his insolent face. But she laughed, knowing there was no winning when the argument took this turn, in a man's world. She had had too much experience to get caught yet again.

'You're probably right. But no, thank you very much, offer refused.'

'Go on, I mean it.'

Give the boy his due, he was entirely amiable; thick, but not vain. Unlike Jeremy, he was good for a laugh. It was a thankless profession, when all was said and done, injury always in wait and luck playing a large part.

The following day, Roly was the favourite. His owner had made a very large bet. 'So has Beryl,' Gin told Rosy, looking worried.

'She going to bet when you're married?'

'Not like she does now. We'll have to save our money.'

'Hope you've told her.'

'Yes, I have.'

If Roly had still been owned by Mrs Palmer, Rosy knew that Jeremy would have withdrawn him, the ground having firmed up too much for him. He looked magnificent in the paddock and his price shortened. Mr Hawkins stood with Artemis and Jeremy as Rosy led him round; instead of enjoying himself, he looked worried sick. The jockeys came out and Rosy had to halt Roly to let them through. Tony winked at her. Mr Hawkins's colours exactly matched his eyes ... perhaps she should have taken him up on his offer. Rosy saw Beryl leaning on the rails and had a sudden instinct that Beryl would accept the opportunity if it came her way, Gin or no Gin. She had an opportunist nature, after all. The wedding date was three weeks away.

'Jockeys please mount!'

She turned Roly into the centre, and stood in front of him to try and keep him still. He was sweating slightly, and too much on his toes for comfort. Rosy knew he was anxious, not merely excited; there was a new edge to his demeanour which she did not like. He swung away from the approaching Mowbray and let out a kick. Jeremy checked the girths, and gave Tony a leg-up.

'Remember what I told you,' Hawkins growled at the jockey.

'You've just got to win, Tony,' trilled Artemis. 'He's

promised me something really lovely if we come up—I'm so excited! I'm counting on you.'

'Yes, ma'am,' said Tony, poker-faced.

As Rosy led Roly back on to the paddock path Tony said to her, 'Them as pays the piper calls the tune, darling.'

'God, that woman—!'

'You look lovely when you're cross.'

'Go to hell!'

She let go of Roly too soon, on purpose, and Tony had a tough few moments controlling him before he got a clear run out on to the course. She half wished Tony would get thrown, the horse bolt and she get the blame, rather than Roly have to run to those orders. Jeremy had said nothing at all.

She went up into the stand with Gin and Beryl. Beryl was chewing her fingernails. She looked about twelve.

'If he wins, it'll pay for my wedding dress, and the bridesmaids'.'

'We don't want bridesmaids,' Gin said. 'A registry office will do, I've told you.'

'Roly'll decide.'

'He can't make all your decisions for you, for God's sake. He's only a horse.' Rosy, worried, vented her temper on the stupid girl her Gin was going to get himself tied up with.

Beryl gave her a contemplative look, and Rosy guessed she would like to have made the same remark as Tony concerning her edginess.

The ground being hard, the field went off at a good pace. The field was not very classy, but there were several horses who, liking the firm, had had an easy winter and were coming to the spring racing fresh, having rested since November. Roly was at the end of a fairly hard season. He lay well back for the first circuit and was left with a good deal to do by half-way. His jockey was depending on his superior class and stamina, and when he went on to chase the leaders the leaders themselves were dropping back fairly fast. Rosy thought his tactics were going to work, but one unconsidered horse, a weedy bay called Smokescreen, kept plugging on, jumping like a stag, and seemed to have no thought of calling it a day. This was where Dave Perkins would have opted for second, but Tony Mowbray, with his large financial interest in winning, started to drive his horse with all his strength, belting him into the second last with more ambition than tact. Roly panicked and took off a stride too soon and went through the top instead of jumping clean, which Rosy knew he would have done if left to his own devices. He pecked heavily on landing, but Mowbray kept his seat cleverly and picked him up with great skill. Smokescreen was at last reaching the end of his tether. Tony picked up his whip again and slammed Roly down the backside. The crowd started to roar.

'Oh, God, I hate him! The pig, the pig!' Rosy was close to tears.

Beryl was leaping about, clutching Gin round the neck, screaming for Roly.

Smokescreen, tiring, battled bravely up to the last, with Roly on his heels. The bay jumped badly but Roly made a wild, soaring leap and caught up in mid-air. They landed side by side and their jockeys both rode them out to the line without mercy. Roly got his head in front in the last fifty yards and won for the fourth consecutive time. The crowd adored him, and Beryl was in tears of bliss, her wedding day glory assured.

Rosy found it impossible to join in the general thanksgiving. If Roly had been fresh and sound perhaps ... everyone loved a courageous battle between good horses. Was she as sentimental as Tony said? This was what racing was all about, wasn't it? With everyone around her singing her dear Roly's praises, she was half proud, half sick, as she ran down the steps to meet him. Roly had no strength left to run on, and she met him at the gate. He came up to her, obviously tender on his off-fore, and exhausted. Everyone crowded round, and she led him into the winners' enclosure to cheers and clapping.

This is what they had always dreamed about, wasn't it? ... winning and success and interviews on the television. It all rubbed off on her, as she could feel herself smiling. Artemis was in raptures, old Hawkins all smiles, even Jeremy looked pleased. Tony unsaddled and managed to pinch her bottom before he went to weigh in. She led Roly away, and watched how tenderly he walked beside her. Mowbray had broken him down, she was sure.

'Lucky it's the end of the season. He'll have all the summer to get over it,' Jeremy said. He came to examine the leg when he got home, running his long, bony fingers down the swelling. 'It was that stumble at the second last, I'm afraid. We'll see what the vet says tomorrow. Keep the hose on it for now and put a compress on it before you go home. I'll look at it again before I go to bed.'

He straightened up, and pulled a fifty-pound note out of his pocket.

'Hawkins gave me this for you.' He smiled. 'Does it make it worth it?'

Rosy looked at it stonily. 'Not really, no.'

'You don't want me to return it?'

'No. I'm not stupid. I just don't like—' She hesitated. She had liked winning, damn it. '*Having* to win, because of the money involved—you know . . .'

'Yes, I know. We'll have to try and educate our Mr Hawkins. But for now—well, the stable could do with his sort of input. We all have our living to make, you know. Would you like to do Spinning Wheel, when he comes here?'

'Is he coming?'

'Next season, yes.'

'Yes, of course. I'd love to do him.'

'You're more conscientious than the boys. These sorts of tips—you deserve them. They can do the hurdlers between them.'

The win had sweetened Jeremy; it was a long time since he had been so talkative. Perhaps lots of winning would make them all into lovely characters.

'Perhaps this is a blessing in disguise for Roly, as he won't be able to race again till next season. He can take a well-deserved rest.'

'Yes, perhaps.'

It was stupid to be so rooted in her ways, so obstinate in thinking she knew what was best for Roly. As a trainer, Jeremy could take the credit for Roly's form; his ego was boosted—no doubt he would get a write-up in next week's *Horse and Hound*. As they stood there briefly in the warm loosebox with Roly between them, the unexpected aura of success was tangible between them, the pride of being responsible for a good horse warming their relationship. Rosy felt it strongly and for a moment a heady vision of the stable's future danced in her mind: cheers all the way and the winning enclosures at Cheltenham and Ascot and Sandown Park becoming second homes. It was a fact that the great horses appeared at random in unexpected stables and shone briefly like unknown comets to bring a few years of glory ... why not Brood House? Spinning Wheel, Roly Fox ... everyone knew that success bred success ... who was to say where it would end? There was another yard, disused, behind the outer yard that the horses presently inhabited, and all sorts of barns and buildings encroached upon by the woodland that could be utilized. The Cutbush fortunes might well be due to flourish anew—and Rosy thought suddenly of Silverfish and the foetus that Letitia swore was fastened snugly in her womb and, in her present state of hallucination, saw a part for herself. Glory all the way.

Jeremy patted Roly's neck and departed. Rosy came off her high, and took Roly out into the yard to start hosing his leg. An hour of that, getting cold and bored, brought the long working day to its end, and she cycled home through the dark spring evening with mixed feelings. The fifty-pound note was folded snugly in her pocket, the only sure bonus in a welter of wishful thinking.

Roly Fox, let down in condition over a week or two, was eventually turned out to grass with Silverfish. This was at Rosy's request. Most of the Brood horses were turned out on neighbouring farms for the summer, the estate possessing only woodland and unfenced down.

Roly's leg recovered. Rosy went to the field in the after-noons and took him down to stand in the stream. She sat on the bank in her shirt-sleeves, holding the halter rope and watching the crystal-clear water flowing over his precious ligaments and tendons. Slippery tendrils of weed and shoals of darting minnows flickered down the current, hypnotic to watch ... the odd trout, drifting, half-seen, half-imagined, merging in the shadows. Rosy called it work, but knew that it was an excuse for dreaming an hour away, doing what she most wanted to. The smell of the water and the damp, flowering weeds in the shadow of the bank cooled anxieties and desires, cold compresses for the hor-monal imagination. She could feel the sun hot on the back of her neck and Roly's kind breath on her hand, watch the glitter of dragonflies and swallows' wings and the tremble of infinitesimal life across the gravel bed where the four firmly planted hooves appeared to dance by the distortion of the water ... enough to occupy the mind and thoughts by the hour, but invoking an overall disillusionment: that this made up her total happiness, a touch of nature and the love of a good horse. God, where was passion and triumph and the sound of trumpets? Sometimes the odd nugget of intellectual awakening stormed her turgid furrow: in her nearly thirty years she had achieved absolutely nothing, not even a relationship that mattered—save with a horse. Even Gin, up to now her comrade in under-achievement, had with marriage become a token success, no longer dis-satisfied and self-questioning but confident and tranquil, a whole man. Was Tony Mowbray's crude diagnosis of what was wrong with her a truth so simple that she could not accept it? Surely life was not so biological?

But when the sun went down and she walked back up the field, she wondered why she had these ridiculous discon-tents. She was happy, in truth, liking her job, her lifestyle. The two horses followed her along the narrow track they had made from the stream to the gate, their shadows long over the grass, tails rhythmically switching to the midges: sweet, trusting Roly in his summer-gloss coat and the dis-

95

dainful, stiff-jointed mare with her lower lip dangling, hiding a secret in her fat belly. Rosy watched for movement—said to be discernible at about four months— but had seen nothing yet. Life was unfathomable, deep in the womb. She went back to her father and fresh nettle soup and pheasant (picked up off the road after being killed by a car. When such delicacies were provided by nature herself, Weeks the vegetarian relaxed his rules). Rosy badly missed Gin two doors down and her cheerful interludes in his mother's kitchen, and the pheasant came as a welcome surprise. She had visited Gin and Beryl at suppertime in their lodge cottage—the 'love-nest' as it had become known by all—but discovered that, however Beryl had found her way to Gin's heart, it was not via the stomach. Beryl was missing her Newbury supermarkets, and as Gin had not yet managed to find a cheap freezer, she was having to do without the convenience food she had been brought up on. Gin had to borrow his father's car and take her late-night shopping twenty miles away, which he detes-ted; the village shop was 'dirty', according to Beryl. She would not go in it, unnerved by the sudden silence that had descended the one and only time she had ventured in.

'She'll get used to it,' Gin said to Rosy. 'I won't have time to take her shopping when the season starts.'

Rosy did not share his confidence. She felt almost motherly towards Beryl, seeing her stranded in the cottage all day, like a kitten up a tree waiting for the fire brigade. But as far as Rosy could see, no fire brigade was to be forth-coming.

'There's no point spending a lot of trouble on this dump, because we're going to get a council house before long,' Beryl told Rosy.

'It might take quite a while though,' Rosy tried to warn her, knowing only too well the dearth of council houses in the district. She would have delighted in decorating the little house, in Beryl's shoes, the rooms so small that the work would have been child's play. Beryl had no nesting instinct, and was content to sit in the bleakly furnished rooms watching the television all afternoon. She only put curtains up in the living-room to get a better picture, and chose bottle-green mock-linen, to shut tight against the sun-shot greenery of the outdoors that poured lavishly into the house while she watched. Racing from Newmarket, from Epsom, from York, from wherever they showed it, on whatever channel. Gin never came in to find her cooking or knitting or making cushion-covers, only watching the television.

'She'll settle down,' he said to Rosy, and boiled himself a couple of eggs. He was noticeably losing weight. Rosy had more sense than to pass comment, but saw Beryl on two or three occasions in the telephone box at the cross-roads, and suspected that she was putting bets on. A girl like Beryl could hardly watch so much racing on television without succumbing to a bet or two. Gin said she had given it up.

'It's all right once in a while, if you get the right price, but the way she goes about it—no one can stand that, when you're saving and getting a house together. I've got to get a car, first priority—I've told her, none of that lark, not now it's my money. When she starts work—well, she can risk a bit of her own money now and then.'

The idea was that she would work for Jeremy when the season started again, but by the time the horses started to come in from grass, Beryl was pregnant. Rosy was appalled. Gin admitted that it was a mistake and was both pleased and worried and Beryl said, 'We'll get a council house now.' As she had a perfectly adequate house already, Rosy did not think this would follow. She felt sorry for the girl, still too much of a child herself to be bearing another.

Roly Fox came in from grass and Silverfish stood at the gate whinnying for him. Lying in bed at night, Rosy could hear her, bereft. The mare was almost certainly in foal and now Rosy realized she might well have a real racehorse on her hands. As she had no money to keep it with, this might prove a difficulty rather than a dream come true, but it was too soon to start worrying on that score. There were other things to worry about—Grace Maddox, for instance.

Grace, according to Gin, who had it from Hugh, was to start work as Jeremy's secretary, with an office in the house.

'She asked him, apparently. He offered her a pittance, thinking she would refuse, but she accepted. So he's lumbered.'

Rosy, who thought she was too old and sensible to feel jealous, now knew differently.

8

Jeremy had been his own secretary for years, carrying everything, computerwise, in his head. He had an ancient typewriter on the end of the kitchen table, and piles of papers on the dresser, kept in place with old kitchen-scale weights.

'I can't work here, like this,' Grace said.

'You can use the old study. Do what you like,' Jeremy said.

Grace knew he didn't want her. The salary he had offered her was an insult. When she had accepted, she had seen the panic flare in his eyes. The job was difficult, for one coming new to it, but Grace was determined to make no mistakes. She went to stay in Lambourn with friends who ran a racing-stable there, and conscientiously learned all she could of the business of making entries; she found out everything she could from Hugh about Jeremy's owners, and how he liked things done.

Her mother was sceptical.

'Really, Grace, you could earn more than that doing a bit of typing for Mr Fosdyke, with half the effort.'

'You don't understand. It's a means to an end.'

Margaret did not choose to. She found Grace's intention to inveigle Jeremy offensive.

'I'm going to make myself indispensable. It won't be difficult, as his life up there is so cheerless.'

'If he didn't like it, he'd have stayed in Australia, surely?'

Jeremy had been to Australia for a month to visit his parents. He had come home tanned but not cheered.

'His parents have separated, didn't Hugh tell you? His

father is living with someone else and his mother has gone back to her old dad.'

'Oh dear!' Such news genuinely upset Margaret, her world rooted in old Hugh. 'I always thought they were rather well suited. Jeremy's father was very reserved—like Jeremy, I suppose, that must be where he gets it from—and that girl, Mary-Ann, she brought him out. She was a driver. She stood up to Letitia, you know. I'm very sorry to hear they've split up.'

'You assume it's a bad thing. It might be a good thing,' Grace said.

'It never occurs to me that a failed marriage can be a good thing.'

'That shows how old-fashioned you are, Ma.'

'I daresay.'

Margaret, clipping her edges, supposed it was true that she was old-fashioned. In her mid-fifties, she was still at heart a cardigan and pearls creature, cast in a country mould, at home with the dahlias and the jam. It was not much to be proud of; Grace's implied scorn was not without foundation. She could at least—even in her chosen sphere—have been Chairman (or Chairwoman) of the Women's Institute, or done something for the local Conservative Association. But she had never been able to put herself forward. Where did Grace get it from?

Grace appropriated a filing cabinet from her father's junk-hole and got Hugh to collect it in the stable Land-rover. She set up office not in the study Jeremy had indicated but in the morning-room, because it led out of the kitchen, which was Jeremy's lair. She wanted to be as close to Jeremy as possible. With the door open, she could talk to him from her desk—or table. The room was furnished with a large table and chairs, but very little else. Grace re-arranged it with furniture from other rooms (although not the drawing-room), and made what she thought of as a workmanlike and homely den. With her own money she bought a Calor gas heater. She wanted a telephone extension installed, but Jeremy would not agree.

'You can use the one in the kitchen,' he said tersely.

Grace did not argue. She was careful to be meek, and as helpful as possible, and to take on as many chores as possible, so that if she went she would be badly missed. She arrived when Jeremy was out with the first string, parked her Mini firmly outside the front door, and went inside. By the time Jeremy came back, she had cleaned the kitchen and got the Aga well stoked, the coffee bubbling at the ready, the post and the *Sporting Life* collected from the box down on the road and laid out for inspection on the table. At first she retreated when Jeremy returned and left him alone at the table with his literature, but gradually she started to add the odd round of buttered toast to her offerings, and after a few weeks she was cooking him a full breakfast when he came in, so that he stopped bothering to make something for himself when he first got up. It was like breaking-in a young horse, Grace thought—adding a little bit new day by day, so that it was accepted without demur. At the first sign of resistance, withdraw and establish what had already been learnt, without starting anything new until all was calm again. Jeremy, from being silent and hostile, gradually thawed and accepted her as part of the furniture. He came in expecting his breakfast, and knowing that the kitchen would be welcoming and cosy, and the post collected.

He even said, 'I don't know why you do this, what I pay you.'

Grace did not enlighten him. He did not offer to pay her any more.

When he was out, Grace explored the house, although without prying. She went up the elegant, curving staircase and visited each bedroom in turn, looking out over the sea of leaves that lapped about the old mansion, high and oppressive at the back, but at the front sliding away sideways beyond the walls of the stable-yard and lying like a great multi-coloured quilt over the undulations of the down as it fell into the valley. The house was like a kernel, the forest its silent protection. Grace, in her mind's eye, opened it out, let in air and ambition and saw a future, not the melancholy that Jeremy seemed to feed upon. The bedrooms were shrines to the past: the master bedroom where his parents had conceived Jeremy in an art-deco bed with cane inlay and— still—a quilt of oyster-grey satin, and vast, convoluted wardrobes inherited from Letitia and Peter Cutbush; and Letitia's dower room with its deliberate return to the past: a brass bed and crocheted valance and a pair of jodhpurs thrown over a chair. Jeremy slept in a monk-like room that had been his from a boy, the Biggles books of his father's stuffed into a bookcase, along with racing year books and forgotten school textbooks, his racing silks still on a hanger behind the door. Grace did not linger here, only enough to get the flavour. Yes, she thought, the house was ripe for a return to life. To be here alone, at night, surrounded by the powerful ambience of past glories, would be enough to depress the thickest consciousness. Jeremy would never thrive without positive removal from the ghosts of Brood. But how tactfully, how gently, he must be prised away ... Grace bristled with mental endeavour, while compelling herself into her unnatural role: quiet, sympathetic, super-efficient. Like a nun. The effort was killing her.

'If you could find time to ride out occasionally,' Jeremy said, 'it would be a great help. That girl of Gin's—I was relying on her, but Gin says she's pregnant.'

Grace forced a smile.

'The second string would do.'

The two new geldings, Peppermill and Needles, were ready to start their hurdling careers; Roly was sound and back in work, and Spinning Wheel arrived one afternoon in October. A bright chestnut all of seventeen and a half hands, he was immediately king of the yard. Rosy took him proudly.

'I still love Roly best, all the same,' she told him as she fed him that evening. 'You're my second string, remember, however good you are.'

But she could not help but be proud of 'doing' such a

good horse. He was easy to ride, strong but obedient. It was like sitting on a rock, the feeling of security a bonus on frosty, skittery mornings when the 'little' hurdlers got the wind up their tails and made life dangerous. Tony Mowbray said he was 'a lazy old sod'; he had to work hard with him during a race, although he was perfectly genuine.

'He needs all of three miles—takes two and a half to get into his stride. Not like your Roly Fox.'

Tony had discovered what Rosy had told him in the first place, that Roly was all heart and no sense, would die for you before he cracked. It did not mean he was never beaten, for his talent was limited, but he was never beaten for lack of trying. He won his first two races of the season and had added two seconds by Christmas. His leg held up by dint of Rosy's dedicated hosing and the punters loved him.

'He's my lucky horse,' Beryl said, showing Rosy her winnings. The bet was open and above board, for Gin had put the money on for her.

Beryl liked visitors to relieve her boredom and Rosy called in when she could. Not that the house was very welcoming. Beryl would not even light the fire if Gin didn't do it, preferring to burn her legs over an electric stove all day. With her pregnancy an excuse, she was fast becoming a slut. When Gin told her to get some exercise, for her own good, she said pathetically, 'Where to? There's nowhere to go.'

'Well, at least when the baby comes, you'll have to stir yourself. You won't be bored then.'

Gin thought Beryl would become a new woman when the baby came. He thought it was what women were for, what they needed. Rosy did not argue with him, realizing that he still saw the whining self-centred Beryl through rose-tinted spectacles. It would take more than a baby, Rosy thought, to make Beryl work. Gin had taken over the evening cooking, in self-defence, and Rosy sometimes peeled potatoes for him, for she knew Beryl wouldn't.

'I see Grace is riding out,' Beryl remarked one evening when Rosy called in on her way home. 'She looks funny on a horse, I reckon. I thought her job was secretary.'

'Lots of racing secretaries ride out, don't they?'

'Yeah, well, she's a funny sort, don't you think? Doesn't fit in somehow. She's too—you know—'

Rosy pretended she didn't. Scheming, ambitious, bigheaded, bossy, clever-by-half ... they all fitted, but she wasn't going to say so.

'She's after him, don't you think? I reckon she'll get him too, the rate she's going on. Six to four on.'

Rosy kept quiet, chilled by the odds Beryl was estimating.

'I asked Gin why he didn't marry you, and he said, no chance, you were in love with Mr Cutbush. Is that right?'

Beryl asked questions like the child she was, ignorant of tact or circumstance. One could not reasonably take offence, the curiosity was without malice.

'Gin and I—it's more like brother and sister, the way we've been. Marriage doesn't come into it. As for Mr Cutbush—yes, well, I've always admired him, I like working for him, but I suppose I don't actually know him very well.'

'You're in love with 'im though?'

'Funny sort of love—'

'Yeah, well, there's all sorts. I mean, I'm not in love, am I, but I'm married—it's a sort of love, you could say. Grace, she's after Mr Cutbush, she must want him, that's a sort too. But hers isn't like yours, I'd say. So yours is another sort. The proper sort, I suppose, but where does it get you, eh?'

Beryl's candid resumé seemed to Rosy more accurate than she could have attempted on the subject herself. Bleak, realistic—it was hardly cheering. Poor old Gin ... so much for his romantic blunder into marriage. He still seemed happy, all the same. Half the battle in life was to make the best of what you'd got.

But she had never even spoken to Jeremy save in the role of employee; she had never said anything other than yes, sir; no, sir. Even in *Woman's Weekly* they moved faster than that.

*

Jeremy sent Grace out in the second string on a horse called Bellboy, belonging to one of his old ladies, and considered a fairly sensible ride. He thought he knew what Grace was after and was not flattered; she seemed to him too much like a student, too young and strident, the edges too sharp. She made him feel staid. He was staid. He resented his rapid progress towards middle age and Grace made him more aware of it. He decided to make a fight of it, conscious that the wooing by housewifery was a clever move and that he was in danger. If she wanted to work for him for a pittance, work she damned well would.

Grace came out from the house in her riding gear with a proprietorial air that irked Rosy. Rosy could not bear to see Grace's Mini parked in the drive and be reminded that Grace was in there making Jeremy's life easy for him; it was a perennial agony. It cheered her enormously to realize that Grace did not want to ride out, and was doing it because she had been ordered to.

'Bellboy's easy,' she said, fetching Roly out for herself. 'And it could be worse—it's not raining.'

This was no longer true by the time they emerged from the wooded ride above Brood and took the chalk road up on to the shoulder. The grey winter turf merged into low cloud and driving rain coming over the top, and it was hard to see for the sharp needles of drizzle. Rosy hunched down into her anorak collar, seeing only Roly's rabbity ears flexing back from the wind and the solid quarters of Bellboy breasting a steep patch ahead of her. They climbed up over the brow and Gin, leading the ride on Drogo, broke into a trot to hurry on out of the worst of the weather on the summit. Behind him Peppermill gave a couple of bucks and Bellboy for no apparent reason shied violently off the path. Rosy saw him disappear and jerked herself rapidly to attention, pulling Roly to a brisk halt. There was a ditch below the road and Bellboy, having lost his footing, was suddenly down in a panic of threshing hooves. Rosy heard Grace scream.

105

'Gin! Gin, stop!' Rosy heard her own shriek furled away by the wind as she flung herself off Roly. She threw the reins at Simon.

'For Christ's sake, get Gin!'

She could see Grace pinned underneath Bellboy, could hear her screaming. Bellboy was upside down, struggling frantically. Rosy jumped down and sat on the horse's head to keep him still, soothing him with a shaking voice, but Grace went on screaming. All Rosy could see was the mud-splashed belly of the horse and above it a hand flung to the sky, clenched in agony, the only bit of Grace visible.

'Jesus Christ!' Gin loomed above her, straddling the ditch.

'Give me your hands, I'll pull you out,' he shouted down to Grace, but she screamed at him: 'Don't touch me! Don't touch me!'

'Are you hurt?'

'Christ, Gin—she wouldn't be making that noise if she wasn't! Can't you get the horse off her?' Rosy dared not move, stroking the trembling neck she was kneeling on, seeing the terrified white of Bellboy's eye and the blood-rimmed nostrils. She could not see Grace's position, which bit of her was trapped.

Gin got down into the ditch and disappeared out of Rosy's sight behind Bellboy's up-ended quarters. The horse, apparently trusting her reassurance, lay still, twitching slightly, his eyes rolling sadly; it occurred to Rosy that he might be more badly injured than Grace. Horses often did not reveal pain; they grazed when their legs were broken or their arteries severed, poor, oblivious creatures ... Grace screamed like a seagull, beating her hands against the white, chalky cliff of the innocent ditch that had trapped her.

Gin surfaced and called Trev to help him, leaving Simon trying to hold four wheeling, frightened horses. They got into the ditch and manhandled Bellboy's backside sufficiently to one side to roll Grace out from beneath. It was vital to get her clear of the horse in case he started lashing

106

out again, yet equally vital that she should not be moved without great care. Gin, with inspired ingenuity, removed his anorak so that she slid across it, then the two of them were able to lift Grace by the anorak slung beneath her.

Whether she was badly hurt or merely frightened Rosy had no way of knowing, for Gin dispatched her to fetch help as quickly as possible. She had an image of Grace's features sharply creased with pain and her skin marble-grey beneath strands of bright blonde hair loosened from her helmet, flung limply on her back on the drenched turf—a dramatic picture which hastened Rosy's journey down the hillside. Gin and Trev had turned their attention to the horse. Rosy rode Roly fast but with infinite care, her horse's legs of more concern than Grace's health. Grace looked as if she had broken a rib or two, nothing worse, please God: the ultimate horror of living out one's life in a wheelchair was a thought that surfaced at such moments, but Rosy had seen enough accidents not to panic, horse-riding accidents being spectacular when occurring at speed but harmless more often than not.

She met Jeremy in the Landrover coming out of the wood and told him what had happened. He swore angrily, revealing little sympathy for Grace, and told Rosy to ring for an ambulance.

'Not that they'll get it up there. I'd better go back for a stretcher, in case.'

There was one in the tack-room, lodged in the rafters. He put it in the Landrover, along with a bundle of horse blankets and departed at speed, leaving Rosy to do the ringing up. The rain pelted down. Rosy shivered, glad that her job was to wait in the warm for the ambulance to arrive. She stood by the tack-room stove, thinking of Jeremy handling the accident and the emotions it was likely to arouse in him, thinking of luck, and coincidence, jealous of Grace taking Jeremy's attention, invoking his concern. Trust Grace. Not for Grace the messy ignominy of a broken nose—the only accident that had ever befallen Rosy—but, congenitally,

107

even in accidents, Grace opted for the dramatic and impressive. Rosy sighed, and rang up Margaret, not wanting to be the one to accompany Grace to hospital in the ambulance.

Grace, it turned out, had broken her back.

Rosy heard in the afternoon, from Hugh. So much for Jeremy's breakfasts. Expressing dismay and sympathy, Rosy felt a wicked spasm of delight spark in her dark subconscious. Even for a jockey, that was at least three months out of action, no doubt twice as long for Grace. Bellboy was unharmed.

Two mornings later, when Rosy was putting Spinning Wheel away after exercise, Jeremy came across to the box.

'I'm going to see Grace in hospital tonight, when I get back from Newbury. Would you like to come with me?'

Rosy was stunned. She felt her jaw sag.

Jeremy, looking nervous, said, 'I've got to go—I feel bad about it—my fault, in a way. But I really dread it. If you come, it'll make it easier. I'm no good at that sort of chat—you know—'

Rosy nodded. 'Of course.'

'I'll pick you up at your house about half-past seven. Will that do?'

'Yes.'

Rosy tried for the rest of the day to work out why he was asking her. She wanted to think that it was an excuse to ask her out, because he could so easily have made the visit with Margaret or Hugh, senior or junior. Was he going to ask her to make his breakfasts for him? If she had half Grace's nerve, she would offer. She tried hard not to pretend that he suddenly had become aware of her as somebody other than a conscientious 'lad'; she made a point of not putting on anything special, or even as much eye-shadow as she would have worn if Gin had asked her out, to play down the 'going-out' angle. It was a job of work, for the stable, like collecting some new gear or picking something up from the vet's. By the time he arrived, she had got herself into such a suitable state of nonchalance that she did not hear his knock. Her father said, 'There's someone at the door. It won't be for me.' He went to answer it, and came back with a jocular, knowing look on his face. 'Like that, is it?' 'Oh, Christ, Dad!' Rosy's venom startled him, startled herself. She fled, slammed herself out of the house and tried unsuccessfully to calm down in the five yards from the door to the gate, where Jeremy waited.

'It's not a nuisance? I'm sorry—'

'No, it's my dad. I'm glad to come. Not your fault—'

In mutual embarrassment they clipped seat-belts and drove towards civilization.

Jeremy had asked Rosy because Hugh and Margaret preferred to visit in the afternoon, and he preferred her company to that of tedious young Hugh, whom he bore manfully during the day and did not want to endure more. The visit was strictly duty, highly charged for Jeremy with everything he most wanted to forget. Rosy was calming and sensible and unemotional, a good antidote for his paranoia. She would make a better assistant trainer than Hugh, but he did not have the nerve to sack Hugh. Hugh did nothing wrong, after all, and it was his parents Jeremy was thinking of, not Hugh himself, in his noble commitment to employing him. One visit to Grace was obligatory, and Rosy's presence would be beneficial, in the same way that it was to nervous horses. For one moment, seeing the expression on Mr Weeks's face, Jeremy had a panicking suspicion that more was being read into the outing than he intended, but Rosy's demeanour quickly reassured him. She was cool and businesslike, carrying a bag of apples from her father's store in the loft and a small bunch of Christmas roses, still wet from the garden. They made scarcely any conversation on the drive, save about the day's racing. Jeremy, not used to actually talking to Rosy, felt at a disadvantage; it was strange how little he knew her, although he saw her every day. But his dread of going into the hospital atmosphere occupied his thoughts more than his unease with Rosy, and when they reached the place and parked, he was glad for her to take the initiative, find the ward and the bed, as if she were finding her horse's allocated box at a race-course stables...

The brightness, the sight of the suspended femurs of unlucky motor-cyclists and white faces on whiter pillows loathing the intrusion of visitors, revived in him such black memories that he had difficulty in resisting his instinct to turn round and run for his life down the wide, rubber-floored corridors and out into the cold, fresh night. God, how he *hated* it!—bringing back the bitterness and the pain and the hot sweat of the eternal, centrally-heated nights when he had lain and cursed each minute away. Why—oh why—had he never learnt to laugh at his misfortune like a proper, upstanding, British public-schoolboy? He was lucky—lucky still to be walking and working, in the only job he knew; he was for ever telling himself so, when the black depression took hold, seeing the innocent Mowbray's face as he came to his fences up the home straight, seeing through the binoculars the light in the eye and the electric, drunken smile at the feel of taking off five or six abreast at a dirty black brush fence with the smacking tattoo of flying timber filling the moment's arrest in the glorious thunder of galloping hooves ... was he still a child, to remember only the glory of it, instead of the muck and the disappointment and the graft? After all the years he couldn't get it right, and grow up, and accept.

Rosy was saying all the right things, arranging the white flowers, smiling, self-possessed. Grace was looking impressively pale and transparent with suffering, smiling thinly. She was not the sort that perked up with visitors and put on a good act, but the sort that suffered visibly, keeping quiet and still and brave. Jeremy recognized the part she played, but was ashamed at his scepticism— damn it, it hurt like hell to break a vertebra, and she had a dreary time ahead of her—yet he felt no compassion, only irritation. He had difficulty in making the modicum of interested conversation. He kept thinking that she intended to marry him, and she always got her own way; and he could never love her—she was too managing. She brought out the worst in him. With luck the accident would put her off horses and everything to do with them. He felt jumpy and sick and left well before the hour was up, as soon as Rosy ran out of the obvious things to say.

'Sorry, I can't—I really hate it—'

Jeremy stood on the hospital steps, taking deep breaths of the outside air. 'I should have grown out of it by now.'

It was the nearest thing to a personal statement he had ever made, Rosy realized. She had no idea of how to answer him; she felt like a schoolgirl. She, too, should have grown out of it by now.

'Shall we go for a quick drink? There's a nice pub two miles down the road?'

His suggestion, her feelings exactly.

After a whisky, Rosy said, 'She wants to marry you, I think.'

'You think? I get that impression too, but why? What have I got to offer her, anybody? I like my own company, I'm morose by nature—'

'You weren't, before.'

'No? Well, it was all fighting at home. I was morose at home, perhaps not when you saw me, at the races. My father had a tough time, being the son of very colourful parents, and carrying on in the same profession. Sons should never put themselves in the position of being compared to a successful father. And for my mother, Letitia as a mother-in-law must be some cross to bear. What I've seen of marriage—it holds no appeal for me. Some day, perhaps, when—if—the stable ever gets on its feet and makes some money, but at the moment it's so precarious. Perhaps Grace thinks she can run it better. She might be right.'

'You're very pessimistic.'

'I suppose I am. It would be easier if I knew where I stood.'

'How do you mean?'

'In regard to the property. With Letitia. Everything belongs to her.'

'Hasn't she made a will?'

'As far as I know, no. Which means it will all go to my father. And at the moment, he seems to need the cash.'

Neither of them expected either to give or receive such confidences over two glasses of whisky, but it happened. Rosy remembered, painfully, the Stubbs. It seemed a good time to mention it.

'She keeps saying to me that she wants me to have a picture—the one called "Horse and Groom in a Landscape". It worries me. I don't want it, not if it's worth a lot. I only want a memento, if she wants to leave me something.'

'The Stubbs?'

'Yes. She knows I love it. But I don't want it. It's yours by rights, it belongs to the family.'

'I ought to talk to our solicitor. It's for him to tidy it all up. But the old girl can be very difficult. If she wants to leave you the Stubbs, she will. It's probably worth more than the estate.'

'I won't have it. It's ridiculous.'

'If she does, I shall have to marry you to get it back.'

Afterwards, Rosy wondered if she remembered this conversation correctly. Having to drive, Jeremy did not prolong the call at the pub, and Rosy had just enough to confuse her, not enough to be bold enough to tell him she would hold him to his suggestion. She supposed Jeremy spoke in jest. He was smiling at the time, not morose at all, but infinitely eligible. She did not reply, the remark leaving her incapable. When she got home and had escaped to bed, she lay for an hour gazing out at the moon-blanched square of light across the room where the Brood woods glittered on the hillside, and ached for lost opportunities. She cried before she went to sleep, wondering if there was something wrong with her, that she was so inept a hand at making things work out the way she wanted them. Grace's plan had gone awry, but at least she had tried; she had nerve and guts. But she, Rosy, like Jeremy, was one of life's drifters. Tonight they had drifted together but she hadn't even the wit to hold on, throw a line, connect, or whatever. She deserved every bit of the nothing she had achieved in her twenty-nine years.

Jeremy missed Grace badly, especially the breakfasts. To be accurate, he missed the home comforts and the look of someone caring that the kitchen had taken on. Not actually having to confront Grace every morning was a great relief. He wanted a housekeeper, motherly, preferably dumb, but nobody in the village fitted the bill, or would come if they did.

He went to see Rogers, the solicitor, who confirmed that Letitia had not made a will, and that the Stubbs was probably worth about half a million.

'But if she hasn't made a will, the girl won't get it anyway.'

'She's written a note, and said she knows I will carry out her few small bequests.'

'That's nothing. The whole lot will go to your father, including the Stubbs.'

'Well, so be it. I reckon he'll sell Brood, in that case. He's hard up.'

'You ought to make a stand, Jeremy. For Brood, at least, else you'll have no livelihood. I'll go and have a chat with her. There ought to be a will, in any case, whatever she decides.'

'She's not going to die tomorrow—probably another ten years to go, by the look of her. It's disgusting to fight over her money. I've never done anything for her. Rosy has more right to the Stubbs than I have if you judge by good works.'

'It's not fighting, don't be ridiculous. You're her only grandson. It should be settled, fairly divided. I'll go and see her.'

'Good luck. Don't be sordid.' Jeremy grinned. He had been at school with Paul Rogers and Paul knew the score.

'If you had three kids at boarding school, like I have, you'd care a darn sight more. That's your trouble, not getting married, starting a family. That mausoleum needs a woman around. What's your problem?'

'Getting a few more winners, basically. Enough to call it a living. I couldn't keep three kids in shoes, let alone at boarding school. At least I've only myself to worry about.'

'Women don't want security these days. Marry a worker, make a partnership. My wife makes as much money as I do.'

No doubt, judging by the office with its carpeting and rubber plant, the car outside and Paul's smooth suiting. Paul had worked at passing exams while Jeremy had been racketing around the race-courses, and Paul could still make good with a bent pelvis; it did not impede soliciting. I'd have made a good solicitor, Jeremy thought, having learned to be careful and prudent and nit-picking. He would be rich, and go racing as a spectator, between making divorces. He raced back to Brood and sniffed in the aromas of dung and old straw and new hay, and preferred to be as he was, a third division trainer with no future. Rosy's two good horses gleaming in the electric light of evening stables could both win at Cheltenham before spring came round and make their spirits take flight. No solicitor had such potential in the filing cabinets. Paper people sending letters of grievances and indignation in stilted prose, winners and losers without thrill or character ... Jeremy remembered that he had been a success once, and felt better. Who would want to interview the likes of Letitia for a living, and try to make her do what he was pretty sure she would decide not to?

Letitia thought Paul Rogers wanted to read the electricity meter and got him a stool to stand on, and a torch.

'No, Mrs Cutbush, I'm Rogers, Paul Rogers, your solicitor. I was passing so thought I'd drop in, as I know you can't get about like you used to. I'm an old friend of Jeremy's.'

'Did he send you?'

'No. Heavens, no!' He gave his professional laugh,

spirits sinking. The ambience of the elderly depressed him deeply, the fuggy aroma of their airless rooms, the intense deliberation with which they spun out trivial chores, losing their glasses, holding on to the furniture, changing the subject ... He knew he should be kind and well-disposed, but the necessary patience was barely within his compass.

'There's nothing wrong?' she asked.

'Not at all.'

'I'll make a cup of tea then.'

He might have known ... he was here for the afternoon and might as well make the best of it. While she was in the kitchen he studied the pictures on the walls and decided that the Stubbs, although smaller than most, was a very decent picture, in perfect condition, the horse posing in a misty, well-wooded hunting landscape with an attendant groom staring out as if for a contemporary camera, painted with as sure an eye for character as the horse. It would surely make a bomb at Sotheby's ... he winced at its vulnerability here in the dilapidated cottage. It should be in a vault.

'Do you lock up?' he asked her when she eventually arrived with a silver teapot on a tray.

'Jeremy asked me that, the last time he was here. There's a key under the flower-pot on the doorstep that Gin and Rosy use when they come. Nobody else comes as a rule. I'm not very popular, you know.'

She smiled maliciously. She was unkempt in a rather dashing style, in clothes that had once been so expensive they had lasted a lifetime, rubbed and faded but indubitably classy. She still had beautiful legs and ankles clad in dark woollen stockings and pointed leather brogues. She looked slightly dirty. On her thin hands, knotted with alarming blue veins, she wore a second fortune in rings, loose now but stopped from falling off by painfully swollen knuckles. For a granny she was far from cosy and homespun, a different kettle of fish from the blue-rinse ladies in apricot courtelle and woolly slippers for whom he was in the habit of making out wills.

115

'I am glad you have come, because I want to make a will,' she said.

Paul Rogers could not believe his luck, having already convinced himself that the visit would prove a complete waste of time.

'My mare is in foal, and I want it legal—that the foal belongs to Rosy Weeks. Also that picture, when I die.' She indicated the Stubbs.

Paul waited hopefully. 'And the estate?'

'That doesn't matter. I don't care. Only the foal and the picture.'

'The picture is probably worth as much as the estate.'

'It doesn't matter. Money doesn't matter at all to me, Mr Rogers.' Her dark eyes, far from faded, widened with contempt and majesty in such a way that Paul's professional patter died in his throat. God, what a harridan!

'The animals—and the picture. We can do the rest another time. I am not intending to die for some time, you know. You can come to tea more often, Mr Rogers, and we can discuss it.'

He was pretty sure she knew that he did not care for this idea at all. Jeremy could do the spade work, persuade the old bat she liked him well enough to divide the spoil in his favour. But Jeremy, he knew, wouldn't. He tried every argument in the book to prevent her willing the Stubbs to Rosy, but to no avail. The deed was done. The visit a disaster. He reported to Jeremy. Jeremy laughed.

'You'll have to marry her,' Paul said. 'What's she like?'

'She'd make a good trainer's wife. I might have come round to thinking about it, but it's impossible now.'

'Don't be so bloody stupid.'

'Not impossible, just highly embarrassing. It's not as if I've ever spoken to her, save to give her orders.'

'Good grounding for marriage. You must go and talk to your granny, Jeremy—she's a nutter. You mustn't let her get away with it. I talked till I was blue in the face, telling her it would all go to the Inland Rev anyway unless she wrapped it up properly now, but she's got a mind above the

116

Inland Rev apparently. It's up to you, lad. I can come round and change it, get it right—just give me a ring and I'll be on my way.'

'Serves me right for meddling.'

Jeremy, expecting nothing, conceded that the news did nothing to cheer him. Better to have drifted, as before, not really expecting much, but with a faint hope. Hope was now extinguished. He had no will to fight Letitia over her money, for God's sake. All now depended on making good with the stable. Good for him, really. High time he came out of mourning for his pelvis and learned ambition. But Rosy, in spite of his instinctive protest, took on a new significance in his life and he could no longer think of her as one of the lads. How exactly he could think of her, he had no idea.

9

'Look.'

Mrs Cutbush pointed to Silverfish's belly as the mare drank ice-cold water out of the field trough, and Rosy saw the indignant thump of the foal moving inside her. She put her hand on the fullness of the belly and felt the wrestling within, and laughed.

'It's an active little beggar.'

'Sharp. Strong. She's never had a sickly foal.' Mrs Cutbush fed the mare and looked after her with renewed interest. With the fresh life growing in Silverfish, the old woman seemed to have taken a new lease on life herself.

'It's a winner!' Rosy was divided between being excited and optimistic about the coming foal, and deeply worried about the responsibilities of rearing and making legal this possibly valuable animal. To put it into training, should she manage to rear it successfully to such a stage, would be financially beyond her, but no doubt between Gin, Mrs Cutbush and herself some plan might take shape.

While the foal inexorably grew to term in the old mare's worn body, Gin worried about the similar growth taking place in Beryl's inadequate frame, and when Rosy tried to pin him down about finding a way of faking the foal's papers to get it registered he said, 'Oh, for God's sake, Rosy, haven't I got enough troubles at the moment?'

Rosy hesitated. She no longer talked to him as she had once done; with marriage he had become more distant, thinner and—now she came to consider the matter—more worried. In looks he had aged five years and his once open, cheerful face was now habitually drawn.

'What troubles? You've never said.'

He shrugged, evasive. 'I'm a family man now. It's not the same.'

'You're a partner in this foal, aren't you?'

'Yes, but—'

'What's up? Is it Beryl?'

They were alone in the tack-room, just before departing for lunch. The boys had gone and Rosy had come to fetch her jacket and found Gin warming his backside in front of the stove. Six months back he had been away back to Beryl the moment the chores were finished.

'I suppose I can tell you. Yes. It's not all roses being married to Beryl, you know.'

'Oh, yes, Gin, I do know. I've got eyes in my head.'

'I don't seem to have made her happy. When I get home she'll be in bed, as like as not, to keep warm, no dinner made, no work done, nothing. She's made me put down for a council house in town, ten miles away—what'll I do then, if we get it? It'll kill me, living there, and I haven't even got a car yet. She's betting with the housekeeping— says it's only a quid or two and she's won more than she's lost, but I know that's not true. When I tell her she mustn't, she sets up this terrible argument—what else is there to do in this godforsaken hole, with no one to talk to, nowhere to go, nothing to think about ... it's getting me down, I can tell you. My family don't take to her, say she's lazy. My sisters—my mother—they haven't time for her. They've nothing in common, nothing to talk about.'

'They might feel differently when the baby is born. After all, it's a grandchild—'

'There's ten already. What's another? It'll be all comparisons. She won't do anything right. This baby's a disaster. I thought it would be great at first, now all I think about is what's going to happen to the poor little devil with Beryl and me like we are. I can tell you, Rosy, life's not much fun any more. I don't know what to do.'

Rosy wanted to put her arms round him and give him a kiss, but thought they would probably both weep. There was no answer to his problem. All she could offer was the likelihood of improvement with the summer coming, the baby born... 'I'll try and drop in more often. Perhaps some of the others would.'

'Who? Albert?' Gin laughed. 'She's right, that's the trouble—it's a lonely spot, and the house is awful—'

'No, Gin. She's not right. If she wanted she could come up here, work, clean tack at least. She could make the house lovely. It's lonely, but she's not tried. Don't blame yourself. It isn't your fault.'

'Makes no difference, whose fault. Putting blame is a useless occupation. It doesn't change how it is.'

'No.'

But there was nothing else to say. Rosy could think of no comfort for Gin. For once her own life seemed promising. She did not want to start getting depressed by events she could do nothing to alter. The difficulty of making the foal a legal member of the British Stud Book seemed, as he indicated, a very small matter beside his domestic problems.

The stable had a winner at Cheltenham in March, to make a season's score of seventeen, the best ever. Roly Fox covered himself in glory and Artemis gave Rosy a gold brooch in the shape of a little Pegasus. Rosy was still torn by Roly's foolish courage in racing, rarely being clever enough to win except by herculean effort. He was far more game than the dour Hawkins deserved. Even with winning the man did not become more lovable, always preoccupied by how much return he was getting from the bookmakers. Such greed disgusted Rosy. The man's life, even in his pleasure—for he declared that racing was his relaxation— revolved around profit.

'If that's what success does, perhaps we don't want it,' Jeremy remarked, as near a joke as he had been known to utter.

But Jeremy smiled more often, and when Rosy heard that the convalescent Grace was being regularly visited by one of her ski instructors, her optimism increased. The threat of Grace taking up her duties again next autumn was the one dark cloud in the sky. Rosy called one afternoon of mild March promise after Cheltenham to visit the recumbent Grace and clashed with the ski instructor by pure chance. He was properly blond, bronzed and muscled, a New Zealander introduced as Ed, and Rosy got the strong impression that Grace now saw her future in a flat in Earl's Court rather than at Brood. She lay gracefully on a sofa in the window overlooking the valley and the forests of Brood, basking in Ed's obvious admiration, and Rosy had to admit that Ed was an impressive catch, far more showy than Jeremy, although possibly he might prove a short-distance performer. He reminded Rosy of the new Brood jockey, who still offered her his sexual services whenever he had the chance, cornering her in Roly's loosebox with roving hands and lips which Rosy deftly fielded. She found Tony childish and funny, but he took no offence; considering his profession, he was astonishingly light-hearted. Rosy had once suggested he try his luck with Grace, but he professed Grace too cool and superior. 'She's not cuddly, like you. I don't like 'em all bone structure—stringy-like. Who're you saving yourself for then? Who d'you go to bed with?'

'No one.'

'You're joking? You have—you're not telling me you never—?'

'No, I'm not telling you that, you cheeky bugger.'

She was old enough to feel maternal over him, tender towards his sky-blue gaze and still-intact white smile. She was past the speedy thresh in the hayloft that his young blood desired. She had gone through that period during her London student days and did not consider herself by any means inexperienced, only inexperienced in true commitment. An affair with Tony did not promise to alter that.

But Silverfish's love-life came splendidly to fruition one dew-dark, freezing early morning, when the mare's strained breathing hung in white clouds and the tiny hooves protruding hesitated before the cold world, so that Rosy pleaded and wept, and swore, and Mrs Cutbush, having waited in the straw for so long that spiders' trails spun from her damp hair, moved at last to declare she would go and make some bacon sandwiches.

'What, now?' Rosy wailed.

'She's always slow. By the time I come back, she'll be born.'

Rosy, familiar with horses' ways, was unfamiliar with the habits of birth and not hungry for bacon sandwiches, only for the whole deliverance of what was presaged by the neat hooves wrapped in their white membrane. Mares, unlike cows, had no heart for difficult deliveries, and died quickly if things went wrong. How could Mrs Cutbush be so casual?

Or, by being so casual, did it mean there was no need for worry? Rosy was in two minds to call the vet, then remembered that there might be difficult questions to answer, like where did the mare go to stud? Deceit, in which before now she had never meddled, was tricky to handle without practice. She sat in the straw with her arms huddled round her legs, shivering with cold and anxiety. Silverfish, who knew far more about it than she did, looked bored rather than distressed, in fact thoroughly sour, her frosty eyelashes veiling her gaze, nostrils dilated with irritation. At intervals she heaved enormous sighs. Rosy felt much in sympathy, and somewhat remorseful to have interrupted the noble old girl's well-deserved retirement to put her through this wretched business again. But practice told: after a deeper sigh than usual, some angry groans and tetchy kicking into the straw, the little diving forelegs of the foal started to slither forward, and Rosy could see a neat little muzzle resting exactly in the right place over the knees, dark-coloured with a small triangle of white between the nostrils. She watched, fascinated, putting her hand on the mare's quivering tail and encouraging her with equally quivering words, half sick with excitement.

'Come on, come on, you old beauty, you.'

And Silverfish crossly made her final effort, and the foal was delivered in a wet, splattery, steaming heap, both hideous and magnificent, to Rosy's incredulous relief and overwhelming joy. If it had been her own delivery, she could scarcely have been more euphoric, or so she thought, as she watched the strange bedraggled creature stretch itself free of its membrane, legs at all angles like a benighted grasshopper's. Silverfish lifted herself up in the straw and looked dispassionately at what she had produced, gave it a careless push in the hindquarters with her nose, and lay back again with another of her world-weary sighs.

Rosy supposed her reaction was a trifle hysterical, and was glad there was no witness to it. When Mrs Cutbush eventually arrived with the bacon sandwiches, Rosy had recovered herself and was cool and collected, guiding the foal to the udder. Both animals were on their feet, the placenta splayed whole on the earth floor ready for disposal, the messed straw forked away. A thin, pearly light was struggling into the barn; thick mist lay over the river, and the cows on the other side, invisible, could be heard munching rhythmically in the frozen quiet. It was too early even for Brood House to show a light, the time only for the crowing cock, a milk-lorry, and a mare's birth, unheeding convenience.

'It's a filly,' Rosy said. 'Like you said.'

'Tiny. She's tiny.' Mrs Cutbush shook her head, but could not help smiling. She gave one of the bacon sandwiches to Silverfish.

'Here.'

Rosy realized that she was very hungry after all. She felt good, having created the foal as surely as the mare herself. All the worries seemed pointless, seeing the little thing now. She was very dark in colour, with a tiny white star and the snip between her nostrils: she might turn out to be a grey, or she might be dark chestnut like Peppermill. She was, indubitably, very small. Like Hyperion, Rosy reminded herself, and Gimcrack, The Little Wonder, Cyllene, The Lamb . . . size was no criterion. She had the blood of classic winners in her veins. Perhaps it was the bacon sandwiches, but Rosy felt a glow creeping into her bloodstream as she stood in the doorway of the big barn. The bleached roof timbers emulating, like poor country cousins, the stone arches of medieval parish churches, pleased her gaze, sheltering the old mare and her equally ancient owner: old bones and general dilapidation relieved by the still damply steaming freshness of the brand new, another miracle, another chance. Rosy was nothing if not an optimist. Mrs Cutbush, who had actually seen The Tetrarch race, could see his descendant now taking her first milk, winners' milk, sweet and hot against the cold white cloud of her infant breath. She watched closely, almost greedily, looking to Rosy suddenly very frail after the long vigil, blue veins showing in her temples, eye sockets hollow with weariness, like Silverfish's own, toast crumbs from the bacon sandwiches clinging here and there to the soft hairs on her chin. A less militant lady Rosy would have instinctively kissed; as it was, she took her arm and said softly, 'You must be tired? I am.'

'She always foals just before dawn.'

'She'll be all right if we leave her now.'

'She can go out when she's ready.'

The barn was open to the field. Silverfish dictated her own coming and going and had chosen herself to foal indoors rather than out. They had been up most of the night. Rosy, feeling her steps spring-heeled, wanting to run with joy, tempered her triumph to the old girl's shaky progress back to the house.

'I'll just have forty winks, till breakfast time. In the chair.'

Rosy made up the fire and brewed tea and they drank together, Rosy sitting on the hearth-rug. The room smelled of old leather and old books and old age.

'She's small but very active. Nothing wrong with that.'

'She's perfect.'

Only seventy per cent of horses bred to race ever saw a racecourse; only ten per cent of those ever won a race. Rosy knew the figures perfectly well, yet her wild hopes would not be dampened.

'I've got to go to work.'

She left the old woman dozing in her chair, and went back home via the field. Silverfish was outside already, walking slowly down to the river, her shadow long over the soaking grass. The mist was dispersing before the fine April sunrise, as sweet a picture of promise that nature could contrive, laced with larks' song and the crunch of frosty grass underfoot. The new filly pressed close to her dam, her eyes wide to the world's perfection, unaware of what she was born for, the merciless effort that would be asked of her, the hopes that were pinned on her delicate, uncertain frame.

Mrs Cutbush felt cold and ill, in spite of the fire Rosy had banked up for her, but she held on to the satisfaction of Silverfish successfully completing her pregnancy to bear her last foal for Rosy. They still had a stake in the future. Yet the past was far more precious to her, and the foal's arrival sparked off memories of similar occasions, playing midwife through cold spring nights with Peter, running and bustling, everything to hand, antiseptic and sparklingly efficient. They had always kept one or two broodmares, out of sentiment. There had been paddocks at Brood then, before the forest had encroached. The night's work with Rosy had jogged the old cells of her memory into feverish recall.

She lay twitching and smiling, shivering, seeing her beloved Peter with his mares and foals; at Royal Ascot in his ridiculous rig-out, carnation in his buttonhole, talking to the King. She saw him in the bedroom at Brood, laughing as he held out his arms to her. Always laughing, smiling. Nothing had ever gone wrong for them, except his getting killed. They neither of them ever dreamed that he might be killed, when he volunteered—'You'd always kick yourself, if you missed it,' he had said, as if it were a visit to Aintree.

It was strange how Peter with his positive, active presence, had not stamped his own son, but produced the silent, stubborn young Peter who had no charm at all, a dark shadow to his father. Letitia had never understood young Peter; all the help she had tried to give him when he

125

took over Brood he had rejected fiercely. Jeremy, born into the ill-assorted threesome left at Brood after the war, had been as difficult. Letitia measured them all to Peter and found them sadly at fault. They would none of them take her advice, pull themselves together, act as he had acted. They had alienated her, turned against her, turned her out. Even Jeremy. Only for the few years on the racecourse, before his accident, had Jeremy laughed like Peter, flowered, responded to her admiration, not been afraid to show excitement and joy. He had been like a plant brought into the light. From being reserved and secretive like his father, he had become bold, confident, funny, just like the old Peter when Letitia had first met him. With the accident had died his new courage and confidence, and the shell that had contained him as a boy had recaptured him. Letitia had aged after Jeremy's accident and lost her old passion for racing, turned to vegetables and dahlias and her dog Jasper. Her reputation for eccentricity had been augmented by one for rudeness. She had become sour in disappointment, and self-centred, and old.

She was terrified of growing immobile and helpless, and had kept the old mare so that she would be forced to go outside every day to feed her and look after her, and she had dug up the large beds in her garden and sown them full of flowers and vegetables and shrubs so that she had to work constantly to keep them all down, at bay, in rows, obedient. It was her boast that nothing grew out of place or rampant. To keep it under her thumb required that she go out and work every day, without fail. She would not give in to the lure of staying in by the fire; it would weaken her outlook. The older she got, the more important it was not to give in. On good days she was filled with pride at her strength and for the beauty and fulfilment of her garden, but on bad days she had to force herself, boot herself into action when her joints cried out to rest. A good day was followed by a bad day, she had done too much and must pay the toll. Every day was a triumph of a kind, the evening her reward when she rested and dozed.

Summer, the period of growth and hard work, was now at hand and her feelings were torn as always by a longing for the kindness of the weather and a dread of keeping the garden from getting out of hand. But as she dozed now, she saw summer only as a procession of sleek-coated mares and foals; the old summers with Peter on the green swards of racecourses, leading in their lovely winners, were bright in her mind. They muddled with the present sun that was rising over the downs and shining strongly through the window, and she dreamed that Silverfish was winning, galloping along the rails, and behind her the foal ran, fresh-born with curling, damp coat, and on her long new legs she ran past Silverfish and beat her to the post to the cheers of long-ago crowds, dressed in the strange cropped clothes of the twenties and waving their toppers.

To Rosy the birth of a son to Beryl was an anti-climax after the night seeing her filly born, but she kept her counsel and made the approved expressions of congratulation and admiration. This was not difficult, for the child born out of such discontent and complaining was a splendid, gurgling, happy creature, in no way the mewling scrap that Rosy had somehow expected. He thrived on Beryl's offerings of tinned milk, tinned soup, chips and Jaffa biscuits and laughed as soon as was humanly possible at the enchanting world he inhabited. Rosy, who had never liked babies until now, was bowled over by Kes, as Beryl called him. ('After a film,' she said. 'Kes was a bird,' Rosy said. 'Oh, no. Kes was the boy.') She volunteered to babysit so that Gin could take Beryl out sometimes, or wheeled Kes down in the afternoon to visit Silverfish and her filly, and the fat, lazy Roly Fox who had been turned out in the mare's field again. The baby slept, too young to take notice, but Rosy was happy enough. Sometimes Beryl went out in the afternoon and would not be back when Rosy returned with the baby, so Rosy fed Kes on the unsuitable concoctions she found in Beryl's refrigerator and sometimes took him up to the stable to carry on with any work that required doing.

127

Beryl said she went for walks on the downs—'It's so marvellous to feel free again,' she exclaimed, and indeed she seemed to have thrown off her grouches and flowered: once more birdlike and spry, with freckles across her nose, back into her jeans and T-shirts. She even made a dab at a bit of housekeeping and made ham salad for Gin, or cooked some beefburgers, and kept the baby clean. Rosy was relieved, and presumed her former sullen laziness had been caused by pregnancy and winter combined. And yet ... there was something other, something breathless and secretive about Beryl's transformation.

Gin bought a car, and said to Rosy, 'Beryl put a bet on—it came up. She put the whole bloody maternity allowance on. If I'd known I'd have killed her, but it came up. I can't get over it! For God's sake don't spread it around. My ma would kill her. I've told 'em I got a bonus at work. Christ, I don't know whether to laugh or cry.'

Cry, Rosy reckoned, if the girl couldn't kick the habit. She knew about betting, was infinitely cautious not to get hooked herself, having seen the unhappiness it caused. It was not for her to lecture. If Gin couldn't stop her, nothing she could think up was likely to make any difference. Was that, though, the reason for Beryl's new optimism, the gleam in her eye? It did not stem from maternalism, for the gleam was brightest when Rosy took the baby and Beryl set off 'to get some air'. 'I have to get out sometimes—Gin never takes me,' she justified herself. It was true that Gin had little time to entertain her for, desperate to make money, he worked for his father in his spare time from the stables, and helped out on a farm when hay-carting came round. Rosy guessed that after her bonanza, Beryl was losing the housekeeping fast. Gin had a strained and overwrought air that nothing else explained. Naturally he would boast of the wins, but Rosy knew that—for someone who bet as Beryl did—the wins were invariably overtaken by the losses.

John Weeks lay on the edge of a small declivity on the

downs watching a family of shrikes posing on a row of stakes that marked the danger for the race horses. He was just high enough above Brood to be clear of the trees, so that he had a clear view of the valley, but a straggle of the Brood vegetation had seeded almost to the declivity, a tangle of thorns and brambles that made a good hide for watching birds. Weeks liked this cup of protection—once, he thought, a small quarry—and settled there quite often when the weather was right, even bringing a flask up with him, along with his binoculars.

On this particular August morning the air was heat-hazy and still, the sky shrill with larks. He could think of nothing more delicious in life than to be doing what he was doing now. (Nothing, a cynic might have said.) But John Weeks, in his voluminous shorts, long socks turned down over the tops of his boots to reveal his stringy brown legs, was never bored communing with nature. The very smell, of warm turf and rabbits and his own sweat, was fragrance to his nostrils; his sense of belonging, of being a natural part of the down, so familiar and loved, never failed to make him aware of an intense satisfaction that could only be provoked in most people by uncommon strokes of fortune. How lucky he was to get such joy out of what was at hand, free, available twenty-four hours of every day! Unaware that people found him intensely boring and smug, he haunted the valley and down, conversing only of habitat and conservation, the nature of chalk and the evolution of the worm, the nourishment in the root vegetable.

He loved the uncultivated forest of Brood, left to its own devices for the last thirty years, the undisturbed nature of the valley, the lack of advancement, and examined it inch by inch through his binoculars, finding pleasure in each eyeful, from the fine little filly galloping down Mrs Cutbush's pasture to provoke its elderly dam, to the extraordinarily large lettuces in the Maddox kitchen garden.

From having been a postman all his life, he already knew each household and its habits. He enjoyed renewing his visits through the binoculars, but did not pry: nature was his business, not people. He did not, on the whole, care for people much, preferring his own company. The only people he saw on the downs were the exercisers of race-horses, and an occasional walker, and he knew that few of them saw him, for he prided himself on melting into his sur-roundings, seeing things that nobody else saw, because he was still and invisible.

Today he saw what nobody else saw, because he was held captive in his shrubbery of gorse by the unexpected arrival of a young man and a young woman who came up through the trees. Walkers always kept to the ridge, the walking path passing above Brood on the crest, and he thought these were walkers who had missed the way. He thought they would pass below him and keep going until their route converged with the route proper. He was going to keep quiet while they came and went. But they came and did not go. They stopped in the depression below him and threw off their clothes and made love with passionate abandon. They were only thirty feet away and John Weeks, who had watched every sort of copulation through his bin-oculars, from fox and vixen to dragonfly, from grass-snake to magpie, with fascinated, biological interest, was horri-fied by the human spectacle. This was nature more natural than he cared to witness. He shut his eyes but the picture seemed to come through his lids and cries of bliss and grunts of consummation were disgusting to his sensibil-ities. He lay helplessly in his hide, outmanoeuvred by Wild Life, unwilling voyeur of a ritual that desecrated this happy place. He knew already that he would never come here again. He longed to slip silently away, but hadn't the skill of the adder to vanish to the thump of a footstep. He had to sit it out until, in the aftermath, he recognized the girl, and guessed who the man was. And could only be grateful that they did not linger, the act their only delight, the contem-plation of nature in its train something that did not occur to them.

He lay back as they departed, staring into the colourless, cloudless sky, feeling the perspiration of guilt and disgust

sliding in drops off his nose. Yet the skylarks were still singing, and the whirr of the combine drifted up from the
valley, life at its most normal, nothing out of place.

The filly foal was Rosy's pride and joy. She was sharp as a
needle and very active, as promised from the moment of
birth. She was pushy and nosy and bold and her galloping
over the uneven pastures of her home was both impressive
and nerve-wracking. Rosy was used to chasers and the little
filly's fine legs looked to Rosy much too delicate for the
wild action they were put to. But there was nothing delicate
about her lifestyle. She thrived, a splendid 'doer', although
she remained small, for her frame was small. By autumn
when she got her second coat it was apparent that she
would be a grey like her dam, but initially she was dark
enough to be almost black. Rosy called her Secret, but the
shy connotation was not very suitable. She decided to
register her as Dark Secret—should she ever get to overcome her difficulties in that direction.

'Look, I'd see to it if I knew someone, but at the moment
I just don't want any more trouble on my plate.' Gin was
uncooperative. 'There's no hurry. It's not as if we're going
to sell her, is it? We'll sort it out next year.'

He had scarcely been to see the filly, too preoccupied to
take an interest. When racing started again he was glad to
get away in the horsebox, growing more cheerful as the
miles clocked up away from home. During the drives he
would talk about Kes with love and joy, and about Beryl
not at all. Rosy knew better than to encourage confidences
in this direction; those days were over. They skirted the uncertain ground, and enjoyed the old relationship during the
long, fuggy hours in the cab, talking about the horses and
racing, but not about love and life, nor betting. Gin still
loved his job, more so now that the stable was getting more
winners. During the hours away, with Spinning Wheel or
Peppermill or Roly Fox dozing to the engine roar that
engulfed them, Rosy producing fruit gums, and coffee from
a thermos to perch on the dashboard, Gin would thaw into

amiability. Mellowing, the nearest he ever came to comment on his situation, was, 'Life is what you make it, I suppose.' Accompanied by a deep sigh. At this, Rosy presumed to herself that she would have to work harder, but in which direction she could not decide.

During the winter, while her filly grew hard in the cold meadow, Rosy devoted all her energies to caring for her racehorses. Mr Hawkins had them each running on average once a fortnight, so that she spent many hours away, and became used to the late nights settling the edgy over-tuned beasts after their hard races, cycling home in the icy dark to feed Silverfish and Secret, yawning into the house to find her potato pie dried up in the oven. A blurred interest in 'News at Ten' with her father, and into bed...

Grace did not appear again at Brood House. As soon as she was fit again she departed with Ed to the snow-slopes of France, to housekeep, presumably, for a more appreciative male. Rosy was deeply satisfied by this turn of events.

Jeremy, working under more pressure for the formidable Mr Hawkins, seemed suddenly more accessible, less anxious to retreat beyond the clock-tower into his fortress. To keep the Hawkins horses racing so hard was a challenge to his skill as trainer, and when they started to get winners at Newbury and Sandown Park and Cheltenham as well as at the more modest courses they were accustomed to attending, his temperament improved along with their results. The work load was heavy in the yard but everyone seemed to thrive on the pressure.

'Except the horses,' as Gin remarked gloomily, when the conversation in the tack-room turned on the subject. 'We might get a rest when he's broken them all down. He thinks they're bloody motor bikes.'

After three runs in six weeks on ground harder than was good for him, Roly's leg was giving trouble. He had gone up in the handicap and his wins were dearly managed. Rosy spent hours hosing his leg in the yard, to keep at bay the dreaded heat. Quite often she rode him down to Silverfish's field and stood him in the river. This was in her own time, during the afternoons, and she did not think of it as extra work. But one afternoon Jeremy saw her as he was driving past, and he stopped at the gate and came across the field to speak to her. Seeing him coming, followed by Silverfish and the curious filly, Rosy recognized an element of fantasy in the encounter—all her prize loves congregating on the riverbank in one magic moment, as if summoned by genie. Pure pantomime, but not to be scorned; rather, savoured: a dark, rain-heavy afternoon, closing early, the earthy smell of the river, swollen and fast-running, the grass churned and trodden where the mare had come to drink. Jeremy approached with his uneasy gait, not quite a limp, his old cap pulled close, frowning.

'You charge overtime for this?' He half-smiled, as human as Rosy had ever known him.

'No. Pure love.'

'It's the best thing going.'

He stood companionably, pulling Silverfish's ear as she pushed at his pockets.

'It's very hard, trying to tell Hawkins his horses are made of flesh and blood. He says he'll take them to someone else if I try to suggest he's pushing them too hard.'

'Would he?'

'Yes. I think he would. Money dictates, I'm afraid, not loyalty.'

'I'd hate to lose Roly.'

'We'll just have to cross our fingers he lasts out. He's done well. He's game as they come. Hawkins doesn't know how lucky he is.'

Jeremy gave Silverfish a Polo mint out of his pocket and the filly pushed in, nipping. He gave her one, cuffed her on the muzzle. He was thinking about the Stubbs. Seeing Rosy sitting there on Roly Fox, he saw them as 'Horse and Groom in a Landscape', entirely appropriate. She deserved the picture; she would get it, for all he intended to do about it, but the business had distanced her in a strange way, singled her out, made her no longer one of the lads. It had made a barrier. He was more aware of her now, but there

133

had been no barrier before. It was one of the quirks of human nature that it wanted what it could not have, did not want what was accessible. There was nothing to be done about Rosy.

The filly nipped him again and he smacked her more smartly.

'Little devil!' He was about to thank Rosy for the extra trouble she was taking and depart, then he remembered the extraordinary disclosure Grace had made over the dinner table, and felt the moment was too opportune to resist.

'Who does she take after? Not her dam, for sure. Who did Letitia get the mare served by?'

Rosy did not reply. In the dusk it was hard to read her expression, but Jeremy sensed her embarrassment. She was too genuinely good to tease.

'It wasn't Peppermill, was it?'

She must have seen he wasn't asking in anger, although she still said nothing.

'Better not let Hawkins know, else he'll want five thousand in stud fees.'

'He doesn't know!'

'No. News to me if he does. It's true though?'

'Yes. I—I—it seemed too good to miss—'

'Stroke of genius. What are you going to do about her papers?'

'Gin was going to find some crook vet but now he's not so keen. I don't know really. It's a bit of a problem. I worry about it.'

'I might find you somebody ... some obscure stallion. Nobody with a good one would take the risk. Perhaps a premium horse. It won't enhance her value, I'm afraid. Are you going to sell her?'

'I don't know.'

Rosy could see Jeremy was amused. It was an enormous relief, suddenly, that he knew.

'How did you find out?'

'Someone told me, who saw you. Pure chance. Don't worry about it.' He stood assessing the filly as, bored, she cantered sharply away up the field. He laughed as she put in a couple of bucks. Silverfish wheeled away and trotted after her. 'You can sell me a share. We'll run her on the flat.'

Did he mean it? Rosy felt the blood rushing to her head, the dizzy vision of sharing the owners' stand with Jeremy almost too much for her composure. But he was laughing, joking.

'I'll do what I can about a stallion. Have to be very careful, but I'm sure I can find someone.'

He departed, and Rosy followed him to the gate. He opened it and fended off the mare and foal while she went through. It was nearly dark, she could not linger. She trotted along the grass verge and turned into the Brood drive. She was excited, warmed by her encounter. She hugged Roly when she untacked him. He looked magnificent in the electric light, hard and fit and shining like a billiard ball. She felt, for once, incredibly lucky at the way things were going.

It was the nature of racing that this state of mind was short-lived. Roly went to Sandown and won, battling his heart out as usual, and came home distressed. The next day there was heat in his foreleg, he left his feed, and Rosy took him out in the afternoon to graze on Jeremy's lawn. Mrs Palmer would have given him a hug and said, 'Give him plenty of time to get over it—perhaps he's done enough for this season,' but Hawkins had said, grimly, 'Sharks, these bookmakers. The best I could get was seven to four on and then he nearly didn't make it. No wonder we're going grey.' He gave Rosy a twenty-pound note. For the hours she had hosed Roly's leg and stood in the stream it worked out at about twenty-five pence per hour. Rosy, huddled in her anorak on the patch of grass (that had once been smooth as green velvet, rolled twice a week when the weather was right, a foreground for the famous rose-beds that were now wild briars on the edge of the woods), bitterly resented that such a man should own a horse like Roly. Most horses—the ones with any sense—packed it in when they were treated as he had been treated.

'You're so bloody stupid, Roly, killing yourself for that oaf. He'll sell you for dogfood when you've crocked yourself up.'

The horse stopped grazing and gave her an affectionate rub with his thick head, nearly pushing her over. She laughed, and scratched his nose. She liked standing on Jeremy's lawn grazing her horse—as if, when she was finished, she could go in and start getting Jeremy's tea ready. Once through the clock-tower and fantasy took over.

Roly was entered for Lingfield in a fortnight's time, and Cheltenham three weeks after that. Jeremy wanted to take him out of Lingfield to give him a chance for Cheltenham, but Hawkins would not hear of it. He had made up a party for Lingfield, entertaining some business friends, and Roly was a part of the entertainment. 'No point, if I haven't a horse running, for God's sake.'

Jeremy asked Rosy to take Roly for a long trot on the road, to see how the leg went.

'The damned horse!—if we can show Hawkins he's not sound he might believe us.'

But Roly, perverse, trotted up sound.

'He'll have to take his chance, I'm afraid. The man's a fool. If he were to lay him off now until next season, he'd get far more races out of him in the end, than doing it this way.'

Rosy put heavy bandages on Roly's forelegs. She watched him go down to the start with a lump in her throat, knowing that all the unbearable things in racing were catching up with her, and the fatal weakness on her part of actually loving her horse was about to have its inevitable repercussion. She stood with Gin as usual, close to tears.

'I'll kill that Mowbray if he rides him into the ground. He *knows*—'

'You've gone through all that before. Nothing's any different.'

There was no way, she knew in fact, that Mowbray could help, the horse having been entered to run. With luck

136

the leg would hold out, or perhaps he would go tender early on and be pulled up without much damage. But Roly did it the hard way, as he inevitably did, jumping like a stag until the second last, when he stood off too far, fiddled a stride, jumped awkwardly and landed very steeply, off-fore leading. Even before he had recovered and run on, Rosy knew the damage was done. Mowbray pulled him up at once—which showed, she realized, how bad it was, for Roly had been in front and looked like being in the frame. The crowd roared with dismay and Tony dismounted. Rosy ran.

'Don't blame me. I couldn't have pulled up any quicker!' He gave her a defensive, almost sympathetic smile.

Roly, all steamed up, danced round them on three legs, not able to stand still, not understanding the pain. Tony took his saddle off and put the sweat-rug on, buckling it in front.

'Sorry, Rosy, honest,' he said, before departing.

Did she look so bad? Rosy had never felt bleaker in her life, but sentiment had no place in public. Jeremy was hurrying through the fringes of the crowd towards her, Gin with him. They were still well down the course, away from the public, a forlorn group Rosy knew—for the scene had been enacted many times on all racecourses, watched perhaps by a few interested parties through binoculars. A horse written off, shoulders shrugged. Memories were only a week or two long in racing . . . on with the next. As Tony had said at the start, there were plenty of youngsters coming along.

Jeremy came up without a word, felt the leg, watched as Rosy tried to lead Roly out. The horse could put no weight on it at all. It hung, almost as if broken. Roly tried, stumbled, and fell to grazing as if he had not eaten for a week.

'Go and fetch the box,' Jeremy said to Gin. 'And get the vet down here on your way. With luck he's already coming.'

Mr Hawkins did not even come to see.

He rang up three days later, and forgot to send the twenty-pound note.

137

Roly was injected with pain-killers, bandaged, cossetted by Rosy. He could not leave his box, fretted, would not eat, grew thin and miserable. Spinning Wheel went to Cheltenham and won a good race. Mr Hawkins came down to see him, actually patted his sleek neck, patted Rosy on the back. She nearly bit his hand. He glanced over Roly's door and shook his head.

'He might as well go to the sales. Ascot in July—he'll be walking sound by then, don't you think?'

'He'll run again, given time. We could turn him out here for eighteen months,' Jeremy said.

'What, and charge me keep all that time? I'm not a mug, Cutbush.'

'It wouldn't cost you much. He's done you well. He deserves a chance.'

'Could you guarantee he'll come back sound?'

'No one can guarantee anything in this game. But there's a fair chance he'll win a few more races for you.'

'I can't wait that long. Get him back by next season, perhaps—'

'Unlikely, I'm afraid. It'll take at least a year.'

'And then it's likely to go again. No. It doesn't interest me. Get him sound and send him to the sales. Someone else can take a chance with him, and I'll get another youngster.'

Jeremy avoided Rosy's eyes.

Later, when he came round in the evening, Rosy said, 'I'd buy him if I could. How much do you think he'll fetch?'

'More than you've got, I imagine. Hawkins won't take the chance, but some people will risk it. He's got a good record.'

'Why's he got to go to the sales? Can't you find a private buyer? He might go anywhere.'

'Why be so pessimistic? He could well get a better home than this—a better owner, at least. He's had a pretty rough deal here, after all.'

'If he's lucky! Why should it depend on luck? He's given everything, all his life. Won't Mrs Palmer buy him back?'

'She's gone to live in America.'

Two days later, as if to placate her, Jeremy told her he had acquired her filly a respectable document. 'She's by Understanding. Look, all down in writing.'

'Who's Understanding?'

'Best I could do. He died of a twisted gut three months ago, the owner doesn't care and the vet who signed the certificate is retiring any day now and did it for a bottle of whisky. The stallion has the same bloodline as Peppermill—goes back to Nasrullah, Nearco, so if anyone ever breeds from your filly they won't go too far wrong. If you sell her, the fact that she's by Understanding won't make you a big price, but beggars can't be choosers. The fact that she's out of Silverfish might make up for it.'

Rosy was greatly relieved. The filly was becoming a worry to her, for she was now a yearling, and if she was going to race she would have to go into training at the end of the year. Time slipped by so fast, and big decisions could not be made on the spur of the moment. The filly was sharp and likely to make an early début. She was tough and hard and fast and everything a budding owner might desire. But Rosy doubted more and more if the budding owner was going to be herself.

'I can tell you, I could do with the money if we sell her,' Gin said.

'What, for Beryl's betting?' Rosy could not help the sharp retort, for Gin reminded her at frequent intervals that he had a half-share in the filly. She had promised him, it was true, when the mating had taken place, but she felt slightly bitter about his attitude now. It was hardly supportive, to talk constantly about selling her. Gin was going down the drain, driven by Beryl's behaviour, no longer the honest cheerful lad he had been formerly, but becoming devious and self-pitying.

'It's an illness, gambling,' he said.

'Yes, well, giving her more money—selling the filly—won't cure it.'

'It's not that. We owe money on everything. It's not for betting, just to clear up some of the debts.'

'You know it won't. It'll go the same way.'

'What can I do?'

There was no answer to that. Not with Kes as part of the set-up. Gin doted on Kes, and Beryl, for all her faults, was not a bad mother. She was good with Kes and he thrived on his strange diet and his outings up on the downs. On mild mornings Beryl pushed his pram up the rutted track through the Brood woodlands, and the wide-eyed baby, parked in the bushes, laughed at the antics she got up to with the man who was waiting for her. He was always in a hurry, glancing at his watch.

'Christ, Beryl, I'm riding in the first race at Wincanton. Let go of me!'

'You're making it up. You're not riding till the third. I've read the paper. There's tons of time.'

'No. There's a spare ride in the first, and I've got it.'

'Keeps you fit, running up here. You are lovely, Tony.'

'Crazy, this weather. I liked it better in the summer.'

'This sleeping-bag's OK though. I got it in a jumble sale. Everest Standard it says on the label. I thought it would be just the thing.'

'You're full of good ideas, I'll give you that.'

'You reckon March Past'll win the first?'

'It'll beat mine, that's for sure.'

'If I give you a fiver, will you give it to Mark for me, to put on Mary March?'

'Yeah, if you want. Shove up, Beryl. I must make tracks, honest.'

'Put the fiver on and I'll give it you tomorrow, when I've collected my Child Allowance.'

'You owe me a fiver from last week.'

'Yeah, well, we win today and you can keep it out of that.'

'I've heard that before.'

They struggled out of the fuggy confines of the bargain sleeping-bag which Beryl folded neatly and stuffed underneath Kes in the pram. She continued her walk, singing, and Tony ran back down one of the old gamekeeper's tracks to where he left his car in a clearing nicely hidden from the main road. The affair was good for a laugh and kept him fit. The exercise in Beryl's sleeping-bag was as good as a sauna. Life needed its little entertainments.

Roly was duly entered for the Ascot July sales and Rosy tried not to think about his departure. She kept telling herself he could have broken his neck instead of done-in a tendon and been departed this life some four or five months, but the argument was no comfort. She always thought horses killed racing at least died at full stretch, enjoying themselves, better than the ones like Roly who, clapped-out, turned to less heady careers in hacking stables or the yards of middle-aged ladies who went in for dressage. If he went to a good home from Ascot she might bear it quite well, or so she convinced herself. He was only a horse. But as the day came nearer she grew more and more depressed, and spent long hours with him in the stream so that his leg would show up as sound as possible. Not that he could be sold with a warranty, but she would do her best by him.

Another summer on, and what had seemed so sweet the summer before was now all doubt and disillusion. Word went round that Grace had left the lovely Ed and was coming home again. If she resumed her wooing of Jeremy... 'That's all I need!' Rosy raged, and the chill river seemed to infect her spirits with a dread of the future, revealing the simple allegiances round which her life revolved as pathetic and insubstantial, all dispersing on the summer breeze: her horses, her dream of Jeremy, even her timeworn friendship with Gin who was growing daily more hard-pressed, bitter and shifty, caught in the oldest trap of all. What narrow horizons, what lack of ambition, what a sad waste of the passions and achievements of which she was sure she was capable ... her life trickling on like one of the lost back-eddies below her, taking no direction. 'What is the matter with me?' she wondered, and went to the doctor to discuss pre-menstrual tension and a course of librium, knowing all the time that the cures were far beyond trendy drugs; Tony Mowbray's suggested cure was probably the answer, but who with? If Grace came back, she would have to get another job, and meet another set of people, and forget Jeremy. Long hours by the river were bad for brooding over her disposition. It was almost with a sense of relief that the date for Roly's disposal arrived, so that her worries on that score could be either alleviated or substantiated. For better or for worse. She dreaded the day, but was glad it had come at last.

She had brought Roly in from the field for the last few days, to get his coat clean and a stable sheen on it. He looked rested and well and trusting. When they loaded him, he thought he was going to the races. He did not know he was never coming back.

Once in the horsebox and on their way, Rosy broke down and wept. Gin was not sympathetic.

'He's only got half my troubles, for God's sake.'

Rosy did not like Gin any more, she decided. She felt much better after a good cry, and knew she was safe for the rest of the day. Jeremy was driving over, and before Jeremy she would keep cool and proud. She would come back happy enough if Roly was bought by someone worthy of him.

Poor Ascot horses, she thought, most of them unwarranted, many going for a few hundred in spite of their decent records and honest eyes. The less glamorous face of racing, Rosy tried to convince herself that she was unduly pessimistic about their fates and that the large majority of buyers were good-hearted and were offering decent homes with clean straw and lots of oats. No doubt plenty were, but there were just too many horses ... the sight depressed her. Why did people breed so many? Was the thrill of racing, at bottom, sheer greed? She never could make up her mind, seeing the way Hawkins's mind worked, and yet knowing that there were considerations and glories way above mere money. Granted, she was a sentimental female groom, but other people revealed mushy hearts—she had seen them, bowled over by the sheer courage of a good horse, crying, for God's sake. She was not the only person obsessed by the likes of Roly Fox. She could not bring herself to lead him round and left the job to Gin, but stayed with him in the stable until his number was near. He had no reserve on him.

'Cheer up,' said Jeremy, quite gently. 'The worst hasn't happened yet. There are some decent people interested in him.'

He had driven over to see how it went; he looked nervous, probably worried she was going to make a fool of them both by crying, but she no longer felt like it, merely cold and sick. They went into the sale ring and sat on the nearest seats and watched two eleven-year-olds go for a few hundred each. They both had decent records, and terrible legs, and their racing days were over. Where did they go? She could see Roly walking round outside in the sunshine. It was a lovely day and he was on his toes, thinking it must be racing, yet he was rounded with summer grass. He looked magnificent, and she knew she was not biased in thinking so. A horse like that must go to a good home! She was so nervous she thought she was going to be sick. Her heart started to pump as Gin brought him in through the entrance, and the auctioneer began to read from the catalogue.

'This is a good horse! The owner making way for young stock, but there's a lot of races in this one yet...'

Roly stared about him as he walked round, surprised, interested, full of goodwill towards the human race. The bidding started at one thousand, and went on steadily. Rosy tried to see who was bidding, but it was very hard to make out. A lot of men stood in the entrance to the ring, and the auctioneer was looking there, and up in the stand behind her. She turned round, craning.

'Who are they?' she asked Jeremy.

'One of them is—' He mentioned a very decent trainer. Rosy's optimism lurched.

'Two thousand nine hundred, two thousand nine

143

hundred, any advance on two thousand nine hundred?'

The invisible man behind made it three thousand, and the price went up again, but more slowly.

Someone behind Rosy said, audibly, 'That's the horse that broke down at Lingfield, isn't it?'

'Is it? Probably. You wouldn't sell a horse like that if it's still any good. I wouldn't anyway.'

The decent trainer dropped out. It was left to the invisible man behind.

'Three thousand two hundred. Are we all finished at three thousand two hundred?'

He waited, nobly, for what seemed to Rosy an age.

The hammer fell. Roly nuzzled Gin's sleeve and Gin gave him a Polo mint.

'Sold to the gentleman—' The auctioneer peered upwards. 'Smith?' He muttered to his clerk. Rosy turned round.

'Who is it?' she asked Jeremy. 'Who's Smith?'

Jeremy was frowning. They got up and pushed and shoved their way outside, into the sunshine. Another horse was already in the ring and nobody was interested in Roly any more. Roly was wondering when the race was going to start. He danced around and Rosy took his rein.

'Who is Smith?'

Gin, glowering, said, 'He's a bloody—'

'Cutbush?'

Smith was a burly, rough-spoken man in a crumpled waxed jacket and a tweed hat. He was fleshy around the jaw and had slitty, shifty eyes.

He said to Rosy, 'My lad will take him.'

He drew aside with Jeremy and Rosy heard him say, 'This leg now…' She was left with the lad, a similarly hulkish, unsmiling boy of about eighteen who produced his own headcollar and changed it quickly. His handling was rough and sharp.

'He's very kind,' Rosy said, belligerently.

The boy grunted.

'Are you going to take him back to the stable, or have

you got a horsebox—?' Now the moment had arrived, she could not bear to part with him.

'I can manage.'

The lad chucked her the removed headcollar and led Roly away without a word. Rosy stood watching. The horsebox that received Roly was a clapped-out scarred wreck, ten times worse than Jeremy's. Rosy, who had vowed not to cry again, felt as if she had turned to stone.

'That's a betting stable,' Gin said dourly. 'Load of crooks. Smith ... you know him. Had that good mare, Blue Eucalyptus.'

'She got killed?'

'Yeah. There was some funny business, but nobody proved anything.'

'What do you mean? How can—'

'Come on, I'll buy you a lunch.' Jeremy was back, speaking tenderly.

'Is he as awful as he looks, that Smith?'

'He's not what you might call one of the country's top ten trainers, no. I'm sorry. I thought Nichols was going to get him.'

Rosy followed the two men blindly into the canteen. All around them sat nice, fresh-faced, middle-aged people who had come to pick up hunters or an eventer, or keen young ladies who wanted a nice hack. Suddenly the place seemed to be teeming with prospective homes, kind and true. There was nobody else like Smith in sight. Why did *he* have to pick Roly? Why on earth had she not alerted one of these ladies to Roly's lovely nature? But Roly, at three thousand two hundred, was almost in the big league. How would he make out in Smith's stables, which she pictured as dirty, with low roofs and strung-up doors? Blind misery overcame her. She pecked at her steak pie, and Jeremy did not offer to drive her home. He let her go back in the horsebox with Gin.

Jeremy felt too bad to drive her home. Roly had stood a good chance of getting a fairish home, handsome and kind

145

as he was, duff leg or no. But it was just in the nature of things that, when it mattered so desperately to Rosy, the likes of Smith had picked on him for his nefarious plans. Not that one could prove anything against Smith, but he was not a man who boasted owners who were in the game for pleasure and the sport. They were all of Hawkins's ilk. Jeremy felt uncomfortable about Hawkins, not wanting an owner like him, but needing his support. If Rosy thought she had problems ... oh, Jesus, who would be in the racing game! It was so magnificent at its best, seedy— to put it kindly—at bottom. Human greed ruined it; the exploitation of one of the kindest, gamest animals on earth for money. But without the money motive, racing would not exist. All industries were about money. And in most stables the horses lived like kings while they earned their keep. Not for them wet winter nights in unsheltered fields, thin tails tucked against the north wind. It was a game of contradictions from top to bottom, materially, emotionally and every other way you could think about it. Unfortunately—or, contrariwise, not—the bug bit deep, and did not let go. Jeremy had thought a lot about getting out, but knew he couldn't.

As he drove now, remembering Rosy's bleak face, old agonies of his own flooded back, of a much-loved pony he had outgrown at sixteen which, sold on to slapdash owners, had died neglected in a field, of tetanus. Even at that age he had wept every night in bed for a week when he found out, and the memory still brought back a dreadful ache. They had done such deeds together, that pony and himself. Sentiment? It was no good thinking that the animal brain worked in the same fashion as the human brain, for that was patently rubbish. The sentimentalists made that mistake. But he had failed that pony, by any standards, just as now he was thinking he had failed Roly. Hawkins, no doubt, would not even inquire as to who had bought him, as long as the cheque went through.

The day was not one to remember with pride and joy.

10

Smith had a small stable of about twelve horses on the out-skirts of Wolverhampton, and ran most of his horses in sel-lers and ill-paid handicaps. Asking around, Rosy built up a picture of a meanly run establishment from which horses ran with great variations of form, ridden mostly by a weasel-faced jockey called Roberts who was known to be suspect and got few rides otherwise. Why she troubled to find out these details which caused her only distress Rosy had no idea, save through a sort of perversity. Much as she admired and cared for her other horses, Spinning Wheel and Peppermill, she knew there would never be a horse for her like Roly.

To distract herself she spent a lot of time with the filly, now registered with Weatherby's as Dark Secret. So quickly did the highclass thoroughbred mature, the filly would be ready to race the following spring. Dark Secret was very forward, and Rosy wanted to get ahead with handling her so that she would be easy to break in when the time came. She weaned her from old Silverfish and kept her up at Brood in Roly's old box, leading her out every day and getting her to accept a bit, and saddle and girths. Jeremy would not accept any money for her keep, but said no more about his proposition to go shares in racing her. No doubt he had forgotten he had made it. When the jump-ing season started again and work stepped up, Rosy reckoned she could put Dark Secret back in the field with Silverfish and consider her relatively civilized, till the time came for her to be broken in properly. Then—who knew?—perhaps she would emulate the ways of her classy mother. She was promising: intelligent and kind enough, although she had a will of her own and would never, Rosy reckoned, come into the 'quiet and lazy' category. Silverfish, in her youth, had been neither quiet nor lazy.

'A touch of the Sun Chariots,' Letitia said.

'You think our filly's a Sun Chariot?'

'I think she's a good one.'

But Jeremy made no further offer to take a share in her, or train her. Gin wanted to sell her.

'Neither of us can afford to put her into training.'

'We might if Jeremy were to take a third share.'

'The guv'nor? He won't. Have you asked him?'

'No.'

Rosy knew she must ask him. Like Grace, she must get what she wanted. She could not wait all her life, hoping that things would pan out right. She wanted this thing for herself, but was not used to getting what she wanted. Jeremy had friends who trained on the flat ... he could fix it ... perhaps.

'Sir, can I have a word?'

She was grooming Peppermill at the time, having tried to make this purposeful statement several times during the last few days, to no avail. Her voice shook. Jeremy was on his way back to the house, the moment opportune.

He said, 'Come to the house with me. I'm expecting a phone call.'

She dropped her tools in the manger and darted after him. She had never set foot in the house before and was stunned by the portrait of Letitia, hesitating, struck by the spark of the old Jeremy that she saw in the portrait's expression.

'She's like you!'

She shouldn't have said it. Jeremy was amused. 'God forbid! I don't seem to hit it off with the old lady these days. Not like you.'

Rosy was embarrassed, thinking of the Stubbs, thinking he thought she was after the old girl's money. Everything was going wrong. She followed him into the kitchen, trying not to stare, to take in his lifestyle. It was harrowing to be on his home ground, painful beyond expectation. Everything that she pretended was a joke, seemed suddenly not to be a joke at all. She had forgotten what she had come for, seeing all the homely things: his battered typewriter, socks hanging to dry on the rail of the Aga, some Alpen shaken into a bowl and a bottle of milk on the table.

'Excuse the mess. Do you want coffee? I'm going to make one.'

'Yes. Thank you.'

'What's the matter?'

Everything, she thought desperately. Doing a Grace was painful in the extreme.

'It's the Silverfish filly. I don't know what to do about her.'

'How can I help?'

'I don't know if you can. It's worth asking—I just thought—I mean, it's worth a try, whether you could— you want—to have a—a share in her, to race her? I can't afford to put her into training. I thought you might—' It sounded quite dreadful, worse than any proposition Grace might have dreamed up.

She pulled herself resolutely together. 'I think I've got to sell her, but I thought I'd ask you first, if you can think of any way I could afford to race her myself?'

There. In a nutshell. Train her for me free. For love. Help me. I love you. Love me, love my horse.

'Have a seat,' Jeremy said.

Did she look as if she was about to fall over? She felt like it. Her knees were trembling. Jeremy was fiddling with the coffee percolator.

'You mean—if I train her? You'd like me to train her?'

'I just wondered if it was possible—if I did all the work? Would I have enough money? I know it costs a fortune ordinarily.'

'Well, I've got a licence. Why not?'

149

He wasn't shocked, offended, embarrassed. Not even put out.

'Why not?' he said. 'Do you take sugar?'

'One please.'

'We could try it, couldn't we? See if she's any good. That's where the money is, after all, if the legs run fast enough. Old Letitia would love it, eh?'

Rosy could not believe it. Jeremy put the coffee down on the table and came and sat opposite her.

'She's very well bred.' He smiled.

Rosy could think of nothing to say. All these weeks of worrying and now Jeremy taking up the cause for a lark. She shook her head.

'One thing about you, Rosy, you go for what you want. I had been thinking for the last couple of years that Silverfish was being wasted, and didn't lift a finger to do anything about it.

Is that how he saw her? She who went irresolutely through life, achieved nothing ... She drank some coffee, wished it was brandy. Now was the moment to propose, obviously. Grace would have ...

Jeremy moved the milk-bottle away from her elbow and said, 'Sorry this place is so scruffy. All will be changed when Grace gets back.'

He spoke with irony, but Rosy heard no more than the actual words.

'Grace is coming back?' The dismay in her voice could not be concealed.

'So she has announced. Give her a week and we'll be all shipshape and shining. She is very efficient is Grace.'

So. The euphoria was short-lived. Grace would get him this time. Rosy sat back, trying to hurry with her coffee— but it was hot—not wanting Jeremy to divine her thoughts. He was being uncommonly nice this morning— was it the prospect of having Grace back? Perhaps not. He had been thawing gradually over the last couple of years, whether because of Hawkins and the success the stable had achieved, or because he was mellowing anyway she did not know.

'Talk of the devil,' Jeremy murmured.

Outside on the gravel Grace's Mini was parking in its assured place hard outside the front door.

'Yoo hoo! Jeremy!'

It was worth it, Rosy supposed, to see the expression on Grace's face when she came in and saw the two of them drinking coffee together. Shock, fury and blatant cover-up—brittle smile and fluttering eyelashes.

'Jeremy! Why, Rosy! How lovely to see you again!'

Insincerity shone from her gorgeous blue eyes. Jeremy stood up like the gentleman he was.

'Can I help myself to coffee? Just like old times,' she said.

'I'm just going,' Rosy said, swallowing fast.

'Oh, no. Have another.'

Rosy suspected Jeremy was enjoying himself at her expense. Grace took a mug and filled it for herself, very obviously not refilling Rosy's. She turned the full glare of her beauty on Jeremy and gave him a smile that cut Rosy right out of the kitchen.

Jeremy said, 'Rosy's got new status, Grace. She's an owner. We're going to train her filly for the flat.'

'You mean Silverfish's filly, by—'

'Understanding. That's right.'

In that moment Rosy realized who had told Jeremy about Peppermill's visit to Letitia's.

'How exciting!'

Grace was having a hard time. Her eyes raked over Rosy, seeing her afresh, her status enhanced. One could see the challenge accepted; Grace loved a challenge. Rosy saw her, in that moment, setting a time limit for her intentions—next June, say, the reception in the garden just when the roses were at their best. Time to get settled before the horses came back into training. Did Jeremy read it too? He very deliberately refilled Rosy's coffee cup. Grace noticed. She passed the sugar nobly.

'Hugh tells me you've lost your Roly Fox. To a not very nice stable, he said.'

151

Sweet smile. Her dart nicely on target. Rosy, her mind now tuned to Dark Secret, felt the wound opened, remorse sprung. There was no glib answer. Jeremy said nothing and there was a long silence, during which they each considered the other, and the implications of what had been said so far. Rosy could see Jeremy retreating into his moody bastard frame of mind and it gave her deep satisfaction that Grace had caused this, when to her he had been uncommonly cordial. But Grace was a formidable opponent. There could be no lasting satisfaction, knowing she was back.

Rosy made her exit as soon as possible, her mind hammering to new possibilities. The season was just getting under way, the horses all back in work and fit to race. Dark Secret was back with Silverfish. Come the cold weather she would have to be brought in and started in work. She would be extra, worked for love. But the prospect was glorious. Working with Jeremy, her place with the owners and trainers, not out in the back, taking a tip, touching the forelock. *My* filly, my colours ... the mind soared. She called in the field on the way down for lunch, and caressed her little racehorse, all sweetness for a handful of oats, fickle, still tiny, but all quality. Her winter coat was steel dark, but with splotches of paler grey over her quarters, a hark-back to The Tetrarch, or to Peppermill. Gin said she would lose the marks when the summer coat came through.

'The guv'nor said he'll train her!' Rosy told him, when they came back for evening stables.

'You're joking?'

'No. "Why not?" he said.'

'It'll cost us a bomb.'

'No. He didn't say so. We can do the work—I can, anyway.' Gin was becoming more and more a liability in the venture, giving nothing and—now—not even pleased with the news of Jeremy's co-operation.

'It's bound to cost us! Entry fees for a start. It's not like jumping, you know.'

'Oh, Gin, come on—we'll see what she's like, that's all. She'll probably never be any good, but we'd kick ourselves if we never found out. Where's your spirit of adventure?'

'It's all used up, being married to Beryl.'

'Suppose the filly's a winner—think of that!'

'Well, that's where the money is, on the flat. I could certainly do with the money.'

Gin had become very boring, Rosy thought. She wished he wasn't involved, but he was not going to relinquish his claim, he made that clear. She knew he wanted to send the filly to the December sales, and make a few quick thousand. It was gratifying to think that this was possible— they had come that far. But without Gin she would never have gone through with the mating; no good regretting his involvement now. She only wanted his enthusiasm, nothing else. It was plain who was going to put the hours in.

Grace took up where she had left off. She too put in the hours: to catch Jeremy, to get Jeremy organized, make herself indispensable. She got him two new owners, and set to work charming Mr Hawkins—to woo owners was a clever move, Rosy admitted, and Jeremy was bound to be grateful. He was not very effective in that area himself, and no doubt it was one of the reasons for his lack of success. Trainers needed to be out-going, plausible, smart and charming; the deviousness of a politician helped. Jeremy was too blunt and only liked owners who liked their horses.

'You *need* Hawkins,' Grace told him crisply.

Hawkins took to calling, taking a drink with Grace and Jeremy in the newly-primped kitchen, now sparkling clean and boasting magazine touches of colour and character: a string of onions and a bowl of lemons. Artemis, apparently, had got the push, like Roly Fox. Hawkins inspected Spinning Wheel, Peppermill and Needles and Rosy got a twenty-pound note for pointing out which was which.

Jeremy, knowing exactly how he was being manipulated, knew that if he married Grace he would go from strength to strength. Largely Grace's strength. She was ruthless and highly efficient. It was very difficult to resist

153

what was happening, especially as she could turn on a relentless charm to order, and when he was being pig-obstinate, sulky and plain rude, she retreated with extraordinary skill into a sympathetic silence, and managed to do exactly the right things to soothe him, even if it meant disappearing altogether. She never lost her temper or her cool. To marry her would be to coast on her capability: it would be very nice, the easy option. In her role as secretary she was, in effect, only running on one cylinder—the thought of her being given *carte blanche* to run the place, and himself, entirely, through marriage, was awe-inspiring. Jeremy knew that he was mellowing with time and success, his hankering to be back in the saddle dissolving with age—for he was now at the age when most jump jockeys retired—but whether he would ever mellow enough to take Grace as a wife he doubted. And yet ... his life was his work, and Grace ... God, she was impressive in her will to get herself installed! She did not appear to be in love with him, any more than he was in love with her, but perhaps that area was mapped for future operation; he did not suppose she had neglected this vital ingredient. Certainly one felt a goodwill towards the creator of this vast improvement in his working life, in one sense; in another, the sheer evidence of her willpower was paralysing. One could never relax with a woman like that. He did not want to become a complete passenger, after all. She did not have the ultimate cleverness: to run the show and make it seem that he did. She ran it and it showed.

But Jeremy was content to let things run. He had found, in this life, that problems tended to solve themselves. He did not have to consider whether to marry Grace or not. At the moment, not. Things might alter but he would do nothing to make them alter, unless, as seemed likely, Grace got too managing to bear. For now she managed, but he kept her firmly in her secretary/housekeeper role, and talked to her like an employer.

Strangely, to Rosy he now talked less like an employer, more as an accomplice.

Grace noticed this and throttled back. She grew quieter and less obvious, and wore skirts instead of trousers. Jeremy noticed the improvement but was too guileless to guess the reason why. He thought life was looking up, and nobody called him a moody bastard any longer.

On racing days Rosy looked out for Mr Smith of Wolverhampton, or thereabouts, and was not cheered by what she saw. His horses were undernourished and scurfy and ran mainly in sellers, losing when they were expected to win and winning when they were expected to lose. He always had a plausible excuse for the stewards but, if he was a crook, he was too petty to cause a lot of trouble. Of Roly Fox there was no sign.

Usually his horses were attended by the surly youth who had taken Roly from her at Ascot and another man who looked like Smith's brother and seemed to be his head lad. Once Rosy asked the youth if Roly Fox was all right and he said, yeah, he's OK, and walked away, scowling. But one dark December day at Towcester the horse running in Smith's name was attended by a girl, a depressed-looking blonde in very tight jeans called Tracy, and when she brought her runner back to the stables, Rosy accosted her. She was washing her horse down in a very inefficient fashion, the horse restive and exhausted. She had no help and Rosy tactfully offered to hold the horse for her.

'Thanks awfully.' She looked as exhausted as the horse.

'You got a horse in your yard called Roly Fox?'

'Yeah, I think so.'

'How is he?'

She looked surprised. 'Why, he's all right, I suppose.'

'I used to do him.'

'Oh.'

'Why doesn't he run these days?' Rosy knew perfectly well, but had to use ignorance to goad the girl into speaking.

'He's got a bad leg.'

'He's not in training then? Is he turned out?'

'No. He's in training.'

155

'How can he be?'

'Mr Smith swims him.'

'Oh.' Rosy knew this was an accepted system of training these days, but did not suspect Mr Smith had a stable swimming-pool, a very expensive piece of equipment. 'Where does he take him?'

'He swims him in the river.'

'In the river! This time of year?'

'Yeah. He tows him from a dinghy.'

'Does he like it?'

'Not much, I shouldn't think.' The girl giggled. 'I wouldn't, would you?'

'Christ! What about the cold?'

'He dries him off in the pig-barn. It's heated, for the piglets. He ties him up there when he gets him home. S'warm as toast.'

Rosy considered this amazing information, not knowing whether to be furiously indignant, or admiring of the ingenuity. If Roly was standing up to the unorthodox treatment, it should be doing his leg a lot of good.

'When's he going to run then? This season?'

'Oh, I think so.'

'Will you let me know when, in advance? So's I can make sure I see him.'

'Yeah, if you like.'

'I'll give you my phone number. Here.' Rosy scrabbled in her pocket and wrote her phone number on her race-card. She had a fiver in her purse. She tucked it in the card and gave it to Tracy. 'Put it in your pocket. Don't forget. I really mean it.'

'Looks like it. Thanks.'

Rosy was torn by Tracy's information. She could not stop thinking of old Roly being towed along behind a dinghy, in an ice-cold river. She reported to Jeremy, who was intrigued. 'Well, he's a tough old bugger. It might work a treat. I wonder what he's planning for him?'

'When he does run, please—please—can I have the day off to go and see him?'

'Why not? With that leg—river or no river—I honestly can't see him running for a while. Not without breaking down again.'

By Christmas the Brood horses had won ten races. Hawkins gave Rosy a hundred pounds, which she put to her Dark Secret fund.

Grace invited Jeremy for Christmas. Rosy invited Letitia. Neither invitation was accepted. Christmas was no holiday at the stables, with three runners on Boxing Day, but Rosy cooked a turkey herself and asked Gin and Beryl down, and took a plateful down to Letitia. It was not a success, her father not approving of the turkey, nor—apparently—of Beryl, to whom he was very cold. Gin was in an equally sour mood. Beryl did not help matters by studying form for the Boxing Day racing—she was going to have a bet because it was Christmas. The atmosphere was deadly, overlaid by loud television *bonhomie*. The little sitting-room was steamy with cooking and the smell of sprouts and boiled-over milk on the stove; Gin was dozing by the fire and Beryl had drunk too much parsnip wine and kept clicking channels on the television to the obvious annoyance of Mr Weeks. Rosy, aware that it was through her invitation that this gruesome afternoon was taking place, chickened out and went out with Kes in his buggy, ostensibly to give his mother a break, in reality to give herself one.

It was a raw, cloudy day and the village was deserted. The roads were wet and greasy, verges muddy, the day already drawing in. Rosy wheeled Kes down to the church, deserted now between morning and evening services. She went and looked at her mother's grave which was covered with a vast species rose which had embraced several other graves around it and whose thorns notoriously captured every passing victim—her father's tribute to his mate's thornless lifespan, a triumphant marvel of blossom in July but a damned nuisance for the rest of the year. There had been much acrimony about the filipes Kiftsgate—an unholy row, in fact, which deeply amused Rosy, seeing that

157

it was intended as a tribute to peace and love. She left all such arguments to her father, who moved through them unperturbed, not capable of understanding that a simple rose could give offence, although the plot he owned measured six feet by four and the rose was catalogued as covering thirty-five by thirty-five. Of such stuff was village life composed.

The church was warm and smelt of flowers and disturbed damp, and Rosy lifted Kes out of his buggy and showed him the crudely constructed crib surrounded by flickering candles. The occupants were well bedded down, and had a serenity that had been markedly lacking from the domestic scene she had just left. Kes was fascinated, and Rosy held him in her arms to take it all in, feeling— suddenly—much soothed by the silence and tranquillity and aware of the ache that churches always gave her, of wishing it mattered to her as it did to the people who used it. Its sheer antiquity, the massive walls impervious to the outside mayhem, impressed the sensibilities: one felt the better for absorbing it. What bliss to be one of the faithful, to believe ... how sordid her profession seemed at that moment, fed by gambling and money-lust. Would she change anything? She gave Kes a quick hug. He was totally innocent, yet raised on squalid altercation and discontent. It was bliss to stand there with her arms round the untouched child, as the atmosphere of ancient religion seemed at that moment to hold her in a similar embrace, and inhale well-being and uplift along with the lingering scents of newly-opened talc and expensive novelty soap, exotic Christmas aftershave, damp and woodworm and cheap candlegrease. What a charade it all was, both in and out of church; she was confused by this surge of love for the smell of religion, and bundled Kes back in his buggy, tucking the rugs close, ridiculing her sentiment.

She walked briskly home, but could not bear to go back to that overfed and overwrought atmosphere so soon. She went on past to Letitia's, opening the door with the key under the flower-pot. The house was in

darkness, but the room warm, the fire glowing and spit-
ting.

'Mrs Cutbush?'

The old lady was in her chair by the fire, Rosy could see
her by the light from the small flame, her eyes glittering.
Tears ran down her cheeks.

'What is it?' It seemed harsh to turn on the light. Rosy
crossed over and knelt down in front of her.

'Are you all right?'

'Yes, dear.'

'Why are you crying?'

'It's time I was dead.'

'No. Oh, no!'

Rosy had never seen Mrs Cutbush without her fight. It
frightened her.

'I want Peter.'

'Look. Don't cry.' Rosy scrambled up. She put on a small
wall-light and went back to the front door and pulled the
buggy inside. She lifted Kes out and took him over to the
old lady.

'I've brought you a visitor.'

She sat on the floor and held Kes up so that he stood by
Letitia's knee. With impeccable manners he held his arms
up to Letitia, not minding her fierce face and her whiskers
and her old-ladies' smell. He was undoubtedly an enchanting baby, in spite of being by Gin out of Beryl.

'Who's he then? Or she? It's not yours, is it?'

'No. It's Gin's. You know Gin.'

'Yes, I know Gin. Well. Fancy.'

Letitia considered Kes and the baby stared back,
unblinking, entirely well-disposed.

'That's a nice child.'

'Yes. Here.' Rosy knelt up and lifted Kes on to Letitia's
lap. Kes reached for one of Letitia's rings, pulling the finger
up to his mouth.

'Well,' said Letitia, and smiled.

She had been a very bad mother in her day, by all
accounts, but Kes charmed her. Rosy felt bad, that she had

left her all alone, after delivering the dinner, but at the same time impatient, having tried—and failed—to make a good day for other deserving causes. Letitia was Jeremy's pigeon, for heaven's sake—certainly on Christmas Day.

As if the message had exploded in some way in the ether, Jeremy appeared, like the good fairy in a pantomime—a tentative knock at the door and an uncertain hail, 'Gran?'

He came in. Rosy felt herself tremble and go scarlet in the gloom. She scrambled up from the floor, seeing Jeremy equally as startled, and embarrassed. Her emotions stretched already by this curious afternoon, Rosy felt a surge of pure, stinging, sexual love overtake her with a violence that she could scarcely credit; the religious yearning in church had been as nothing beside this crude lust for person, an agony of wanting—of having wanted for so long. Her heart raced with copybook passion, robbing her of both speech and sense. The gloom was blessed, covering her bedazzlement. She had to turn away all the same, staggering into the log-basket, which she turned into a wild stoking of the fire.

'You've got company then? Here, shall I put the light on? Wait a sec.'

'Fancy,' said Letitia again. 'All these visitors.'

Jeremy turned on the light, too soon for Rosy who kept her back turned. He saw Letitia's tears still wet, felt furious to be found wanting on Christmas Day, and as if by instinct his eyes turned to the Stubbs painting, as if seeking reassurance in the eternal peace that obviously abounded in the landscape of his ancestors. Rosy saw the direction of his glance and her acute embarrassment over her sexual disturbance was immediately replaced by an equal embarrassment to be caught in the act of courting the old woman for her possessions—or so it could be construed. Jeremy noticed her reaction and knew what she was thinking. His happy visit was disastrous, even before a conversation was started.

'I've come to drink your health, Gran. Apologize for my neglect and all that.'

160

The bottle of Cointreau he had brought was a life-saver in more ways than one, the fire of spirits to cauterize raw nerve-endings. Rosy fetched the glasses from the cabinet and set them on the old brass trivet in the hearth. Her ferocious assault on Letitia's stove had resulted in a cheerful burst of flame, and Jeremy poured the drinks generously and tactfully turned the light off again, so that they sat on the hearthrug in the firelight reviving the festive atmosphere. It worked, gazing into flames having a distinctly soothing effect—indeed, glowing, after the Cointreau.

'Marvellous stuff,' said Jeremy.

'Reminds me of hunting. I always put this in my flask,' said Letitia, and Rosy saw her again as the Munnings girl, fearless across country. Fearless too in old age, except on Christmas Day. Rosy took Kes off her, and he lay quietly in her arms watching the fire, sleepy after the cold air outside, the warmth within. Any likely conversation being spiked with danger, nothing was said. It did not seem out of place, the festive silence save for the fluttering of the flames. And just as Rosy saw Letitia's eyes close and the empty glass fall sideways in her lap, she felt Kes grow heavy with sleep in her arms. She was effectively alone with Jeremy. Momentary panic slithered into amusement and pleasure and the ominous—a touch inebriated—shiver of desire; the ill-tempered day had flowered ... how unpredictable it all was. She could not move, for Kes, and sat cradling him, smiling into the flames.

From where he sat Jeremy saw Rosy crouching on the hearth with the Stubbs picture on the wall behind her like a balloon over her head. The way he felt at that moment it could well have had a caption inside it warning him off. He too was aware that they were virtually alone in a distinctly inviting situation, but it was as if old Stubbs was on guard.

Strangely, Rosy with the baby in her arms was somebody quite different from the reliable girl in the stable he had taken for granted for the last few years. Taken out of context, he saw her suddenly as someone entirely congenial, sympathetic and attractive. She was strong, trustworthy, loyal and unstrident. All the virtues. With the spirits coursing through his bloodstream he felt an ardour over-taking him unknown since the days of Judith Partridge. Yet such was his perpetual condition of self-doubt and self-denial he could not overcome habitual caution, even given the amazing ambience that surrounded them. In fact he felt that his uncommon stirrings of sexual interest were per-haps more a sentimental weakness due to the combination of its being Christmas Day with all the memories and nostalgia inevitably aroused and of having had too much to drink before lunch. His feelings astonished him.

'I haven't fed Jasper,' Letitia said suddenly, and sat up, the Cointreau glass falling into the hearth. It smashed on the flags; Kes woke and started to cry.

'I must go back. Beryl will wonder what I'm doing,' Rosy said.

Jeremy swept up the glass. He thought nobly of asking Letitia to go back home with him, but abandoned the idea immediately. Brood House did not appeal, with or without Letitia. He had been out all day and lunched in a hotel with racing friends, and when Rosy departed with Kes in his buggy, he felt bereft and abandoned. He knew the godly. thing to have done was stay and get Letitia's tea and watch television with her, but even while the thought was going through his head he was putting on his coat and departing.

Out in the garden he felt smashed.

He peed on his grandmother's splendid leeks and walked down the path.

Rosy Weeks! He wanted babies and a warm home to go back to and someone in bed to talk to. He wanted the assu-rance of Paul Rogers the solicitor, rose-beds like Fred Winter, a family car with a dog in the back. What was he doing with his life, whining over his dicky leg and his mean-spirited owners? He had to go back home and feed because everyone had the evening off, and when he had done that he drove to the Maddoxes very fast, and introduced himself into their post-prandial torpor.

Margaret had opened up the whole house and lit fires in

the downstairs rooms for Christmas, which was lucky, she thought, greeting Jeremy. Grace wildly reached for her high heels which she had kicked off as they were killing her and raced upstairs to do her face before Jeremy saw her, and Hugh did up his waist buttons and smoothed his tartan waistcoat and yearned ineffectually for fresh air without moving out of his armchair. Margaret was genuinely pleased to see Jeremy, because he was so nice. The Beaumonts were coming, friends of young Hugh's and stultifyingly hearty and boring, and she was dreading the effect of being civil when she was so tired—Christmas seemed to her one endless round of chores and cooking and overindulgence, when she longed to be quiet and remember what the point of it all was, and go to church in peace, without being hurried because of getting the sprouts on and the bread sauce ... she never seemed to get it right. Neither Grace nor young Hugh lifted a finger, and old Hugh hunted all day on Christmas Eve and again on Boxing Day, and slept—understandably—most of the day in between.

'Oh, Jeremy!' She couldn't help herself giving him a hug and a kiss, and he looked a little surprised, and she hoped he didn't think she was pre-empting the role of mother-in-law. How she would love him in the family! But, poor lad, not as Grace's husband ... why had she not produced him herself, instead of dull Hugh? How extraordinary genes were, the deadly strains they chose to perpetuate instead of doubling up on the virtues. Even with horses, all done on paper, it hardly ever came out right. Jeremy sometimes had an uncanny look of the fierce Letitia, yet self-expression had been Letitia's strength, and Jeremy was reserved sometimes to the point of embarrassment. Old Hugh was full of lovely characteristics that had completely passed his children by. How very odd was nature. She kissed Jeremy again, and realized she had had a little more sherry than was good for her.

'Let me get you a drink. What will you have?'

Jeremy loved being kissed by Margaret and made to feel one of the family. His yearning for family comforts was

163

suddenly granted: this gracious house, full of Margaret's comfortable touches, warmth and affection ... he felt pleased to belong, having merely appeared at the door. When Grace came down she stood in the doorway showing herself off, simulating surprise, and then offering a welcome both effusive and sexual, pressing her lips softly against his own, so that he realized that all he wanted was perfectly attainable. If he were to ask Grace to marry him, tonight, she would accept. It would be in *The Times* and the *Telegraph* the moment they were back in business.

The trouble was, he preferred her mother.

'Racing tomorrow?' Old Hugh bestirred himself, offered a cigar. 'Kempton? I'm going hunting, you know, else I might be interested.'

'Kempton, yes.'

'No holiday for your trade, eh? Can't move at Kempton as a rule.'

'That's right.'

The Beaumonts arrived and Margaret and old Hugh took more drink to sustain them. Ida Beaumont trained eventers and was into flat work, impulsion, diagonals and leg-yield even before Hugh had produced the ice for her gin, and John Beaumont sold cars and was equally eloquent on suspension, acceleration, cornering and road-holding. It all sounded to Margaret like exactly the same thing and she broke it up to play scrabble, which she liked. Jeremy proved brilliant, to her delight, producing quirky words, so that she tried to remember what sort of an education he had had ... perhaps he would have made a better barrister than trainer. One never knew until too late. But he seemed happier tonight than she could remember seeing him, and not only on the drink. They adjourned and ate mince pies, and young Hugh put on some music and old Hugh went out for some more logs. Jeremy went to help him, but he insisted on going alone. Grace was in the kitchen, starting to make coffee, and she called out to Jeremy as he crossed the hall so loudly that he could not possibly pretend not to hear. Reluctantly he pulled up.

'Do you want some help?'

'I want company.'

Oh well. Jeremy went in and sat on the table. He noticed that the kitchen was the parent product of what Grace was gradually turning his into: the pine-plated country-living style, somewhat dishevelled after its heavy day but smelling amiably of present coffee and past roasts. Grace wore a frilly apron and was flushed and looked rather magnificent, the bright blond hair tumbled. It could be like this for me, Jeremy thought, with Grace, and when she came up to him he slipped off the table and caught her in his arms just as she was obviously hoping he would, with perfect timing. Her kiss was far more passionate than his own, so that he had to adjust, allow his natural impulses to take over and stop thinking about the consequences. They could wait. Her skin smelt delicious and she trembled and moaned in a very excited fashion when their lips parted and grasped his hand and pressed it to her breast. He kissed her neck, feeling the pulse fluttering under his lips, and started to work his way down, but the coffee boiled over just as he was moving into the mysteries of her decolleté, and Hugh could be heard thumping the log-basket down in the hall so he had to come up for air. He was surprised and rather pleased with himself.

'Oh, Jeremy!' Grace was looking ecstatic as she dived for the coffee.

Whatever had he been wasting his time for, he wondered? Grace at home all day doing nothing while he had worried about entries and corn-bills and owners' bills, when she harboured all this passion and goodwill ... He had not been entirely celibate since Judith Partridge, but certainly had forgotten the taste of passion and excitement.

They made the coffee together, giggling, and carried it in to the music and chatter. Ida Beaumont had forgotten her leg-yields and was castigating a hunter judge whom Jeremy had been at school with, which he found quite interesting, but he kept thinking about Grace's rather flat breasts and could not stop wanting to know more about that long-legged, slender body. Christmas certainly had something to answer for. Margaret was looking at him curiously, rather sadly, he thought, but he had another Cointreau before leaving and forgot that he preferred the mother.

11

Roly lifted up his head and whinnied. He swung round in
the box and looked out over the half-door with a look in
his eyes that made Rosy's heart turn over. From behind
someone hit him a thump and he flinched.

'Roly!'

There was no mistaking that he recognized her. No
mistaking that he was miserable, that he was tucked-up,
too thin. That his heart had lifted at the sound of her
voice—sentimental though it might seem, Rosy knew that
this was true, just as it was true that at the sight of him the
lump in her throat swelled up and threatened to choke her.
She went up to him and saw his nostrils flutter with his old
whicker of welcome, and he pushed his head at her, his
hard old bonehead that made his welcome positively painful. She pulled his long ears gently. The knowledge of how
far she had failed him was overwhelming.

The youth who had taken him over at the sale, the
younger Smith, looked out to see what the disturbance
was.

'What do you want?'

'You've got him sound then?'

He grunted.

'Who's riding him?'

'Parkins.'

The stable wally, a jockey not known for his honesty.
Rosy could not make conversation with this dour young
man, and could only lean on the door and watch how

roughly he bridled the horse, how Roly pulled nervously away from him and put back his ears.

'Want anything?' he inquired coldly.

She shook her head. She had guessed she would feel bad, but nothing like as bad as this. All the hours she had spent on this horse, all the summer standing in the river, the mornings over the downs with the skylarks twittering in the cold clear sky, the evenings in the box, the shadows from the swinging lightbulb dancing over the deep straw ... a vast nostalgia for everything remembered about Roly Fox engulfed her. A nervous dread for his future lay coldly in her stomach. Roly, the most honest, willing horse that ever looked through a bridle, now partner—she was convinced—to some dubious enterprise.

She had brought Villanelle to Leicester with Gin, and he had run, not badly, in the first. Gin wanted to get home early but Rosy stayed on to see Roly run. Tony had promised to drive her home. He was riding a horse in the same race that Roly was in.

'The way that leg was, I can't see him getting round,' he had remarked in the car.

'The guv'nor reckoned it would take eighteen months at least.'

Whatever happened, Rosy knew her day was going to prove disastrous, probing into old hurts. She was only a spectator in Roly's life; had never been anything else. A horse's lad was the least regarded of human species in racing, yet possibly meant more to the horse and its success or otherwise than owner, trainer and jockey. If any human rang bells in Roly's plain head, Rosy knew it was herself.

It was a mild day with the feel of spring to it, the season coming to its last leg. She leaned on the paddock rail watching Roly led round, and noticed that all his zest and bounce were now extinguished; he walked lethargically, not pulling at the lead-rein as he once had, and hardly bothering to remove his gaze from the buttocks of the horse in front. He was favourite, because of past endeavours, but anyone who bet on the look of a horse in the paddock was likely to give

168

him a miss, in Rosy's opinion, and she heard a few remarks made to this effect. Tony had arranged to get a bet put on for Beryl—'She says he's her lucky horse'—and Rosy did not try to dissuade him. Beryl was a hopeless case.

They went down to the start. Roly moved easily, his heavily-bandaged forelegs flicking over the soft ground. He carried top weight, the race a two-and-a-half-mile handicap. Roberts was a graceless jockey, heavy-handed, ferret-faced. Rosy did not enjoy the depressing face of racing and huddled miserably into the collar of her anorak, not wanting to meet anyone she knew. She had no binoculars, but could make Roly out by the lime-green Smith colours—the trainer ran the horse under his own name.

She did not expect Roly to win and was not surprised to see him run a lack-lustre race and pull up three fences from home. Roberts got off him and walked back, but Roly appeared to be sound, as far as Rosy could make out. Smith, no doubt, would have a plausible story for the stewards. He met Roberts in the unsaddling enclosure and did not appear to ask him any questions or to be put out. Rosy distinctly got the impression that the result was as he expected, and probably ordered. When Tony had changed and come to find her, he confirmed that Roberts had made no show at all.

'He said he pulled up because the horse was making a noise. Said he swallowed his tongue. If he did, I never heard him, and I was close enough most of the time. Smith has told the stewards that and got away with it.'

Rosy shrugged, less interested in the mysterious ways of Roly's new owner than in the sight of his dejected hindquarters disappearing up the ramp of the battered lorry that transported him.

'You shouldn't have come, mate, if that's how you feel. If we all got fond of our nags, where would it get us?'

'He knew me all right.'

'Well then. You'd have felt worse if he hadn't.'

They drove home, Rosy refusing a nice cuddle in the car-park of the Rose and Crown at the half-way mark. 'Don't you ever give up?'

'I could cheer you up, Rosy, if you'd give me half a chance.'

'You're out of luck.'

'Be miserable then.'

The story of her life. She could not get out of her head the sound of Roly's anxious whicker when he saw her, and the sight of his resigned plod round the paddock.

A week later, starting at ten to one, he ran again and was pulled up for the second time. *Sporting Life* reported that all was not well with the once reliable Roly Fox—'His trainer reports breathing problems and a tendency to choke on his tongue.'

Beryl had lost two lots of family allowance and three weeks' milk bill on Roly, her lucky horse. 'He's not lucky any longer,' Rosy said bitterly. 'Whatever you do, don't bet on him again.'

For once, Beryl did not argue.

Jeremy felt bad about Rosy. The two or three minutes sitting on the hearth with her in his grandmother's house had made an impression so that the moment of arousal, so fleeting, silent, elusive, was remembered quite clearly. Whether Rosy had been aware of anything he had no idea. His arrival had clearly embarrassed her, presumably because of the boss and employee status, possibly because of the awkward situation over the Stubbs painting, which he had done nothing to alter or resolve. He had avoided speaking to her since, because he did not know how to treat her. He felt bad about Roly Fox too, and not too good about the Silverfish filly which Gin desperately wanted to sell, being so deep in debt—not a sound start for a partnership. Jeremy knew of no way to help Gin, and reflected sadly on the perils of marriage. Which brought him back to Grace.

Grace wanted to marry him.

'Why?' Jeremy asked her, lifting his head from between the disappointing breasts on one of the evenings he had taken her upstairs to occupy Letitia's amazing marriage bed ('Staying late to do the entries'). 'What difference would it make?'

'It would regularize the situation.'

Such utterances from Grace were one of the reasons he jibbed at the idea of her becoming his wife.

'I am a very indecisive person. I like it as it is now.'

'Oh, Jeremy, that's the trouble with you. You would get on so much better if you—' she hesitated, remembering that people did not like to be told what was wrong with them.

'Married you?'

'Went for what you really wanted. I could help you in so many ways.'

'You do.'

This was true. Even now, lying in Letitia's bed, there was an electric blanket beneath them which made the whole act possible. The house was actually inhabitable now Grace had possession. There was hot water in the tap, bread in the bread-bin, a new ribbon for the typewriter. The well-ordered household was beguiling, and undermined his resistance. The whole business of marrying Grace would be simple and undemanding. The Maddox family would embrace him; from being friendless and undernourished he would thrive, inherit lovely Margaret and old Hugh, throw off the last of his inhibitions and make good. Grace would enchant owners and cook them delicious lunches, look good in the paddock, and keep immaculate books. The marriage was obviously meant.

He turned away from Grace and lay with his hands behind his head. He played with the words on his tongue: 'All right. Let's get married.' But said nothing.

Grace waited, frowning. It was hard work not talking, playing herself down. It was bad for her health, making her irritable when she got home and unable to sleep well. She found Jeremy infuriatingly elusive and longed to pull him together. Sometimes she wanted to shake him. But she took long calming breaths, and turned to him, pressing herself against his slender, ribby body (a pity he was a little on the small side, but with jockeys this was usually inevitable) and smiling tightly.

'I do love you, Jeremy.'

She had had a lot of lovers, he knew. He did not hold this against her. He did not think she knew the meaning of the word love. Remembering Judith Partridge, he knew only too well that the essential ingredient was lacking between them. He did not say anything.

'Have you always been so undemonstrative?'

Her eyes glittered in a strange way, as if she were under some sort of pressure. He smiled at her. She was mareish, he thought. He stroked her hair gently, knowing he must get up in a minute and do his round of the horses. This ten o'clock at night habit was apt to annoy Grace.

'Does your back hurt?' Something solicitous was demanded, he thought.

'No more than your pelvis,' she snapped back.

Certainly the exercise his pelvis had been getting lately had done him no harm. How unrelaxing Grace was!— even in bed one was always nervously alert for the next loaded remark. Cautiously he slid away from her, with a casual, 'Must go and do the rounds.'

Grace gritted her teeth and buried her face in the pillow.

Going out into the night, Jeremy felt the spring-touched breeze off the downs fresh in his face, and his whole being gave an impulsive shiver of delight. What it meant he had no idea, but he whistled as he made his way to the first loosebox.

Pushing her way through the paddock crowds at Towcester, Rosy cursed her compulsive determination to see Roly Fox run again, knowing how it would distress her. He was entered for a three-mile handicap and was now so ill-considered that the bookies were offering him at twenty to one. Even Beryl did not want to know this time. Brood House had no runners, but Rosy had asked for the afternoon off and begged a lift from a friend of her father's who was going to Northampton on business. How she was going to get home she had no idea.

'I'm round the bend,' she thought, 'in love with a bloody horse.' She had tried not to think about him, but his stupid, honest face haunted her. She had tried earnestly to shift her allegiance to Dark Secret, but the filly wanted no friends. She was as haughty as her dam, and no one would ever do her down. She had no will to please, to do her best, like Roly; she was all hot blood and give-me-my-way.

'Why do I do this?' Seeking out Roly in the paddock was no joy; seeing his sad eyes as he went past was misery indeed. She tried to convince herself that it was all in the mind, that she read sentimental meanings into horses' demeanours where none could possibly exist, that animals required only their food and a certain degree of comfort to live satisfactory lives, that she was an idiot woman of the type she most despised, who fawned on overfed pets and gave them human attributes ... she tried every argument in the book, and remained unconvinced. Roly was unhappy and so was she.

Smith senior, she thought, looked dead worried. The field was not a classy one; in his prime Roly could have beaten them with ease, but Roly was now a has-been. Horses came and went, as Tony Mowbray was fond of saying. Before the jockeys mounted Smith produced a strap from his pocket and buckled it through Roly's mouth and under his lower jaw. This was a device to prevent the tongue-swallowing that Roly was reported to be suffering from, but Rosy watched with interest, knowing that the horse had never choked himself in that way during any of the races he had run from Brood. There was a long, animated discussion with the jockey, Roberts, and then Roly was led through and cantered down to the start. Rosy, on an impulse, followed Smith and his spotty son, and stood by them in the stand, waiting for the off.

It was a mild spring day, the sort that spurred optimism in the heart, smelled good, gave lift to the twittering skylarks in the sky. As she watched the horses go past on the

173

first circuit Rosy was aware of why she liked it. The ground was soft, which suited Roly, but she could not believe his leg was going to be improved by the day. He was running well enough, pushed by Roberts, and by the time they came round the bottom on the last circuit and hit the hill again he was in the lead. But the testing course was cruel to horses not in the top of condition and horses he could once have shaken off with ease lobbed after him only a couple of lengths adrift. Rosy could see that it was going to be a hard race, and a glimpse at Smith convinced her that Roly was intended to win this time—Smith was tight-lipped and tense and muttering oaths.

On this, the day that Roberts should have pulled up, he now started to ride like a demon, legs and arms flailing. Roly came to the last and jumped bravely, but was virtually on three legs as he made his way to the post. Two other horses hung to his girth and the crowd roared; Roberts's whip whistled into the dull hide, and Rosy wept.

'You bastard!' But Smith did not hear her, white from the tension. At twenty to one he had made his pile and had a good excuse for the stewards' inquiry. Rosy saw it all now as plain as daylight. Roly, like the good servant he was, had played his part, and could now go on the scrap-heap which was all he was good for. Rosy, masochist to the last, pushed her way through to the winners' enclosure and saw Roly limp home, bewildered by pain. Smith made a show of concern over the leg; young Smith held Roly's head, and Roly stood heaving. Rosy pushed her way through and went to Roly and, even in his state of distress, the old horse lifted his head and shoved his muzzle into her outstretched hand. But young Smith pulled him roughly away and said, 'You've no right here.'

He swore at her. Rosy opened her mouth to reply in what would have been an unwise fashion, but a hand descended on her shoulder and a voice said tersely, 'Shut up.'

It was Jeremy.

'Come away or you'll get yourself into trouble.' He put his arm round her and steered her firmly out of the enclosure and away from the crowd. Rosy, all screwed up, was ungrateful and said angrily, 'Are they going to get away with it? Did you see what happened?'

'Yes, I did, and I daresay they will get away with it. That's the way of the world, Rosy. Come and have a drink.'

'Don't you care?'

'They are very petty crooks, as crooks go. I'm sorry about the horse, that such a decent animal should be used in that way, yes, but now that he's played his part I daresay he'll be turned out and have a rest. He certainly won't be able to race again for a while.'

Rosy tried to pull herself together, much surprised by the arrival of Jeremy out of blue. She should have been bowled over with pleasure, but the day hurt too much. She followed him to the bar, not too sure how she felt about anything.

'I know you think I'm a fool, but that horse—he's not like any of the others. He's special.'

'It happened to me once. I know how you feel. We're not all made of stone, after all.'

'I get too emotional, I know.'

'Think straight, and you'll see that nothing's as bad as it seems. He's worth pretty well nothing at all at the moment. Perhaps you could scrape up enough cash to make an offer, if it means that much to you.'

He left her to go and buy the drinks, and Rosy stood staring out of the window towards the paddock, where the horses were already circling for the next race. Could it be as simple as that? With Hawkins's tips she had saved up a thousand or so, which was meant to be going towards running the filly. She was not a complete pauper.

When Jeremy came back she said, 'Can we go and talk to him, before he goes?'

'No. Give him a day or two. You have to sleep on these things. Cool it, Rosy, or he'll take you for a ride.'

He took her to a table and sat her down, and Rosy wanted to ask what he was doing at Towcester, but did not like to. Perhaps Grace was lurking somewhere. He smiled. 'You should have had your money on.'

Rosy had a mental vision of Beryl reading of Roly's win at twenty to one and this the first time she hadn't bet on him, and nearly choked in her whisky.

'Poor Beryl! I persuaded her he wasn't worth it!'

Jeremy laughed. 'Do her good! Do you want a lift home, or are you with anyone?'

'No. I'm not. Thank you.'

Sitting beside him in the fuggy interior of Jeremy's Audi, Rosy was aware that the events of the day were rather special, but the mixture was wearying, and she could not remember, when she got home, whether anything significant had taken place, or all had happened according to chance. Jeremy was a changed character these days, considerate and positively outgoing, and Rosy put it down to the relationship with Grace. He was as good as married, it seemed, and only a matter of time before the union actually took place. He never said how he had come to be at Towcester.

When she got home she felt very depressed and restless. She ate and washed up and it was still too early to go to bed. She went out into the garden and stared up at Brood House on the hillside. But all was in darkness, and Jeremy—no doubt—out galivanting with Grace, his beloved.

Beryl turned on the radio at four o'clock for the racing results. She had been Copydexing a patch on to a pair of Gin's jeans and her fingers were all rubbery, and Kes, unfortunately, had got the brush and put it in his mouth and was now making faces at the taste.

'Come here!' She pulled it off him and screwed the bottle up. Doing the patch made her feel highly domestic and virtuous. If it wasn't for the betting she wasn't a bad wife, except for Tony Mowbray ... well, except for a few things ... She grimaced to herself and reached for the fag-packet. At least she didn't drink.

The television set had gone. The hire-purchase people had taken it back, which was a terrible drag. However racing wasn't on as often as it used to be, and the afternoons could no longer be passed so pleasantly. It said something when she was reduced to mending.

Kes was pulling Copydex off his tongue in white strings like chewing gum. He didn't like it and started to cry.

'Results from Towcester. The one-thirty...'

'Oh, shut up!' Beryl said to him.

'The three-thirty. First, number four, Roly Fox. Second...'

Beryl, in the middle of drawing on her cigarette, stopped in mid-breath, transfixed. She heard the urbane voice intone, 'Starting price, twenty to one.' She choked, flung the cigarette in the hearth. She jumped up, took hold of the transistor and flung it with all her might across the room. It hit the window, smashed it, and disappeared into the undergrowth from where it went on calmly disclosing the winners of the last.

Kes, entranced, laughed with delight, clearly wanting a repeat performance. Beryl flung herself full length on the floor and howled. Kes was puzzled and sat looking at her for a while, then he laughed again and made for the abandoned Copydex jar, to see what he could make of it for the second time.

While she was undressing to get into bed, Rosy heard the phone ring downstairs. No one rang so late—although late was only after ten o'clock by Rosy's reckoning—and she went downstairs to answer it with a slight apprehension. She lifted the receiver and spoke, and heard the sound of money going into a call-box.

'It's me, Trace.'

'Trace?'

'You gave me a fiver once, to tell you about Roly Fox.'

'Oh, yes, thanks. I went to Towcester today. I saw him.'

'Yeah, well. I thought you might like to know, he's going to the knacker's in the morning. Lorry's coming at nine.'

The receiver was replaced and the phone went dead.

Rosy stood with it in her hand, frozen. What had Jeremy

said? Sleep on it, cool it. But the likes of Smith, having got what they wanted, did not hang around. Roly was only fit for the knackers, after that race, and every oat spent on him now was money down the drain. Lackadaisical Jeremy, who was never known these days to act on impulse, did not realize the ways of sharks, the greed of parasites like Smith. If she'd had her way she would have approached Smith on the spot. Rosy put the receiver down and rang Jeremy's number at Brood House. The ring went on and on. He was in bed with Grace, Rosy guessed, and let it ring. On and on.

At last, an irritable voice, 'Yes? Cutbush speaking.'

Rosy, shivering, said, 'Roly Fox is going to be put down in the morning.'

'What? Is that Rosy?'

'Yes. At nine o'clock.'

'Oh, Jesus. The swine. What do you want then? To go up there?'

'Yes. Yes, please, I do.'

There was a long silence. Rosy willed him.

'OK. Suppose I pick you up at—say—seven-thirty. That should do. I'll ring Hugh and he can see to things. We could be back soon after ten. Suit you?'

'Yes. Oh, yes.'

'I'll call for you. That'd be best.'

'All right.'

She would be ready. She was ready now. She did not even want to undress. Suppose Jeremy got a puncture, or overslept? Suppose the knacker came early and they missed him? Rosy went back to bed and lay awake, watching the stars in the sky through the window, shivering under the blankets. Either it was very cold or she had something wrong with her. She had Roly wrong with her. Roly on the brain, Roly in the heart; she was demented, Roly was only a horse. Yet Jeremy had not scoffed, nor even debated coming. That thought helped. She thought she would never go to sleep, but in fact slept heavily when dawn came, and awoke to the alarm feeling drugged and heavy. She dragged herself out

178

of bed and went to the window. The air was full of moisture, mist lying thickly over the valley, yet the downs above shouldering out into the sky like icebergs over an ocean. Brood was hidden and she thought of Jeremy lying in bed (with Grace?) seeing only mist and hearing the drops of water pattering on the leaves, sliding and pattering and murmuring in the gutters. She could hear the stream that ran through the village—where she had stood Roly all through the summer—gurgling through the culvert where it crossed the road, and she could smell the damp, strong promise of spring. Life was full of promise, but Roly was for the knacker's today.

Rosy pulled on her working clothes and went downstairs quietly, not waking her father, who never stirred before nine. She made herself some coffee but could not eat anything. She felt sick, like—when she was at school—before exams. The worse she felt, the more she despised herself. All for a bloody horse!

Jeremy arrived on the dot. He was bright-eyed and freshly-shaved, business-like and unsentimental. Rosy got in the car and fastened her seat-belt.

'What are we going for?' Jeremy asked. 'We must know what we intend to do. You want to make an offer for Roly, to buy him?'

'Yes. I've got more than carcass money, which is all he's going to get.'

'That's right. He won't get the insurance to pay if he has him put down—although I doubt if he insures his horses. What if he asks a big price?'

'Why ever should he?'

'Oh, Rosy, don't be so innocent! You want him badly. It shows, you know, arriving before nine o'clock with a cheque book in your hand. You're dealing with a shark.'

'I've got a thousand pounds. And Dark Secret. That's all.'

'That's more than he'll get from the knacker. We'll just have to keep our fingers crossed. Play it by ear. Perhaps I'm doing the man an injustice.'

Jeremy drove fast, like all racing men, hurtling through the spring morning, past fields of lambs and dripping woods and brimming water-meadows all smelling of new life and rebirth and the optimistic future. Rosy sat in silence, in a turmoil of doubt and despair, hating herself for her rubbishy feelings.

Smith's yard was not very different from how she had envisaged it, a muddle of do-it-yourself buildings round a muddy yard, a shaggy manure heap prominent, a squat bungalow by the gate, guarded by a mangy, barking dog chained to a kennel. Half a dozen horses were about to go out on exercise, and Smith was emerging from the bungalow as Jeremy pulled up.

'Shall I do the talking?' Jeremy asked. 'I think it would be best.'

'Yes.'

'Stay here then.'

Jeremy got out and went to greet Smith. Rosy sat shrinking in her seat, shivering. She saw the two men talking for a minute or two, then Smith gestured to one of the lads to lead out on exercise without him, and he went back into the house with Jeremy. The string came past Rosy, and Rosy recognized the girl Tracy on one of the horses, but Tracy did not acknowledge her. When they had gone, the dog stopped barking and went back into its kennel. For a few minutes the yard was empty and silent. Then a lorry came up the road and turned into the drive. The name on the front was the name of the slaughterer. The driver got out and went to the bungalow and knocked on the door, and the dog started barking again. Smith came to the door and said something to the driver who went back to the lorry, got in the cab and pulled out a packet of cigarettes. The dog went on barking. Rosy watched all this as if she were watching a play on television.

When the lorry-driver was about half-way through his cigarette Jeremy came out of the house alone and came back to Rosy. He opened the door and got into the driving-seat.

'I told you,' he said.

'What is it?'

'He wants the price he paid for him, three thousand two hundred. I've knocked him down to three thousand. It's up to you, Rosy. I can help you out for the time being, but in the long run, I can't afford to pay two thousand out for a dud horse. I wish I could.'

'I would have to sell the filly.'

'We could stall. Let him load Roly and go to the knacker's. At the last moment, he might change his mind. But then if we were to follow, and be there, he'd know how badly we want the horse. I'm afraid it's a bit of an impasse.'

'Three thousand? The filly would fetch enough, wouldn't she? I know Gin wants to sell her.'

'Oh, yes, I reckon she'd fetch that.'

Jeremy did not press her. He did not tell her how stupid she was, what a waste of money it was, that Roly was worth nothing. That she was going to throw all her hopes out of the window, get herself into debt for a worthless crock. But there was a stubborn bit of her that—seeing what a fool she was quite clearly—could not give in. What was bloody money, in the end? To sell the filly might prove, eventually, to be the best course.

'Yes, tell him he can have the money. If you can loan me the two thousand until we sell—'

'That's no problem.'

Jeremy got out and went back into the bungalow. He was away for about ten minutes. Then he came out with Smith and Smith went to the lorry-driver and said something to him. The driver put out his cigarette, started up his engine and departed, and Jeremy came back to the car.

'That's it then. Three thousand pounds, and he'll deliver him tonight, after racing.'

Rosy smiled.

She felt wonderful. Having thrown away her hard-earned tips, all her hopes of the filly, she felt marvellous.

'I'm sorry I'm such a fool,' she said. But she couldn't stop grinning.

Jeremy glanced at her and smiled too.

'Money isn't everything.'

12

Roly's leg was as bad as Rosy had seen in her lifetime, and for a couple of weeks the tacit opinion in the yard was that it would have been kinder to have let Smith have his way. Only Gin was delighted at the way things had turned out, with the decision to sell Dark Secret. The filly was entered for Tattersalls next sale at Newmarket early in May and Rosy hardened her heart against what might have been, only grateful that she had the means to pay Jeremy back. Or assumed she had the means ... it was hard to foresee what sort of price the filly would fetch, the stated sire being a nonentity as far as getting winners was concerned.

'I think you're crazy, honestly,' Grace announced, pausing to regard Rosy in her eternal chore, playing the cold water hose over Roly's swollen leg. 'Throwing away all that money, and the filly too. Still, I suppose you'll never be short, not with the picture.'

'The picture?'

'The Stubbs Letitia is leaving you. It must be worth a bomb.'

'Who said she's leaving it to me?'

'She's made her will, saying so. Hasn't she told you?'

'Not that she's made a will. I don't want it—it belongs to the family.'

Grace laughed. 'Oh, Rosy! You must be joking! You don't want it? You don't expect me to believe that?'

'I don't mind a memento or a hundred quid or something. But not the picture. It's too valuable, it's a family thing. How do you know about the will? Nobody's told me.'

'Jeremy told me.'

Grace was feeling at her most bitchy, Jeremy having taken to treating her more like a secretary than a lover lately. She was making no progress with him at all and was trying to screw herself up to give him an ultimatum. She could not afford to waste any more time on him if the state was not to be made a permanency. She was tempted to go away for a month and leave him to find out how much he now relied on her, but she was afraid of what might happen if she took her eye off him.

'You don't believe everyone thinks that you do all that for Letitia out of neighbourliness? Even Jeremy can't stand the sight of her. She's such a bad-tempered old bag. But she needs someone to help her, and I suppose if you're prepared to put the time in, you deserve what she—'

Without thinking twice, Rosy switched the hose and turned it on Grace's face. She had her finger over the sprayer and the jet had considerable force behind it, hitting Grace full in the mouth and turning her further conversation into a choking howl of anger. Rosy stood staring, astonished at her own impulse, even more astonished by Grace's accusation. It was like being back at school again, ragging in the girls' cloakroom. She took her finger off the jet and the water fell away, soaking Grace's tweeds and filling her shoes and gurgling down the drain.

For a moment Rosy thought Grace was going to hit her. Seeing her rage, barely controlled, stunned by her malice, Rosy felt a heartening swoop of pure joy, aware that someone as sound as Jeremy would never marry a bitch like Grace. It just wasn't possible.

'I'm sorry, but you asked for that. Sorry, sorry, sorry.'

She went back to Roly's leg again, turning her back, trying to shut out her feelings. Her role in life was as spectator: a stable-lad had no opinions, touched his forelock in time-honoured style to guv'nors and owners and did not answer back. Grace flounced away, and found herself in

184

the path of Mr Hawkins's Rolls just scraping through the gateway. The window purred down and Hawkins said, 'Grace, my dear! How are you?'

Glancing up, Rosy saw his expression change to concern when he saw the state Grace was in, and she saw Grace make a great effort to look as if being soaked by a cold water hose was part of everyday occurrences at Brood.

'Just a slight accident with the hose—I must go in and change.'

Even in such an extremity it came naturally to Grace to toss her wet hair back and smile brightly, because Hawkins was a male. For pure effort, Rosy reckoned, she deserved to win her man.

'Thought I'd just look in on Spinning Wheel—passing near, you know. Aren't you my girl, eh?' He smiled at Rosy as she untied Roly to lead him back to his box. 'This isn't one of mine, is it?'

If he was to produce his twenty-pound note, Rosy thought she would throw it back in his face. Hawkins did not even recognize Roly Fox, the gamest horse he was ever likely to lay eyes on, who had won him a small fortune in bets. She turned her back on the man and led Roly back into his box again to rebandage the bowed tendon.

'People, bloody people!'

She crouched in the straw, her fingers working neatly and tenderly on the damaged leg, trying not to think of Grace discussing her with Jeremy, finding out about the picture. Surely Jeremy did not think she had helped Letitia with an eye to a reward? Grace might, but not Jeremy. God, she wished she had never set eyes on the picture, if people were going to jump to such cruel conclusions.

She finished the bandage off, much disturbed, and laid her cheek briefly on Roly's neck, sniffing his hide gratefully. He was poor and skinny and dead lame, but the misery had gone from his eyes and his rabbity ears were interested in life once more. He butted her with his bone-head, and Rosy gave him a last caress before hurrying on to attend to the horses she was paid to look after, as opposed to the two she did for herself. She needed Hawkins's tip, damn it, and she went in to Spinning Wheel to change his rug, and brush his mane and make him look as if he wanted for nothing—to make it seem the groom was worth its keep ... it might have a fortune in the offing, but at present was deeply in debt, and needed every penny it could get.

Sitting on a strawbale outside Dark Secret's box at Park Paddocks, Newmarket, waiting for customers, Rosy had to admit that a spring day in the heartland of racing England had much to recommend it. The silken grass lawns rolled gently between yards of beautifully appointed looseboxes; old brick archways led into older, mellower yards; wide asphalt paths ran downhill past the neat parking into modern complexes where visitors could stroll to their hearts' content, reading their catalogues, requesting this colt or that mare to be led out, shown off. This was the smart end of racing, where horses raced on summer turf and race-goers strolled in summer dresses and shirtsleeves and sat out on flower-bedecked terraces clinking the ice in their drinks. Rosy had had visions that she too might grace a paddock with Jeremy this summer, but her visions were now away in the clouds with the rest of them: her assets were for sale.

It was how she had chosen. No complaints.

'Tell me why, with a mare like Silverfish, Mrs Cutbush put her to a no-hoper like Understanding?'

An elegant woman studying the catalogue was talking to her companion, an expensively-suited, dark-skinned man. Rosy had overheard this remark several times, but had not actually been asked it, nobody assuming that she was other than the menial lad.

The man said, 'I'm not interested in an Understanding.'

'Pity,' said the woman, looking at Dark Secret over the door. 'She's very nice. They say the old lady is very eccentric these days. She never goes out. My mother knew her, when her husband trained. She was said to be rather amazing as a girl.'

They strolled away, leaving Rosy depressed. Dark Secret was well grown and very good-looking, her conformation not to be faulted, and Rosy could only hope that it was on these qualities she would raise the bids, along with her illustrious dam. The less said about the bogus sire the better, she gathered.

'Funny time of year to sell a two-year-old. "To Dissolve a Partnership".'

An incredibly handsome, blond youth with a gnarled, broken-nosed older man paused by the box.

'That can mean anything. She looks fit, doesn't she? Sharp.'

'The dam's got a lot of form. Grand-dam won the Thousand Guineas and the St Leger. Herringbone.'

'She didn't get anything of note, Herringbone—not that I can remember.'

'Perhaps the genes are ready to spring again, Dad. That's how it works sometimes.'

'Or the line dies out, more often. We'll have a look at her, if you like.'

Rosy sprang up and led Dark Secret out into the yard. She stood to be examined, lipping at Rosy's hand. Nobody could fault her looks and condition, her fine appearance all down to Rosy's hard work. Her spring coat had settled on grey, a dark steel grey still mottled over her quarters with faint splashes of light and dark. Some viewers had not liked this oddity, but the more discerning ones were impressed by the apparent throwback to The Tetrarch through six generations.

Rosy walked and trotted her, and she went obediently, all spring and contained fire, action long and smooth. How could they not admire?

They did. 'Very nice. Very nice.'

Pencillings in the catalogue.

Rosy put her away, encouraged. The boy looking after the mare in the next-door box came back from lunch and said he would show Dark Secret for her to any interested parties if she wanted to go and get a cup of tea, so Rosy wandered off and looked at some of the competition. Gin had disappeared, in spite of promises to relieve. He was utterly unreliable these days and sickened her with his eagerness to exchange Dark Secret for hard cash. Jeremy had nobly backed out of the partnership—'I was only in it for the trainer's name, after all, to make it convenient. I've no claim to any cash. Only if we'd won some!'

Jeremy had said he would come.

Rosy leaned on the paddock rail where the animals soon to go into the ring were paraded before entering. She thought how smooth and well-mannered appearances were, compared with her winter game ... perhaps, when Jeremy married Grace and she herself left Brood, she would turn to flat-racing. There were plenty of girls at Newmarket. The loudspeaker intoned the bids from inside the ring: the voice of inexorable selling, the smooth professional patter that hid all the human folly, ambition, chance and glory that underlaid the thoroughbred breeding industry. She, through chance and opportunity, had perhaps produced as good as any—on potential, at least. But was selling because sentiment preferred another horse, worthless and futureless. She would not have changed anything, but it did not do to dwell on the logistics of the operation.

'Rosy?'

Expecting Gin, Rosy found Jeremy.

'Had many customers looking?'

'Yes. Quite a few.'

'That's a good sign. She shows herself so well.'

Rosy no longer called Jeremy 'sir'. She was not sure why this was, and assumed that it was his attitude to herself. Over the past year something subtle had altered in their relationship. The business with Roly, now with Dark Secret—a working partnership ... it seemed to carry on outside work, to have led them into—what seemed to Rosy—a special kind of friendship. She did not suppose in her wildest dreams that Jeremy thought there was anything significant in it. He was now, it seemed, engaged to Grace.

But he no longer treated Rosy as just a lad, more of a head lad, if it had to be declared in racing parlance. They got on well, in the same way as she had once got on well with Gin. At thirty, she thought she was beginning to grow up.

'You never know your luck,' he said. 'She's ready to run, after all. She looks good. You might be able to retire after this.'

'Do you think?'

'Well, perhaps not to be too hopeful. Understanding does your cause no good. Sorry about that, but it was needs must. Have you eaten?'

'I was going to get a sandwich and go back. I don't want to miss any buyers.'

Jeremy escorted her to the bar and bought her sausage rolls and coffee, and then said he had people to see and would come back when the filly was due in the ring. Rosy supposed Grace was around, but when it came time to take Dark Secret out to the parade ring he came back with Gin. No sign of Grace. It was evening, fine and warm, and the crowds were back from the races and filling the sales building. Rosy discovered that she was nervous.

'Shall we go and find a seat?'

Gin had charge of the filly. They left him and climbed up the staircase into the sales-ring and took a seat opposite the entrance. There were four lots to go before Dark Secret, and Rosy sat in mounting apprehension while Jeremy scanned the buyers for any likely faces. It was a much smarter milieu than the Ascot Sales where poor old Roly had met his fate; Rosy had no qualms this time about the filly going to a bad home.

When Dark Secret came in she hesitated at the strangeness of her surroundings, but Gin soothed her and she then walked on boldly, showing off her swinging walk. Looking down on her, Rosy reckoned she had done a good job, engineering such a filly. Her pulses were starting to thump uncomfortably. The auctioneer read out her description and dwelt on the erstwhile fame of the dam as instructed, listing Silverfish's other winning produce, ignoring the sire,

189

and then vigorously pointing out the good action, conformation and condition.

'A two-year-old, in training and ready to run straight away for her new owner. This is a great opportunity...'

He tried to start her at five thousand, dropped to four, to three, and got his first bid, by which time Rosy was in a sweat of agony. From the three the bids climbed steadily to six, to seven, where one bidder dropped out. There was a long hold up, the auctioneer very patient, pleading and cajoling, then someone else came in at eight and the bidding climbed steadily to twelve thousand. By this point Rosy had stopped sweating with apprehension and now was feeling quite sick with excitement.

Jeremy glanced at her and grinned.

'I reckon you'll be retiring after this.'

'I can't believe it!'

She had been so terrified the filly would not make her even the two thousand she owed Jeremy. Now, splitting with Gin, she was four thousand to the good.

'Twelve thousand five hundred? Thank you, sir. The bid is on my right...'

Dark Secret had her admirers. The price danced up to fifteen thousand, and hovered there. Rosy had her eyes on the ticker-tape figures spluttering on the indicator-board, hardly dared to breathe. Gin was looking poker-faced as he hurried round to the filly's long, powerful stride.

'Sixteen thousand? Thank you. I am bid sixteen thousand.'

Rosy thought, six thousand pounds. I have six thousand pounds for myself. It was a fortune.

The bidding went to another five hundred. And another.

At seventeen thousand five hundred it stopped. The auctioneer did not spend much more time waiting, but brought his hammer down after it was obvious no other bidder was coming in.

Rosy looked at Jeremy, jubilant, and he put his arm round her and gave her a little hug.

'Well done! I'm really pleased for you.'

Rosy found it hard to believe. Nothing like this had ever happened to her in her life. She went down the stairs behind Jeremy, walking very carefully, trying to stop the idiotic grin bursting over her face. Outside the exit doors Gin was waiting with Dark Secret. Grace and Mr Hawkins were standing with him.

'What a splendid price!' Grace called out, all smiles. 'Wasn't it much better than you expected?'

'Yes. A lot.'

'Well done, Gin. Congratulations,' Jeremy said. Gin looked happier than he had done since he was married. Perhaps the thought struck Jeremy for he added, 'Don't let that wife of yours spend it all now.'

'I will not, sir. It's great news. Eh, Rosy?'

'Oh, Gin!' Rosy gave him a hug. 'Isn't it lovely?'

'Yeah—until she wins the Oaks!'

Laughs all round. An elderly groom came up to take Dark Secret... 'For Mr Pemberton's stable. We'll be taking her home right away. Two miles up the road—she's not got a long journey.'

He was kindly, gentle, a real groom, not like the boy who had taken Roly Fox.

Mr Pemberton, apparently, was the man with the broken nose and the blonde son.

'I know him,' said Hawkins. 'He's a customer of mine.'

Grace, with two men in attendance, drinks and dinner in the offing, was in her element. Rosy, watching her, knew perfectly well that she was toying with the idea of telling Hawkins how Dark Secret had been bred. If Hawkins had been able to tell one horse from another, it should have struck him how like Peppermill the filly was; he would not have needed Grace's advice. But Jeremy, sensing the same mischief, took Grace firmly by the arm and said to Rosy, 'You'll go back in the box with Gin?'

'Yes.'

'A good day's work. Well done.'

With which he departed with Grace and Mr Hawkins, and Rosy was back to her station again. She took her leave of her lovely filly, thinking of the money and not of the cold morning Silverfish first took the little thing out into the frosty air ... *my* filly, she thought stubbornly, whatever happens afterwards. And made for home with Gin, perched in the familiar lorry, trying to realize that things weren't quite the same any more, although what difference the money made, she wasn't quite sure.

'You haven't been out for years. Will you come to Ascot with us, if we take you in the car? To see Dark Secret run?'

'Eh?' Letitia was at the field gate when Rosy came in the evening to check Roly Fox.

'We've just been talking about it. It was Gin's idea. We're going in the car and he said ask you. Like old times. It's Royal Ascot week—Dark Secret is entered for the Queen Mary Stakes. Can you believe it? What do you think?'

Excited herself, Rosy knew the old lady could not make head nor tail of what she was talking about. Jeremy had entered the filly months ago, for old times' sake, without telling anyone, in case she came good. Now the new owners had decided she could take her chance.

'We'd look after you, so you won't get too tired. We'll get seats in the grandstand, do it properly. What do you think? When did you last go to Ascot? Silverfish won at Ascot, didn't she?'

'Hmm.'

Beryl had said it would be too much for the old girl. Rosy and Gin had disagreed, knowing how she laboured in her garden, fetching and carrying, trundling her wheelbarrow up and down the slopes.

'She's like the old mare—go on for ever. She'd love Ascot again.'

'We'd have to dress up,' Beryl said.

'We're not going in the Royal Enclosure! I'll wear my wedding suit.'

'I'll have to buy something.'

'Trust you!'

The eternal bickering, even in general agreement, made Rosy smile. It was arranged they would go together.

'Mrs C can have the front seat. Ask her, Rosy. It'd be a lark with her.'

They had got so excited about the idea that Rosy was now impatient for the old lady to show the same interest. But she chewed her lips and frowned into the evening.

'Peter won't be there.'

'No.' For God's sake, Peter had been dead for forty years.

'Someone will have to feed Jasper.'

'We can leave his food down. He'll be all right.'

'I'll think about it.'

'You must! You'll love it, to see it all again. The Queen and everything.'

'The King. He spoke to us, you know. He shook hands with us.'

Was it cruel, starting old memories? How could you tell, trying to figure how the tiring brain worked, what was good for it, what bad? She had the physical strength, if they looked after her. They were carried away by the idea.

'Fancy, our filly going for the Queen Mary! They must think highly of her. It's a Group race.'

Dark Secret had run once, at Newmarket, and been fourth in a large field. Jeremy had been very impressed. Their horses were all turned out now for the summer and there was no work to do, save tidying and maintenance. With Roly now at grass and no Dark Secret, Rosy was lying in bed till eight o'clock in the mornings and reckoned she was putting on weight. She was thinking of getting driving lessons and buying a car. Her money was in the bank, untouched. She kept thinking about it, warmly. If they had kept Dark Secret, would she have come fourth at Newmarket and be trying for the Queen Mary? Who could tell?'

'I'll sleep on it,' Mrs Cutbush said.

'You do that. And say yes in the morning.'

'I've got to feed the dog.'

Once Jeremy had bought his grandmother another dog

to replace Jasper, but she had kept putting it out of the door and complaining that Jasper was bringing his friends in and she didn't like it. Jeremy had had to find the dog another home.

Rosy walked down towards the river and Roly came towards her, friendly and accommodating. His leg was improving very slowly. He had put on weight and the old sheen was back on his hide. He was now as happy as a horse could be, back with his old companion; even Silverfish had lost her sour demeanour in his presence. Rosy still found walking through this field in the evening or early in the morning, to see the horses, gave her pleasure out of all proportion. If she left and went to work elsewhere, there would be a great loss. She felt she belonged here, on this ground, where Dark Secret had first seen the light, and the old horses found solace. It was a part of her. How stupid, mocked her common sense, loving a field. Even worse than a horse. Tony Mowbray would have plenty of pithy comments to make on her latest folly. She kept meaning to look for a new job. Every day. But never did.

When she called on Mrs Cutbush the next day she was astonished to find her wearing a full-skirted dress with short sleeves in white cotton with a pattern of red tulips splashed gaily over it. On her head was a red straw hat with a wide brim, a bunch of cherries with dark green leaves decorating one side, the dirty grey hair escaping in loops from beneath. Her sticklike arms which Rosy had never seen uncovered protruded from the caped shoulderline to reveal the pathetic frailty of the ancient frame; equally spindly legs in shiny stockings supported the strange edifice, shod in dirty white satin shoes of ancient design.

'The shoes don't fit any more. They pinch me,' she said. 'I wore this rig-out the last time I went to Ascot. It will do again, except for the shoes.'

'It's fantastic!' Rosy was touched. It was funny, but not to be laughed at. 'You look marvellous!'

Letitia allowed her to take the dress home to wash and iron, and Rosy tactfully shortened it a little at the same time. To her great relief, Letitia agreed to wear one of her classy but equally ancient long cardigans over the dress—'You aren't used to having your arms bare. You don't want to get a chill.' It was a deep plum colour, and calmed the initial impact of the bright tulips considerably. A pair of leather sandals, found in the back of the wardrobe, completed the picture, still eye-catching but—Rosy hoped—no longer grotesque. Bizarre. It was OK to be bizarre, after all, especially when, in the past, you had led your own horses into the winners' enclosure.

At the last moment Rosy panicked about the outing and mentioned it to Jeremy.

'I should have told you. You don't think it'll be too much for her? We just thought it would be such a splendid day out.'

'God, Rosy, it's a fantastic idea! I'm ashamed the thought never crossed my own mind. If it had, I couldn't have faced taking her anyway. I think you're a saint.'

'She's really very tough, the way she works in her garden.'

'Yes, she's amazing. Actually, I thought of going with Grace. She likes the idea. Shall we arrange to meet? You bring Gran out to the paddock to see the filly, and I'll try and find you. Get a place in plenty of time and you can sit her down.'

'I'll try. Yes. I'll look out for you.'

'It will be terribly crowded, that's the trouble in June. All those society ladies trying to get on the telly.'

'You wait till you see your grandmother. She's fished out her forties Ascot gear. The telly will go wild when it sees her.'

'God, Rosy, I do admire you! I might not find you after all.'

'You should be proud of her. She's fantastic.'

'You're right. But old memories die hard. Why do you think my parents emigrated?'

Rosy smiled. 'For the sunshine? I can imagine.'

Rosy, sorting over the best of her own unexciting wardrobe, realized that such a conversation with Jeremy could never have happened two years ago. One had to admit, like it or not—and she did not—that Grace had had a good influence on him. And the heartless Hawkins, supplying good horses. Two really nasty people had unlocked Jeremy from his bitterness and gloom. So much for life's rich pattern.

On the Wednesday morning of Royal Ascot week the motley race-goers from Brood packed into Gin's ancient Cortina. Mrs Cutbush sat in the front, holding her hat, while Gin in his wedding suit and a rather dubious blue satin tie fastened her seat-belt solicitously. Beryl read *Sporting Life* in the back, noting that Dark Secret was offered at ten to one.

'Seventeen runners. It'll take a good filly to win.'

'She is a good filly.'

Suppose ... Rosy did not dare, for all sorts of reasons. She was excited and, for once, without qualms of apprehension. A mere spectator. There was a lot to be said for spectating.

Kes had been left with Gin's mother.

It was a perfect day, clear and cloudless, a slight breeze keeping the temperature at a comfortable level—Rosy blessed it, having been afraid that Letitia might be tempted to shed her cardigan. When they arrived Gin set his passengers down at the entrance and arranged to meet them when he had parked the car. Rosy and Beryl took Letitia to the nearest bar and got her a seat and some sandwiches and coffee, no small feat in the mêlée, and Gin joined them as planned, ready for his first pint.

'There's no point the four of us being tied to the old girl,' Rosy whispered to Gin. 'Leave her to me. You and Beryl go and do your own thing and I'll meet you here after the last.'

Rosy took Letitia up into the grandstand to watch the royal party arrive down the course in their horse-drawn coaches. She gave her her own binoculars, and Letitia peered diligently in all directions, muttering and exclaiming. Her eyes glittered like a child's. Rosy sat back, thinking that in Letitia's day it had been no different: the throng of racing's richest participators, a galaxy of obvious wealth and privilege from the rows of Rollers in the car-parks to the champagne corks popping in the bars: the sport at its most picturesque, enough to make a good Socialist turn to the dogs. Yet behind the glitter, in the stables, at home, on the gallops, the whole business worked in exactly the same way as they worked at Brood. The top dressing was incidental ... a charade that—to a real race-goer—cluttered one of the year's very best meetings. The crowds were a pain if one seriously wanted to watch the racing. Yet one had to admire the picture as the runners for the first race cantered out on to the sacred turf and bounded down past the stands. The course was as handsome as its crowds, the heath fading away into distant blue woods, apparently remote from the antlike activity in the foreground. Rosy had worked here in the winter when a much thinner throng came to watch the jumping; it bore little resemblance now to those bleak days. Yet, with a little thump of anticipation, Rosy remembered that she did have a horse here today. Dark Secret was hers as much as any horse could be. Already, she felt herself break out in a sweat at the thought of her race.

Getting Letitia to the paddock to meet Jeremy was a major operation in the crush. Holding her firmly by the skinny arm, Rosy took her down the stairs and out across the crowded lawns. She got to the all-important oval of tree-shaded turf before the preceding race finished, and seated her on one of the toadstool-like seats in front of the rails. Already three fillies were being led round. One of them was Dark Secret.

'Look, that's her! Silverfish's filly!'

Behind them the crowd roared its winner home, and Dark Secret paused in her step, her ears pricking up to the noise. She was as beautiful a thoroughbred as Rosy had ever set eyes on. I'm not biased, she told herself. She was perfection, and her condition hard and shining, her action keen, impatient. The groom who had taken her from Park

Paddocks was leading her, smiling, gentling her with words.

'Hi, Gran, you made it! How does it feel to be back here again?'

As good as his word, Jeremy joined them before the crush started, with Grace at his side. He was wearing formal dress, and Grace was bedecked in canary frills, showing a lot of flat brown chest. Rosy saw her eyes rake Letitia's splendid show of tulips and the resplendent hat, saw the mirth bursting, suppressed, felt the malice. She could hear the voice: 'My dear, she looked an absolute fright! You should have seen her!' Grace, seeing Rosy's face, froze over.

'She's doing fine. She belonged here, after all, once.'

'Your grandfather won the Queen Mary before the war,' Letitia said to Jeremy. 'With a filly by Mr Jinks. His grandsire was The Tetrarch, you know. He did like that strain.'

'Perhaps the filly will do it again. Doesn't she look good?'

'Silverfish looked like her, as a two-year-old. She was as dark.'

The other fillies came in, nervous, flirting with their bits, eyes staring at the bright crowd. The paddock filled with owners and trainers. Rosy glimpsed the blond young man in grey tails, and his broken-nosed father. Their trainer was one of the top five, and their jockey a household word. Bright as a parakeet, he flipped up into the saddle and rode down past Letitia on the rails.

'Good luck, young man!' she called out boldly, and the crowd around them stared and tittered. The jockey touched his cap, to Rosy's amazement. They were not normally given to hearing remarks from the crowd.

'You'll never get her back into the grandstand in time,' Jeremy said as the fillies left the paddock and the huge crowd surged back to their vantage points. 'Shall we go and stand on the rails? We'll see the finish, at least, and we can watch them come back.'

'Oh Jeremy, you'll see nothing from there!' Grace said tetchily.

'You can go back to the stand. I'll meet you afterwards.'

'Not without you. I'll never find you again.'

'Very well. Stay here then.' Very tart. Unloving.

They guided Letitia across the grass to the railside, where indeed they would see nothing until the finish itself.

'It's only five furlongs, after all. Hardly worth going into the grandstand for a minute's worth of racing. We'll hear the commentary.'

'Silverfish's produce always stayed,' Letitia said. 'Five furlongs is too short.'

'She's only a baby, Gran. Far enough for a baby.'

Grace stayed with them, sulking, studying her race-card. Rosy leaned on the rail, listening to her heart pounding. She had never been so nervous about a horse racing, not even dear Roly. She'll end down the field, she told herself— a high-class race like this, don't hope for anything. It's impossible. The prize money was nearly thirty thousand pounds. We're in the big league. She'll win because we sold her . . . 'They're under starter's orders!' Oh, God!

'They're off!'

Rosy felt the blood thundering in her ears like the thunder of hooves on the hard turf. For the whole minute before they came into view she stood hardly breathing, screwed up with praying, eyes shut tight. She felt desperately sick. The name Dark Secret was somewhere in the jumbled commentary, but the voice was all at sea, as she was herself. She felt fingers digging into her arm, Jeremy's voice bawling.

'Come on, my girl! Dark Secret!'

Rosy heard screaming, and realized that it was herself.

The familiar, heart-wrenching crescendo of flying hooves overlaid the great crowd's roar as the field exploded into view, a tangle of colour and action. One filly came clear. She shot from the pack like a bullet fifty yards from the post and went on flying when the others had spent their strength, hurtling away down the wide green course and round the bend as if she had another circuit to run.

'Dark Secret wins by three—four lengths! White Hyacinth second, Amritzar, Pagan Princess . . .'

'She's won!' Rosy flung herself into Jeremy's arms. He hugged her, kissed her, danced a wild circle, picked his grandmother up and kissed her.

'Your Silverfish has done it again, Gran! What a mare! What a filly! What a breeder! Congratulations, Rosy!'

Rosy found she was crying—tears of joy, half hysterics. She was shaking like a tree in a gale. The brilliance of the turf, the jockeys' silks, and Ascot dresses, whirled in circles round her head, and she was reaching for the fragile Letitia, thinking giddily, The excitement will kill her! 'Are you all right, Mrs Cutbush?'

'I'm very well, thank you.'

'Shall we go and see her in the winners' enclosure? Oh, please!'

The crowd was thronging back. Rosy took the old lady's arm on one side and Jeremy took the other, and they hurried, half-lifting the old lady over the grass. The officious gateman put a rope across their way to stop the crowd pressing up from the grandstand and they were caught on the wrong side. Jeremy went on shoving.

'This is Mrs Cutbush, the breeder of the winner. Please let her through.'

'Sir?'

The gateman raised his bowler. 'Mrs Cutbush, congratulations, madam.'

He lifted the rope back to let them through, and put it back just before Grace could make it.

'There, Gran, you're back in the winners' enclosure, where you belong.'

Jeremy introduced her to the excited, handsome boy, and his equally excited father, and the famous trainer, all waiting for their winner. Rosy was introduced too. 'She broke in the filly. She handled her from a foal.' They were enchanted with the amazing figure of their filly's breeder, her black eyes sparkling, the red straw hat tipping rakishly over one eye with the cherries failing to counterbalance on the other side. Watching her, Rosy ached suddenly for these smart people to see her as Munnings had seen her in

200

the golden landscape of her youth, with her beautiful, imperious gaze from the back of the prancing beast in Jeremy's hall, her lovely, sensitive hands and radiant red hair. Even with the sober cardigan, she really did look something of a freak. The newsmen were enchanted and camera bulbs were popping all over the place.

They drew back when Dark Secret was led in, to keep out of the picture, slipping away to a decent distance to admire their famous filly as she danced and cavorted in Ascot's place of honour. Rosy was embarrassed now at having pushed in, but Jeremy had done it for his grandmother; her name was a small part of Ascot's history. In her dotage she had not lost her touch.

'If I don't go to the lavatory soon, dear,' she said suddenly to Rosy, 'I'll wet my drawers.'

'I'll take you. We'll go now.'

She explained the situation to Jeremy. 'Then I'll take her back to the grandstand.'

'I'd better go and find Grace. I'll look for you in the grandstand for the next race then. Which end will you be?'

They made the best rendezvous they could, and Rosy set off with Letitia on her mission. The queue was enormous. 'You can go through, I'll take you,' Rosy said. 'I'll ask the attendant.'

She battled her way through and a kindly attendant held the next door open for her, ahead of the crowd. Rosy slumped against a wash-basin, still wrapped in the dream of winning, seeing that tremendous burst of speed that had taken Dark Secret clear. She had beaten the best in the highest class of racing, and was bound to be entered for further good races, at Newmarket in July, or Goodwood, at Sandown Park. She would be quoted for next year's Thousand Guineas. She had the right antecedents. Rosy still felt faint at this magic stroke of success, trying to take in the true tragedy of the afternoon: that she had bred a triumphant winner and sold it in order to buy the old crock that was Roly Fox. When the gloss of this amazing day had worn off, she was going to be left with something close to heartbreak. If a filly like Dark Secret carried through with the promise she had just shown, she was likely to make half a million racing and command three times that to go to stud when she was finished. Gin might have thrown away a million, to pay off Beryl's paltry debts. She herself, Rosy Weeks, had thrown away the chance of becoming a millionaire.

In the bustle and crush, Rosy felt as if her head was bursting. It was unbearably hot. Whatever was Letitia up to?

'Your gran's a long time in there, dear,' said the attendant. 'Do you think she's all right. Do you want to give her a call?'

Rosy looked up anxiously, unaware of how long she had stood gazing into space.

She tried the door but it was locked.

'Mrs Cutbush? Are you all right?'

No answer. Rosy knocked heavily, and shouted.

'Perhaps she's fainted. It's so hot,' said the attendant. 'I'll fetch a chair and we can look over the door. It does happen sometimes, you know.'

Everyone was agog, staring. Rosy was deeply afraid, the old girl unused to going away from home, having had such an exciting day. Her own head was whirling.

'I'll climb up. Give it to me.' She took the chair from the attendant and shoved it against the door. By hauling on the top of the door she could just lift herself high enough to see over. Below her, huddled against the door, lay a heap of white and scarlet, like a shot bird. The crazy hat covered the face, the bright cherries flung forward, dipping on the tiles.

'I'll fetch some help,' the attendant said. 'Just give me a moment. I'll ring through to the First Aid.'

'Please, if you give me a bunk up, I can climb over.'

Strangers giving advice, a flurry of excitement, faces peering up. A large horsey lady in grey silk pushed forward and gave Rosy a professional leg-up, so that she got a knee over the top of the door. There was space enough, and an upright to hold on to. Nowhere to land. She crouched there, considering.

'If you can just open the door, dear. That's all we need.'

Rosy lowered herself with infinite care, one leg reaching for the lavatory seat, to take her weight. Balanced, holding the partition, she could reach forward and unlatch the door. But Letitia lay against it, and it could not be opened.

'You shouldn't move her, dear! Wait for the First Aid men. They know what to do.'

They hustled in, practised, important, the crush giving way. They looked over, appraising the situation, while Rosy stood on the lavatory seat. They took the door off its hinges and lifted it gently away. Letitia rolled forward and the hat slithered sideways showing a paper-white face, blue lips. They knelt over her, feeling for her pulse amongst the bright tulips.

'She's alive? She's not—'

'Yes, she's breathing, dear. Not too good though. Let's have some room, please. Can we clear a space?'

'Perhaps she's just fainted . . . the heat?'

Rosy felt desperate, seeing the birdlike limbs straightened out on the stretcher, the gnarled hands with their resplendent rings tidied down at her side. She longed for Jeremy to know, to come, but in this crushing, gaudy throng, however to find him? She felt appallingly responsible.

'Oh, please—'

'Steady on, young lady. We're doing our best. Make some room, please! We'll have her out of here and into the air. We've got the ambulance right outside.'

Between them they secured Letitia on to the stretcher and lifted it. Rosy kept close, following them out, pushing and shoving to keep at its side. An ambulance with its blue light flashing was waiting, and curious crowds staring.

'Where are you taking her?'

'We'll just run her into the hospital, to be on the safe side. It looks like a bit more than a fainting fit, the pulse isn't good.'

'Shall I come?'

'You're welcome, dear. We'll want her particulars.'

'But I must tell her grandson—he's here, I must find him. We were meeting him in a minute—'

Rosy's panic would not go away. In an emergency, when she needed to keep calm, she was like a frightened hen. She needed Jeremy, not only for Letitia, but for herself.

'You come along when you've found him, love. We'll take her on in, I think that's best.'

For all the calm voices, they were not wasting any time, the stretcher in place, doors closed, engine running. The ambulance departed, and Rosy was left distraught, blindly making for the grandstand. *She's going to die and it's all my fault. I should never have thought ... the excitement ... the filly winning...* She saw again the brightness of Letitia's eyes, the bloodstream alight. From the stands the crowd was roaring again, the commentator's voice raised, cracking with excitement. It had taken no time at all for Letitia to pass unconscious out of the whirl of Ascot, only the interval between races. The same crowd, oblivious, cheered and applauded and surged down towards the winners' enclosure.

Rosy fought her way back to the grandstand. As it emptied she forced her way back up to the place she had arranged with Jeremy and, to her infinite relief, saw him standing just below, with Grace, talking to some people. She ran down again.

'Whatever's the matter?'

'Mrs Cutbush—your gran—she's been taken ill. They've taken her to hospital—'

'Oh, no!' Jeremy's face contorted with genuine, unrehearsed anguish.

'There,' said Grace, 'I said it was stupid.'

'I shall have to go. Excuse me.'

'Jeremy! For heaven's sake! Not this minute, surely?'

'Yes, Grace, of course. Are you coming?'

'Oh, no! It takes all day, waiting around in hospitals. Won't afterwards do?'

'I'm going now. You can get a lift home with someone, I'm sure.'

204

'I arranged to meet Gin in the bar after the last,' Rosy said. 'He'll take you back.'

Jeremy was already hurrying down the steps. She ran after him.

'I'm coming too. I can't stay.'

'Fine.'

They pushed their way out, Jeremy taking Rosy's arm to guide her. She was in tears, seeing Jeremy's distress.

'It was all my fault! I thought—she's so strong—'

'Don't blame yourself, Rosy! Didn't you see her face? She was loving it. The day of her life! Whatever happens, don't regret anything.' He paused in his hurry, turned to her and gave her a little shake. 'It was lovely of you to arrange it. She'll never forget. Whatever happens, it wasn't a mistake, Rosy.'

Rosy was comforted. Jeremy spoke not as a comforter but as a man stating the obvious truth. 'It's so hot, for heaven's sake—I daresay she'll be as right as rain in the morning.'

But the hospital said she was still unconscious when they got there. A doctor spoke to them briefly. 'It doesn't look too good. A slight heart attack ... she's been taken up to intensive care.'

A nurse asked them for her particulars, which Jeremy gave, then they sat waiting in somebody's office, were offered cups of tea. Eventually the doctor came back and said, 'There's nothing you can do for the time being. Perhaps you could come back later, say, at six o'clock, and then we might be able to tell you what the situation is. If she's stable by then, you could go home.'

'Very well.'

They went back to the car.

'Grace was right, I suppose,' Rosy said.

'Grace is always right,' Jeremy said, without joy. 'I don't fancy going back, do you? We would make the last race, I suppose.'

'I wouldn't see anything.'

'No.'

They went back to the car and got in, winding down the windows.

'We'll go somewhere quiet.'

The roads in and out of Ascot all seemed to lead through woodland and heath. They found a convenient lay-by and parked the car, and were able to walk off it along a path through bracken and tangled trees. The late afternoon was now very hot and still, but the woods were mercifully cool. It was silent, save for the distant swish of a passing car, and seemed light-years away from the milling crowd they had so recently left. They came to an opening where the turf was fine and dry, and a large oak had fallen. Jeremy dropped down and settled himself with his back to the trunk, pulling off his tie and unpopping the studs.

'This wretched gear! I'm sweating like a pig. Poor old Letitia—she did look amazing, didn't she? She's a real character. Shame I never could get on with her. My loss, not hers.'

'Oh, God, I hope she's all right!'

'Stop worrying, Rosy. Everything's for the best, whatever.'

Rosy dropped down on the turf. Her brain was in a turmoil; the peace of the woodland was blessed, after the shocks and confusion of the day. She lay curled on the turf, smelling the scent of the hot grass and the crushed bracken, the crumbly, peaty soil. On the still air, from the distance, came the faint voice of the commentator from the races and, presently, the sound of distant cheering as the last finish was decided. Rosy saw Dark Secret again, and shivered.

As if he knew, Jeremy said, 'We should have kept that filly.'

'Yes. But it's what you just said. Everything's for the best.'

'It has to be.'

'Roly was going to the knacker's.'

'Money's not everything. We said so before.'

The race was over. On the still air now there was only the humming of a bee, the whine of a mosquito.

206

'If Letitia dies, I shall lose Brood. I shall lose everything. I've never done anything about it, all my fault. Whatever will Grace say?'

'Doesn't she know?'

'She thinks it's all mine.'

Rosy smiled into the turf. If Letitia died, she would inherit the Stubbs which was worth half a million. Suddenly, the afternoon was unreal. She had dozed off in the heat, and when she awoke she would be back in Roly's field, lying by the riverbank, as she did sometimes on a warm afternoon. She did not want Letitia to die.

'I shall have to find another place. Or give up,' Jeremy said.

Rosy concentrated on taking long, steady breaths, to make her pulses stop thudding. Her veins seemed suddenly to have grown too small for their purpose. Her mind could not absorb everything calmly, not least that she was alone with Jeremy in a peaceful, lonely place, and he was confiding to her whole regions of his private life, of which Grace knew nothing. When she turned her head, she could see him from a strange angle, low down, his shoulder turned away from her, and above it the outcrop of his cheekbone, the slight gaunt shadow beneath it, the hair cut short in front of his ears. His eyes were looking away and she could not see them, but in her mind she could see the pale grey-green irises with the dark rings round them, the dark eye-lashes and well-defined eyelids in their hollow sockets. He had a hard-used look, youthful and yet with the beginnings of wisdom, a touch wary, a thread or two of grey. She knew she loved him as much as she had ever loved him; nothing in her was cured or discouraged or—after all this time, it seemed—ever would be. Perhaps now—this half-hour or so—was the most she would ever have, and it was taken up with preoccupations of life and death, and larger things than mere infatuation. She would love him if he had nothing, if she had nothing too, if everything was bleak and hopeless in front of them, if they had to live in a field without a roof to their name. She thought she had a touch of the sun, or premonitions of death. She shut her eyes and said nothing.

From the road, the hiss of traffic from the races now made a rhythmic interruption to the silence. The day was over, fortunes lost, fortunes made, trainers triumphant, trainers in despair. The breeze had gone and the sun was brazen in the evening sky. The hot roads throbbed to the queues of cars. Their fumes hung heavily on the sweet air. 'Please don't let Letitia die!' Rosy's prayer thumped to the swish of traffic as she lay with her face turned into the turf. 'Please don't let Letitia die!'

Grace sat peevishly in the back of Gin's Cortina in the crawling, pulsing, sweating queue making for the M4 and listened irritably to Gin's boring agitation over the state of Letitia Cutbush.

'God, if she dies! And we thought it was such a great idea! Rosy'll be in a terrible stew. She'll think it's all her fault.'

'It will be, as I see it,' Grace said. 'It was her idea.'

'Yeah, but she saw Dark Secret win, didn't she? It must have been fantastic for her. I dare say that's what did it, the excitement. I reckon a lot of owners damn near have heart attacks when their horses win.'

'You'll be wishing you hadn't sold that filly, I imagine?'

'Yeah—well—'

Beryl had already had her say on that count, Gin did not want to dwell on it. Beryl's greed had been assuaged somewhat by the return her hefty bet had brought, but every time she thought of the prize money the filly had won, and her enhanced value, tears came into her eyes.

As he sat staring at the backside of the car in front, drumming his fingers on the wheel, Gin's mind turned to other permutations on the day's happening.

'If the old girl dies, we might be out of a job, Beryl. Did you think of that?'

'Good riddance to that place, I'd say.'

'Why d'you say that?' Grace inquired.

208

'She owns the place, doesn't she? And she always told us she hadn't made a will, she wasn't going to die, there was plenty of time. So I suppose it will all go to Mr Cutbush in Australia.'

'Are you sure?' Grace's voice was sharp.

'Only going off what she said. Might not be true, I suppose. You can never tell—she used to ramble quite a lot. Say one thing one day and another the next. You know what they're like, when they're old.'

Grace did not speak again. She felt the heat was killing her, the sun burning her up as her thighs clung sweatily to the plastic seat. If she said anything, she would spit gobbets of fire.

13

Rosy and Jeremy went back to the hospital at six and sat with Letitia until she died, at ten o'clock. She did not recover consciousness, but lay quite still, smiling faintly. For some reason the red hat with the cherries was perched on the radio over the top of the bed.

It was a happy death, if such a thing could be, apparently painless, apparently happy. She only stirred once in the four hours they watched her, and said, 'Feed Jasper.' Just before she died she said something else. Rosy thought it was 'Peter'. But Jeremy said it was 'Jasper' again. Rosy stuck to her belief, and hoped Letitia was indeed going to meet her beloved husband, forever fixed in her mind at the age of forty-five. If it had not been for Jeremy, Rosy would have been devastated.

'Nobody could go better than that, Rosy,' he said gently. 'Think of it—how she might have become. She would have hated to be dependent, you must see that, and in a year or two...'

'What have I done?'

She could not help thinking that she had lost him Brood, but Jeremy did not mention it again. Letitia had always said she would make a will when she got older, and perhaps she would have willed it to Jeremy. Rosy felt that the old woman meant it for Jeremy.

Rosy took the red hat, and the nurses wanted to give Jeremy the rings but they would not come off.

'Later.'

They accepted cups of tea instead. The doctor and the

sister were kind in the course of duty: Royal Ascot week tended to be busy, with a fracture or two, heat-stroke, drunken drivers smashing themselves up and the odd coronary. Rosy felt the day had gone on for a very long time. When they went back to the car the air was cool and still and it was the twilight dark of midsummer, the stars faint and the moon gauzy. They drove back past the silent grandstands and the empty course, with the windows open, the night air blowing in, and Rosy felt the tears trickling down her cheeks. The smell of the woods in the half-dark, Jeremy's profile beside her, watching the road, the memory of Dark Secret flying past the winning post, Letitia's face in the winners' enclosure ... it was all a tangle of triumph and disaster, joy and grief, which overwhelmed her as the car sped on out towards the motorway. Jeremy glanced at her, wound up the windows, and drove in silence, fast along the empty roads.

Rosy woke at the usual time the following morning, and got out of bed to go to work. She had a blinding headache and did not want to think about what had happened. Jeremy had said not to come in, but there were several jobs that needed doing, and Roly to check. It was still very hot, and she remembered Jasper's dogfood in Letitia's kitchen: it must be cleared away before it stank the place out. She cycled down there on her bike. The morning was bliss, going to be a scorcher, but still fresh, cloudless, the sky almost without colour, alive with skylarks. The horses were down by the river, Silverfish lying down, Roly cropping the wet grass beside her. His leg was improved, but he was still lame. By rights he should still be in his box, but he deserved the summer grass. The midges were rising already, the horses' tails switching. Rosy left them and walked up to Letitia's garden gate, and to the front door. The rose over the porch was in magnificent bloom, its drooping pink heads too heavy to hold up, scattering petals. The garden looked splendid—poor Letitia!

'Oh, damn!' Rosy swore, groping for the key under the

flower-pot, feeling the wretched grief flattening the beauty of the morning. Letitia was old, she was ready to go, she died happy ... she kept telling herself, as Jeremy had told her. Oh, Jeremy! Rosy wept. Last night she had loved him agonizingly; half the tears had been for Jeremy, if only she had been honest. If they had been together in that way for any reason other than Letitia's heart attack, she thought she would not have been able to stop herself from flinging herself into his arms, asking for his love. Just like Grace.

She let herself into the house and went through into the kitchen. She cleared the dogfood, wrapping it in a plastic bag and putting it in the dustbin. Poor old ghost Jasper, he would now be forgotten for ever. She tidied up and threw out a few bits of food that might go bad, and went back towards the front door. Halfway through the living-room, she realized that where the Stubbs picture had hung on the wall, there was now a blank, an empty patch where the wall had faded to the exact size of the picture.

She stopped, put out. *Her* picture. Not that she had ever thought of it before as her picture, but now that Letitia was dead, it presumably was. Or had been. Had Jeremy taken it for safety? He always said it was foolish to leave such a valuable object so poorly guarded. A burglar? Rosy felt her panics rising, her head throbbing with renewed zest.

She locked the house behind her and cycled up to Brood, running and panting up the last zigzag. Gin was in the yard, clearing out the haybarn ready for a new delivery. Rosy had rung him when she got home and told him about Letitia, not realizing how late it was.

'Have you been into Mrs Cutbush's? The picture's gone, the Stubbs.'

'No. Of course not. Bloody hell, the valuable one?'

'I must tell Jeremy.'

There was no sign of Grace, or her car. Rosy ran under the clock-tower and to the front door, went inside, called out.

Jeremy was in the kitchen, making his own breakfast.

'Hi. I thought you were Grace. She doesn't seem to be coming today.'

'The picture's gone. The Stubbs.'

'What's up? What do you mean?'

'Someone's taken it. Did you take it, for safety?'

'No. Why ever should I? Never crossed my mind.'

Jeremy pulled out a chair for her. 'Sit down, take it easy. It's gone missing—your picture? Your fortune, Rosy?'

'It's not that. I never did want it. But I didn't want it stolen either.'

'And now it's gone? We're not doing very well between us. We've lost quite a few fortunes in the last twenty-four hours. Does Gin know anything about it? He knows about the key.'

'He said he didn't.'

'I'll call him, see if he's any ideas.'

Jeremy went out and Rosy leaned her elbows on the table, feeling as bad as she had the evening before. Sunlight filled the kitchen, polishing the new pine surfaces, glowing on a jugful of roses. There had been no roses before Grace. Jeremy came back with Gin.

'Have you seen Grace? Did you bring her home last night?' Jeremy asked him.

'Yes. I brought her here, to collect her Mini. Then she drove home.'

'I rang her this morning, but no signs of life.'

'She wouldn't know about it. She's never been in the cottage,' Rosy said.

'I wasn't thinking that. I'm just wondering where she is. I can't believe the Stubbs could have been stolen. Did many people know Letitia was going to Ascot yesterday?'

'I suppose the news got around,' Gin said. 'Yes, I imagine quite a few people knew. My ma knew, and my family; they knew in the shop. And lots of people knew the key was under the flower-pot.'

'Oh, hell, I suppose I'll have to ring the police. I've got to ring my father in Australia, and find out about undertakers and all that sort of thing. I thought Grace would be in. If the police come up, they'll take hours asking questions. I can't believe anyone nicked it though. Is Hugh in today?'

213

'He was going up to Newmarket, to look at that animal with Hawkins.'

'Oh, that's right. OK, Gin, carry on. I'll ring the police.'

Gin hesitated. 'Perhaps you should wait until Grace comes. She might know something.'

'All right. That's a point. I'll try her again.'

Gin went out and Jeremy rang the Maddox number. It was answered. 'Hullo. Margaret? Is Grace around this morning? I thought she was coming in?'

Long pause.

'Yes. It was all a bit of a disaster. She told you? Yes, she died in the evening. I got back too late to ring ... yes, yes ... thank you.... Grace? She left an hour ago? Oh, no, I expect she's called in somewhere. Thank you. Yes, thank you. I'll call later and talk about it.' He put the phone down.

'Bloody Grace. Just when I really need her.'

Rosy sat slumped in the kitchen chair, thinking that Jeremy did not speak of Grace as if he loved her.

Perhaps Jeremy thought the same, as he said, 'Sorry. I've just come to depend on her, rather. She's good at arranging things like funerals, long distance phone calls, all that. What to say to policemen. What shall we do about that, Rosy? Your picture. Your fortune. She really did leave it to you, you know. She made a will to say that, but not about anything else. She said she'd do all that later. Perhaps some one is playing a trick.'

'Are you really going to lose Brood?'

'I think so. My father never cared tuppence for the place, and is frightfully short of money. It'll be on the market as soon as he hears.' He sat on the edge of the table, looked at Rosy thoughtfully, for a long time. A lot of flippant remarks went through his head, about marrying her for her Stubbs, but now she hadn't got it; they none of them seemed very tasteful, considering how she looked. She was the least material-minded person he had ever met. She had not touched the money she had received for the filly, nor even yet voiced any regrets about selling Dark Secret. It was the first thing that had occurred to Grace, when he had rejoined her after the race: she had kept saying over and over how dreadful to have sold the filly—not how great that the filly had run so splendidly, but just how absolutely ghastly to have passed up all that money. She really had wanted to get her hands on Brood. Rosy was not like that at all. Even now he guessed that if she was given the choice again between Dark Secret, knowing how valuable she was, and saving old Roly Fox from the knacker's, she would opt for Roly.

'What are you thinking about?' he asked her.

'It's awful you losing Brood. It—it belongs to you.'

'What about you losing the Stubbs?'

She shrugged.

Jeremy could not help laughing. 'Look, I've got to do all these things, ring my father, and the solicitor and that, but let's just go down to the cottage again first. I'll have a look round. I can't believe just any old burglar walked in and took that picture.'

'All right. I'm not dreaming though.'

Rosy got up. The panics had subsided, now that it was in Jeremy's hands. She got into his car and he shouted to Gin, 'Won't be long,' and they drove away down the steep hairpin turns through the tunnel of trees. The sunlight needled through the leaves. Outside Gin's cottage, Kes sat in the middle of the drive. Jeremy pulled up.

'I'll take him in.' Rosy scrambled out and picked him up, hugging him. 'Where's your mum? What's she up to?'

Beryl came to the door, surprised. 'Where you going to, with the guv'nor?'

'We're going to the cottage. Someone's been in and pinched the picture, the Stubbs. He's going to have a look, and call the police.'

Beryl swung Kes into her arms, and laughed. In a mock whisper, she said, 'I reckon his ladylove took it! She wasn't half narked when Gin said the guv'nor would lose Brood if the old girl died. She thought it was his! I could tell—she didn't say anything the rest of the way home. But her face!

215

That was a picture an' all—I don't know about Stubbs though! I won a monkey on our filly—wasn't that great?'

Rosy got back into the car. She was shocked by what Beryl had said, but could hardly repeat it to Jeremy. Grace had been very bitter to her about Letitia leaving her the Stubbs that day in the yard when she had been hosing Roly's leg. Grace was very keen on money, after all. And yesterday, Jeremy had not been at all loving to her, on all the evidence. And going home, not with Jeremy, but with Gin and Beryl in the old beat-up Cortina—she must have hated it. Rosy was silent on the short drive, preoccupied with these disturbing thoughts and followed Jeremy reluctantly up the long path between the riotous flowerbeds and the serried vegetables where bees and butterflies were tumbling—it was getting very hot already. The peace, compared with yesterday at Ascot, was incredible. No wonder Letitia's system had been unable to cope with the contrast—what a fool she had been!

Jeremy had unlocked the door and was studying the blank space on the wall.

'Well, Rosy, you weren't dreaming.'

He looked serious.

'It's probably worth more than Brood.'

'We're equal then,' Rosy said, and grinned.

'Damn it, I don't know why you're laughing!'

'It's better than crying.'

If he went on standing there, looking at her like that, Rosy thought she would pass out. Every time they met in this cottage she found his presence overpowering and all her faculties undermined as if by some magic nuance in the walls and the furnishings. She had to retreat, or he would have to hold her up, the closeness of the small room and all its memories pressing in on her unbearably. She went out of the door and round the side of the house to the gate into the field. She leaned on it, looking down her beloved field to the two horses grazing, the ridiculous axis of her life. Jeremy came after her.

'What's wrong?'

216

'I love you.'

'What?'

'I just love you. I can't bear it. It's awful.'

'Do you feel all right?'

'No. Not really. Too much has happened. But it doesn't make any difference.'

He leaned on the gate beside her, looking down the field. She supposed he was thinking about Grace. Grace, after all, was pretty unreliable. She, Rosy, had done a Grace, staking a claim, proclaiming her need. But she could not regret it. The relief was balm.

Jeremy put his arm round her and gave a little squeeze as he had done on several occasions, when she had been upset about Roly, about Letitia. But the arm did not relinquish her this time. The fingers caressed the nape of her neck, her hair, an ear-lobe, very gentle, tentative. Rosy felt her hormones taking charge, her control faltering, the sun burning, the field shaking.

'Rosy?'

She turned to him and he put both arms round her very quickly, no longer gentle, but as quaking as she, remembering—did she but know it—Judith Partridge and the bliss she had imparted all those years ago. And not only remembering, but experiencing again with an anguished sigh of realization—everything that was absent from his coupling with Grace, the illusion of the sky coming down, the sun burning, the field shaking. Not the illusion but the conviction that this was how love ought to be, flowering out of want, money no object.

They neither of them said a word, but kissed passionately in the morning sunshine, until the two horses came up and nudged them over the gate, and they remembered they were on the way to the police station.

14

Letitia's funeral was the biggest social occasion in the village since the Maddox wedding in 1950. Not only did the whole village attend, including all the good ladies she had repelled with her rudeness, but many elderly racing people from her past, most of Jeremy's owners, including Mr Hawkins, the new owners of Dark Secret and, last but not least, the suntanned Peter Cutbush junior from Australia, her son and heir. Margaret and Hugh had offered their home for a reception afterwards, and Margaret had made a buffet lunch; it was more suitable than Brood, and much closer to the church, within walking distance. Grace had helped her, and now sat in the church between her parents and Mr Hawkins. Rosy sat at the back with her father, resisting Jeremy's invitation to sit with him and his father. She did not want to give the village anything else to gossip about: they had enough with Letitia's dramatic departure and the theft of her Stubbs.

It was not an unhappy occasion—how could it be? The general opinion supported Rosy and was not against her ... what a way to go, they all said, the perfect end of a racing lady. A pity it was in the lavatory, but that was beside the point, it was only the initial collapse. She had died dramatically and with dignity, as she had lived. The vicar stood up and said all these things, not at great length, and the congregation sat eyeing each other, looking forward to the chat and food and drink to come, enjoying the spectacle of the ancient church with the sun streaming in through the stained glass, and the impeccable organ-playing of the young man who was imported for important occasions.

Rosy sat in a state of trance, the service drifting over her head. Since his father had arrived, Jeremy had confirmed that Brood was to be sold. Peter Cutbush was claiming all that Letitia had left, except her old cottage which he said Jeremy was welcome to—'Don't let it be said I didn't even leave you a roof over your head!' He was a hard but quite jovial man. There had been no falling out. He wanted the money and told Jeremy he would try and leave him a reasonable pile when he went, but for now, he could use it. Jeremy was philosophical. No, he did not want to go to Australia. He would get by. His father was relieved to see that he was a lot happier than he remembered him in the past, even when on the point of losing not only his home but his livelihood. 'For all you think you're hard done by, mate, remember what I suffered with the old lady. For all that happened to you, you never suffered like I did in that house. Good riddance to it, I say. And the money she's left, I've earned it, mate, believe me.' Jeremy could not disagree.

So Letitia departed, having made her impression deeply for better or for worse on those she had had to do with.

The Pembertons, owners of Dark Secret, eating vol-au-vents on Margaret's immaculate lawn in the crush afterwards, said to Rosy, 'What a character! We shall never forget her, standing there at Ascot in those amazing tulips—the expression on her face! She was like a queen. If I was eighty-something, you know, I wouldn't mind going out like that. The only pity is, she won't be there to see the filly run again.'

'At Epsom next year,' said the blond son, grinning. 'She'll be an Oaks contender, we hope. We're going to nurse her for the big one. A pity the old lady won't see that.'

Rosy was pleased to talk to them, wanting to avoid all the people she knew best—Jeremy, his father, Grace (especially Grace). The Pembertons were owners in the style of Jeremy's now defunct old ladies, racing for the sport, loving the horse, not bothered about the betting.

'Her dam is in a field down the road, if you'd like to see her. I could take you down, before you leave.'

'Great! We'd love that. We'd really love that.'

The sire was also at grass in a field further down the valley, did they but know it, but Rosy was not inclined to say anything on that score. If Dark Secret was destined for fame, how fortunate that Jeremy had declared her sire to be of the same bloodline as was actually the case, for it would matter when she became a brood mare.

'I understand Mr Cutbush will have to give up Brood House with the old lady dying. We have a couple of chasers, to keep us amused in the winter—we wouldn't mind sending them to Mr Cutbush next season, if he gets another yard.'

The magic words all small trainers wanted to hear...

Beyond the rose-bushes, Grace was deep in conversation with old Hawkins. Hawkins and Pemberton ... Rosy, still a touch entranced, saw them together on the lawn, the bad and the good owners. Jeremy longed to give Hawkins his come-uppance, but could not afford it. Grace, Rosy thought, watching her filling Hawkins's wineglass, was extraordinarily assiduous in chatting up Jeremy's owners. Surely she did not have to work so hard at her job on an off-day such as this? She had hardly passed the time of day with anyone else. Beyond them, in the haze of midsummer, the woods of Brood floated from the valley floor to the horizon, hiding the house and the yards and all the industry that happened on the hillside with a panoply of tremulous green, a glorious backdrop to the Maddox roses. Rosy could see her father on his knees in Margaret's shrubbery, only the shiny seat of his best trousers protruding, on the trail—no doubt—of camomile or creeping jenny; Kes was crawling after him, thinking he had found one of his own kind. Beryl had abandoned him to go indoors and listen to the racing results. Jeremy was talking to various remote relations who had come out of the woodwork now Letitia was no longer there in person; they were happy to reminisce and say how wonderful she was, but had not wanted to know when she might have been glad to see them. Unfair, Rosy corrected herself, remembering the lady from meals on wheels. Letitia was as her son described, as he took the money in recompense.

She took the Pembertons down to see Silverfish, and when they departed she sat on by the riverbank in the late afternoon sunshine. It was exactly the same as the day Letitia had died; the weather had remained unbroken, day after day of cloudless skies and strong bright sun. She felt very tired. She had scarcely seen Jeremy, his father having arrived immediately he had got the news of Letitia, but nursed the memory of his embracing her at the field gate. Although ... given her confession, what could the man have done? Even in the name of good manners, he was bound to have made some response. Having thought about it nearly all the time since, she could now not accurately remember just how sincere his response had been, reality and dreams getting muddled. In her own highly over-emotional condition, she perhaps imputed her own passion to him.

On the road the cars from the funeral were departing to their various homes. Rosy saw Hawkins's car go by, presumably on its way to Brood, for it carried Peter Cutbush and Grace as passengers. Not Jeremy. Rosy had not spoken to Grace since Ascot. She lay on her back on the grass, having removed her tights and shoes. She shut her eyes and listened to the soft tumble of the river below her, and the steady cropping of the two horses close by, thinking how inconsequential life appeared to be, nobody much in charge of what happened to them, but making the best of circumstances as they arose. After all his years of hard work, Jeremy's business was down the drain, they had all lost their jobs, their futures, their ridiculous fortunes. Yet she was not unhappy. She was in a state of suspension, not able to think clearly about anything any longer. Her brain needed a rest. I will clear it, she thought, lie here and concentrate on thinking of absolutely nothing at all. Just the sky and the grass and the running stream.

'Rosy.'

Her concentration on absolutely nothing was so determined that she did not hear the voice until it repeated her name. She opened her eyes. Jeremy stood there, against the sun, looking down on her.

'I thought you'd be here.'

She did not say anything. He sat down beside her. He was in white shirt sleeves, the funeral tie discarded. Roly Fox came up and stood nudging his shoulder, then wandered on to take a drink from the river. Rosy sat up and kept her eyes carefully on the drinking horse, his black tail switching steadily from side to side.

'He looks happy enough now.'

'I wouldn't have changed anything. The Pembertons say they'll send you a couple of chasers this season, if you've got a yard.'

'Really?'

'I brought them to meet Silverfish. They've just gone.'

Jeremy picked a piece of grass, and chewed it thoughtfully.

'But I haven't got a yard.' He searched for some edible clover, picked another stalk. 'I thought, while I'm being divested of everything, I might as well divest myself of Hawkins as well. He offered to buy Brood, keep me on there. Can you imagine? I couldn't sink lower than that. I told him to try Hugh.'

'You're better off without a man like that.'

'My feelings exactly. He is my living, though.' He looked at Rosy and smiled. 'I know what you're going to say: money isn't everything.'

Rosy smiled too, shrugged. 'No.'

She said, 'You've got this. You could build a few boxes at the top of the field. There's room. Say yes to Mr Pemberton.'

Jeremy turned round and surveyed the rolling six acres or so of Letitia's field. He rolled over and lay on his stomach, looking up at the level patch at the top, and the decrepit barn where Silverfish had borne her foal. The scent of Letitia's straggling lavender bushes came faintly on the air. He was frowning. He lay still, considering, for what seemed to Rosy a very long time. Roly came out of the stream and walked slowly past, making for the barn where Silverfish had already gone to find shade. They were great mates these days. Rosy's mind, passing on to the horses, went back to thinking of nothing, too afraid to think of Jeremy.

'I would need a head lad,' he said at last. 'Would you take the job?'

'Yes, I would.'

'Living in?'

'Yes,' she said.

'Whoever took the Stubbs,' Jeremy said, 'did us a good turn. I could never have asked you ... I've got nothing.'

'Nor me.'

'Dear burglar.' He smiled at her, and his expression gradually changed, the smile broadening. He seemed to shed his years and to Rosy he was the boy in the curling photos, riding in his winner, passionate and triumphant.

'I'll make you out a contract, straight away.'

'Yes, sir,' she said.

The 'Horse and Groom in a Landscape' lay, as they spoke, where it was to lie for ten years before being discovered: in the loft of Letitia's cottage. Grace, who had hidden it there in a splendid fit of spite after returning from Ascot, was already in Brood House, mentally measuring up for carpets and curtains while Hawkins (she must learn to call him John) clasped her to his paunch.

A crack of sunlight filtered beneath one of the cottage tiles and played on the face of the groom and his timeless gaze fixed now upon the cistern lagged in old horse blankets. No surprise, naturally, was registered. He in his day had been, no doubt, party to vicissitudes of human nature no stranger than those that had brought about his incarceration in this dusty setting.

And his horse cavorted for eternity, the bold eyes for ever alight, waiting patiently for daylight and his just due, once more, of admiration and love.